Worlds Apart

To Stacey—

Best wishes to you!

Kate Mathias

Worlds Apart

Kate Mathias

To order additional copies of this book, contact:
Xlibris Corporation
1-888-795-4274
www.Xlibris.com
Orders@Xlibris.com
117286

Contents

For Josh

I am so thankful that we get to laugh through life together.

Acknowledgements

My warmest thank you goes to my husband, Josh. He has been my biggest supporter throughout this journey. His belief in me kept me going even when I was frustrated. He pushes me daily to be the best I can be and am so thankful to share all of my joys with him. He captured my heart seventeen years ago and am blessed to share my life with him.

A big thank you to my parents, Carolyn and Bill Chase. My mom was one of my beta readers and I truly enjoyed listening to her trying to guess what was going to happen next in my story. Both of my parents have always been my biggest cheerleaders in life and gave me the needed push to take this book onto the publishing path. Thank you, Mom and Dad.

My medical scenes would not have been correct or as believable without the help of my friend and trauma surgeon, Dr. Kris Venkatesh. A huge thank you to both he and his wife, Shayla for letting me bounce ideas off of them on what should happen to my characters. The major scenes wouldn't have been the same without their help.

I appreciate all of my beta readers who were my first set of eyes that poured over my story. My sincere thanks to Liz Todd, Carolyn Chase, Josh Mathias, Kerri and Jeff Williams for keeping me motivated to write more so they could continue to read.

My heartfelt thanks also to Jeff Williams for his help with the cover concept and design. He found exactly the image that I was searching for to create the look that I wanted for the cover of my book.

Thank you to my family and friends for always supporting me and believing in my dreams. I love you with all of my heart.

Prologue

May 2011

"No brakes!" Those words screamed in her head as her neck rolled around and slammed into the headrest. The radio that she had been singing to just a few seconds before suddenly was quiet. The silence was deafening as she watched a road sign slowly pass in front of her eyes. She was in a Mazda Miata and had lost her traction on some loose rocks on the side of the road just as she was pulling off on an exit from the interstate. Everything seemed to be in slow motion as she watched the road sign come inches from the hood of her car for the second time. The third time that she passed the sign, she wasn't as lucky.

The force that propelled her into the steering wheel knocked the wind out of her and left her gasping for breath. The crunching of metal echoed in her ears as the road sign split the hood of the car in two. The dashboard seemed to crumble like tinfoil as it collapsed onto her stomach and legs penetrating her abdomen in one swift movement. The car had stopped moving, but her head was still spinning as she reached down and felt her stomach. She pulled her hand away and looked down at the warm red liquid that covered her fingers.

She had never felt this intense pain before in her life. Her stomach had a gaping hole that blood was swiftly running out of. She tried to move her legs to get out of the car and cried out in pain.

Piper struggled with the seat belt to get it to release but was getting so tired that she could hardly keep her eyes open. She felt herself drifting into blackness with the sounds of wailing sirens fading into the background.

July 2000

leep! Bleep! Piper Samson reached over and slammed her hand down on her alarm. She slowly rolled over and groaned when she saw the bright numbers reading 5:15. It was still dark outside, and she wondered how her family had ever talked her into doing this. She stretched and slowly sat up letting her long legs drape over the edge of the bed. She could already hear laughter coming from downstairs and smell a mixture of coffee and bacon. She couldn't help but smile as she pulled on some shorts and a tank top and stuffed her chestnut-colored hair into a baseball cap.

As she padded into the kitchen still half asleep, she was immediately grabbed by the waist and swung around in circles. She laughed and threw a punch at her brother who looked enough like her to be her twin.

"Nice way to welcome a girl home, you brute!" Piper scolded her fifteen-month younger brother Pete.

"Oh, now, Piper 'Cub.' You know that your brothers are just happy to see that you are home," Henry Samson stated. He walked over and kissed his wife, Claire. "Good morning, beautiful." Henry wrapped his arms around Claire as she flipped the sizzling bacon on the stove.

"Flattery will get you everywhere, Mr. Samson," Claire laughed as Henry nabbed a piece of bacon and pinched her ample rear end.

Piper plopped down in the nearest kitchen chair and pulled her right leg up under her. She smiled back at her two brothers and Dad and thought it was just like old times. Piper was back living at home for a few months before she began her new job of teaching fourth grade at Silver Oaks Elementary School. She had already been teaching for four years at a different school in Nebraska. She had decided to move back home to be closer to her family. She had begrudgingly agreed to help her family with some of the side jobs that her father always seemed to be coming up with.

Henry Samson chartered small planes to business people and also flew packages back and forth to Kansas. He was the small airport's flight instructor on the weekends. He used to fly Piper Cub airplanes, and that is how Piper got her name. Henry could never be satisfied with having just one or two jobs and always seemed to come up with new and exciting (that is how he described them) ways for the family to have time together and also to turn a buck. His latest plan was selling sod that he grew on the thirty-five acres that the family owned on the other side of the pond. Piper had been roped into helping her dad and brothers, but secretly she was pleased to get to spend time with her family for a few weeks before fall semester started again.

Piper leaned across the table and grabbed a piece of bacon before her brothers could eat it all. She poured herself a cup of coffee, and then scooped up a hefty helping of scrambled eggs. She stabbed a forkful of eggs and blew on them before forking them in her mouth. She sighed and thought about how nice it was to be home.

"So fill me in, Greg. How is my cute nephew doing?" Piper asked. Greg smiled and finished chewing his toast.

"Charlie is doing amazing and can't wait to see his auntie Piper again. Anna said to tell you hello and wants to invite you over for dinner tonight. She was bummed that I got to see you first this morning until I told her what time we were starting and said she decided she could wait till tonight to see you." Piper laughed easily and thought about Greg's family. He and Anna had been high school sweethearts, and Anna had been one of Piper's closest friends.

Greg was five years older than Piper and lived about ten minutes away from the house that they had all grown up in. Charlie was Piper's only nephew and was a bundle of energy. He had just turned two last week and was enamored with bugs, dirt, trucks, and the constant question of why. Piper could hardly wait to see him and take him fishing at the family pond during the next couple of weeks while she was home.

Piper smiled as she listened to her brother Pete talk to Greg about his summer course he had just completed at the University of Iowa. He was a senior in engineering and was already so passionate about the buildings and bridges he hoped to build one day.

Pete was the complete opposite in looks from the fair-skinned, dirty-blonde, browned-eyed Greg. Pete and Piper took after their mother's looks. Claire was still stunning with her chestnut-colored hair streaked with gray that she wore tucked behind her ears. Her gray green eyes lit up when she laughed or when she looked at her children or Henry. She had provided a home so full of love and laughter for her children growing up. Piper wished moments like these, where her family was tucked in the cozy kitchen, could last forever.

Henry scooted his chair back on the hardwood floor and stood up. "I don't mean to rush you all, but that sod isn't going to cut itself! We need to get a move on before I have to get to my real job."

"So you are admitting that this sod-cutting thing isn't a real job?" Pete joked.

"It is as real as how I can still take you with one hand tied behind my back!" Henry grunted as he grabbed Pete in a one-armed headlock and forced him out the door. Laughing, Greg scooped up the keys off the table and headed out behind them letting the screen door slam.

"Bye, Mama," Piper called over her shoulder on the way out the door.

"Have a good morning, sweetheart!" Claire blew her a kiss from the kitchen sink.

Piper stooped down and pulled on her tennis shoes. The sun was just starting to peak up for the day. The grass was still dewy from the night before. She looked out over the pond and smiled when her eyes saw the old tire swing that her dad had hung in the weeping willow tree. It swayed slightly in the breeze. She remembered how her brothers had pushed her in that swing until she was so high that she felt like she was flying. She sighed and thought she better get a move on and catch up with her brothers.

The sod farm was just down the road from the main house. In total, the Samson family owned just under two hundred acres. The farm had been in the family since Henry's grandfather and used to be a full-working farm. They leased out most of the land to Dave Whitehead, a neighbor down the road. Henry kept a few acres for himself for his "side jobs" as the family referred to them. Everyone in the community was aware of Henry and his "jobs" and always looked to see what he was doing next. Piper strolled up to the truck that her brothers and Dad were piling into.

"Dad, how long do you think we will work this morning?"

"It should go pretty quickly. I would say not more than four short hours. Five at the most." Henry grinned as he threw some old work gloves in the cab of the truck. "Climb in. We are meeting Dave's nephew, Joe, in about five minutes. He has graciously agreed to help us."

Piper groaned as she hiked her leg up on the running board so she could scoot into the front seat next to Greg. "How did you talk Joe into helping?" Piper vaguely remembered Joe from a few years back when she had met him at a carnival the town was having. He had just recently moved in with the Whitehead's. He started his new job as a financial planner in a few weeks and must be using that time to help out on the farm.

"Simple. I just told him that it was easy work and that he would be able to skip the gym today after helping lift the sod rolls. Or maybe it was the one hundred bucks I promised him?"

"One hundred bucks?" Pete asked his dad. "I didn't hear that you were paying us today. Awesome!"

"Oh, I'm not paying you, just Joe. You are doing it simply for the joy you get in helping out your old man!"

Piper sat back and smiled as she listened to a conversation that she had heard hundreds of times. They bumped over the dusty road, and Piper brushed some loose hair out of her face. She was glad that she had worn shorts and a tank top because she was already warm, and the day had just begun.

The truck came to a stop, and she jumped down onto the dusty gravel patch. Putting her hands on her hips, she shook her head as she saw the sod-cutting machine that she was sure her dad had found at an auction somewhere. He probably claimed to have gotten a really good deal on it too.

Joe Reynolds was leaning against his blue Ford F-150 truck watching the Samson family. He remembered Greg and Pete from when he was in high school and had played their school in sports. What he didn't remember was their younger sister ever looking like she did right now.

Joe watched her move gracefully across the grass. Her well-toned tanned legs looked to go on for miles. She had cut-off jean shorts that hit her midthigh and a light blue tank top on that showed off her athletic shoulders and arms. She had dark chestnut-colored hair that she had balled up and stuffed into a baseball cap. One of her brothers had just said something that amused her. As he continued to watch her, she threw her head back and the throaty laugh that escaped her seem to float on the breeze to him. This sod job had more perks than just that one hundred dollars Joe decided right then and there.

Joe walked over to the family that was already starting to pull on their work gloves. He moved over to Piper first and introduced himself. "I'm your neighbor's cousin, Joe Reynolds," he explained to Piper and took her slender hand in his to shake.

Piper had been looking down trying to pull on one of her gloves. She looked up at Joe through her eyelashes and felt her pulse race slightly. Piper was tall, standing at five foot ten, but she had to look up to Joe. He must be about six foot five inches tall and one of the most gorgeous men she had ever seen. His hair was nearly black and left slightly longer as it curled around the back of his head in tousled waves. His eyes were a clear blue that almost seemed to look right through her. He was tanned and well toned from a summer of working outside doing manual labor. His voice was deep and calm, and as Piper looked down at their joined hands, she felt a little shimmer of butterflies in her belly.

"Nice to meet you, Joe. Thanks for helping my family out today. Although I heard that you were promised to be paid for your work? Hope you got that in writing! My dad is well known for his frugal ways when it comes to money." Piper laughed and turned toward her dad.

"I resemble that comment!" Henry proclaimed and then kicked on the sod cutter. The machine sputtered to life and started to move away from Piper and the boys. They got behind it and began to roll the sod as Henry continued to move down the sod, cutting it into strips. Piper and Pete decided that they should roll the sod while Joe and Greg lifted the sod rolls onto the pallets.

They continued to work for about four hours until Greg said that he needed to get going. Greg and Anna owned the local restaurant, and he needed to get it opened up for the lunch crowd. Greg reminded them about dinner tonight at his house and said he could drop them all off at the house on his way to town.

"That would be great! I want to get back to work on an online course I am taking for some extra hours," Pete explained.

"I need to get cleaned up for an appointment at the airport. Let's head out! There is always more tomorrow." Henry smiled with a gleam in his eyes.

Piper didn't want the morning to end just yet. She looked at Joe and as if he could read her mind asked, "Piper, do you want to go get some lunch?"

"Let me head home and get a shower and cleaned up first. Why don't you pick me up in an hour if that works?"

"That works perfectly. See you then." He smiled at her as he got into his truck and slammed the door.

Yes, it most certainly does, thought Piper. These few weeks at home may just turn out to be the best decision she had ever made.

Two

G reg pulled into the driveway, and Piper bounded out of the truck yelling, "See you tonight, Greg!" She ran into the quiet house and took the stairs two at a time to get up to her room. She began going through her clothes to see what would be suitable to wear to a first lunch date. She settled on a cotton sundress that was pale green with spaghetti straps that crisscrossed in the back. She grabbed the dress and headed into the shower.

Precisely one hour later, the doorbell rang, and Piper could hear the screen door creak on its hinges as her mom swung the door open and invited Joe inside. Claire and Joe were making small talk when Piper started to descend down the stairs.

Joe knew at that moment that he would never look at another woman in his life. As Piper started down the stairs, he found he couldn't concentrate on what her mother was talking to him about. He knew that he had never seen anyone so beautiful in his life. The pale green dress matched Piper's eyes, and the way that it clung to her taunt belly and then flowed out slightly at the hips made his breath catch. Her cheeks were flushed from the shower, giving her a glow. She smelled of vanilla, and Joe caught a whiff of her lavender shampoo as she turned her head to say hello to him. Her hair was down now and hung midway down her back in loose curls, shiny and chestnut brown. She kissed her mom good-bye, and then turned to Joe and asked if he was ready.

"Absolutely." Joe thought that he had been ready and waiting his whole life for her. He took her by the arm and led her to the truck, opening her door for her to slide in.

"Where should we go for lunch?" Piper asked already knowing the answer. There were really only a few spots in town that served lunch. One of the places was more like a bar, and the other one was the restaurant that her brother and sister-in-law owned, Jasmine's.

"I was thinking that we could go to your brother's place if that is okay with you?"

"Sure! I helped develop the menu and can recommend what the best thing to order is."

The restaurant was buzzing with its normal crowd. Business people were out taking advantage of their lunch hour, mothers were there with their children, and high schoolers were enjoying lunch for the last few weeks of their summer break. Greg spotted them immediately and sat them outside on the patio. There was a slight breeze that kept the bugs away, and the shade the umbrella provided helped with the heat.

Anna rushed over to their table, and Piper jumped up before she made it all the way there. They laughed and hugged each other so tightly that Joe could see what the two women meant to each other.

"I was hoping I would see you before dinner tonight. Welcome home! I can't believe you are here. We have so much to catch up on, but that can wait." Anna turned to Joe and introduced herself.

"I remember meeting you a few times over the years when I have been here visiting my uncle. You have the most amazing fried chicken. I talked Piper into coming here for lunch. I played it off like I didn't know what I would order for lunch, but I guess my secret is out." Anna laughed and said that she would bring out two fried chicken dinners since that was Piper's favorite meal too. She smiled and said they would talk later and needed to get back to her customers.

"She seems really great."

"She truly is more like a sister to me than a sister-in-law. She and I were best friends before she started dating my brother. I have known her for most of my life. I am so blessed to have her in my family. They have this amazing little boy too." Joe was watching Piper as she talked about her family. Her eyes lit up and sparkled as she was telling a story about something her nephew had done last time she visited. She laughed easily, and Joe couldn't help but smile as he watched the love that she had for her family flow out into her words.

"So tell me more about you and your family. I could talk all day about mine. My brother says that I talk too much." Piper got a little shy then and gave a sly smile and looked down.

"I could listen to you talk all day." Joe reached over and took her hand that was fidgeting with her silverware. "Let's see, where to start on my family. I have a younger brother, Colin. He still lives at home with my mom and dad. I don't come from a family like yours." As Joe started to tell Piper about how it was for him growing up, he couldn't believe that he was sharing all of this with her. He never really showed or shared his feelings easily, and certainly not on the first date. He couldn't stop himself as he looked into those big green eyes that stared intently at him and listened to his every word.

"I know that my parents love me and my brother. They just never openly showed us. They have really never told me that they love me. They have worked hard for everything that they have. Maybe because they were never really given anything from their parents, they thought that is how we should be raised too. I have had a job for as long as I remember. Growing up I couldn't wait to get out of the house and make something of myself. I think I am almost there too. I know that they are proud of me in their own way."

As Piper listened to Joe talk and quietly ate her chicken, she thought about how different families were. She felt blessed for hers but was starting to feel slightly protective of Joe. She wondered where this might lead.

Joe paid for lunch and suggested that they go to the corner ice-cream shop if she was up for dessert.

"This girl never turns down ice cream!" Piper practically skipped out the door and headed to the Ice Cream Stripe. Joe laughed as he watched her practically dance ahead of him and shook his head to try and make sense of what he was feeling just from being close to her.

Piper ordered a double dip of chocolate peanut butter ice cream in a cup, while Joe stuck simply with vanilla. Piper razzed him for being boring, and he explained that vanilla was a classic and shouldn't be underestimated.

They decided to take a walk around the town and all the while talked about everything under the sun. The hours seemed to tick away as mere minutes until Piper glanced at her watch.

"Shoot! I am supposed to be at Greg and Anna's house for dinner soon. Why don't you come with me?"

"I don't want to intrude on your family dinner."

"Not at all. Besides, after dinner we usually end up playing cards, and I could use another person on my team, assuming you don't stink at cards," Piper teased and pulled him in the direction of his truck.

Eight minutes later they were pulling into Greg's driveway. The house was a pretty little red brick ranch with white shutters. There were flower boxes on the windows overflowing with petunias of all colors. The yard had been freshly mowed and edged. It was easy to see that the home was well taken care of. The windows were open, and music flowed outside and greeted them on the sidewalk.

"Knock, knock!" Piper called thru the screen door. Charlie was sitting on the family room rug playing with his trucks. He looked up and saw Piper and squealed with delight. She swung open the door, and he jumped into her arms. She swung him around and around until he was laughing so hard that he got the hiccups.

"Put that boy down before he throws up!"

"Hi, Pops!" Piper kissed her dad's cheek and, still holding Charlie's hand, headed into the kitchen where the rest of the family was in a lively debate about some band that was playing in the next town over.

Piper walked over to Anna and asked, "How can I help? I hope you don't mind that I brought Joe."

"I would've never guessed you were bringing him by the way I saw you looking at him at lunch," she giggled and turned back to slicing the watermelon and pointed with her knife at the kitchen table.

Piper turned her head and laughed when she saw that the table had been set for seven people and a high chair.

"Was it that obvious?"

"Yes. Now go get everyone's drinks and tell them that dinner is almost ready."

Once everyone was seated and chattering away, and the food was being passed from left to right with Pete taking three helpings, Joe leaned into Piper and whispered, "Your family is amazing. You are amazing."

Funny, Piper had been thinking the same about him. After the dinner dishes had been cleared, and dessert and coffee were served, Claire pulled out a deck of cards. *Here we go*, thought Piper.

"You aren't going to make Joe be on your team, are you, Piper? You cheat!" Pete insisted.

"I do not! You're just a sore loser because I beat you every single time." Piper smiled sweetly. "Bring it on, brother. Bring it on."

The drive home was relaxing following a day that seemed perfect. The windows were rolled halfway down, and the breeze that blew into the truck smelled faintly of fresh cut grass. The crickets were chirping, and off in the field to the right were lightning bugs, blinking their little lights. Piper leaned her head back on the seat and gave a content sigh.

When the truck came to a rest, Joe popped out of the truck and tried to get over to Piper's door to open it for her. She beat him to it but smiled and accepted his hand as he helped her step down.

As he walked her to the door, he told her what an amazing day he had. They stopped on the front porch. They stood just looking at each other for a few seconds.

"Can I kiss you, Piper?"

She didn't trust her voice, so Piper just shook her head yes. He slowly reached his hand up the side of her neck causing her to tremble slightly just from his touch. With his other hand he slowly pulled her close to him until their bellies were pressed together. He brushed a loose piece of hair out of her face and bent to take her lips onto his.

At first his lips felt soft and warm. She felt herself slipping into him and finding safety and comfort in his kiss. As the kiss deepened, so did her need for him. He must have felt it too because the kiss became hungrier and more forceful. She heard a moan escape her lips. Joe quickly pulled away.

"I'm sorry. If I continued, I don't know if I would be able to stop." His voice was husky. Piper felt the same way. She was warm and tingly and had never felt so quivery after just a kiss.

Piper leaned in to give him a hug. She whispered in his ear, "Thanks for a wonderful day." She gave him a kiss on the cheek and let herself into the house.

"Good night." She smiled and gave a little wave through the screen door.

"Night." Joe returned the smile and moved toward his truck hating to leave.

Three

The next day Piper practically floated down the stairs. Claire was standing at the kitchen sink looking out into the backyard. The sunlight was streaming through the window, and a slight breeze made the cheery yellow curtains twirl lightly.

"Good morning, Mama. Isn't it beautiful today?"

"I have seen that look before, lovey, but never on you. He is something special, huh?"

"I don't know what it is, but I feel a connection with him that I haven't ever felt before. We will just see where it goes. What are your plans for the day?"

"I have a dentist appointment in about twenty minutes. I was just looking at my flowerbed over there. It needs a pop of color. Maybe after I finish at the dentist we could plant some flowers together?"

"That sounds great! I will be here. I may go for a run while you are gone."

Claire grabbed her purse and headed out the door. "I will see you soon."

Piper went upstairs to change into her workout gear. On second thought she decided to go and get some Asiatic lilies to plant and surprise her mom for the flowerbed. She picked out a pretty assortment of red, orange, and pink ones from the nursery down the street and headed back home.

She had been digging for a few minutes when she began to feel strange. Her stomach started to get queasy. Her heart began to race, and her pulse sped up. She felt as though her heart was beating right into her chest wall. She lay down and noticed that everything seemed to get *glimmery* around her. Items in the yard were moving slightly, and her vision was becoming blurred. She closed her eyes for a few seconds. When she opened them, she sat up feeling slightly better.

That was strange, she thought. Maybe she should get a drink and cool down. She walked back to the house and went in the kitchen door. She looked around at the familiar kitchen and noticed that things were different. There were new paintings on the walls, and the tablecloth was different than it had been moments before.

She began to wonder if maybe she hit her head and went to the sink to get a glass of water. She held the glass to her lips and was slowly taking a sip when she heard a voice that sounded like her own.

"Hey, Mom! You will never guess the deal I got on these flowers."

Piper turned from the sink and stared at the woman that walked into the kitchen with Asiatic lilies in her hand. She looked identical to Piper, pale green eyes and the same body. The only difference was this woman's hair was cut into a bob that just grazed her shoulders and had hair the color of sun spun blonde.

Piper was still standing at the sink with the glass in her hand. The two women stared at each other. It was like they were looking in a mirror. The glass slipped from Piper's hand and, seemingly in slow motion, fell and shattered onto the kitchen floor into a million pieces.

Piper opened her eyes and was lying on the grass. *What just happened, and who was that woman?* She got up quickly and ran into the kitchen. She slowly looked around and looked at each item in the kitchen that had been there since she was a little girl. She was back in her house now, but where had she just been, and who was the woman that looked just like her?

She was feeling a little sick to her stomach and plopped down into the kitchen chair and placed her head into her hands. Her mind was reeling. She was still in that position when her mom walked through the door.

"I got a clean bill of health on my teeth, and that cute dentist says to tell you hi. I think he wants to ask you out to dinner," Claire was chattering on as she walked into the kitchen and placed her purse on the table. She took one look at Piper and immediately went to her side.

"Honey, what is wrong? You are as white as a ghost. Are you feeling all right?"

How could Piper explain to her mom what had just happened without sounding crazy? She had just experienced it, and it sounded crazy to her. She didn't want to cause her mom any undue stress when maybe all that happened was a hallucination of some sort.

"I was trying to surprise you with your favorite flowers, Mama. I was out planting them in the back when my heart started racing. I got sick to my stomach and felt kind of dizzy. I am feeling better now."

"I'm so sorry. You know your father has that heart arrhythmia since he was a kid. He always said that it felt like his heart would skip a beat, and then race. Maybe you have it too. I think we should set up an appointment for you to go to the doctor. I could never talk your stubborn dad into going and having his checked out. He always claims that he is in perfect health, and that is usually after he eats a whole dozen of my chocolate chip cookies."

Piper looked up at her mom who was stroking her arm all the while, making her feel better. Claire's eyes were full of love and concern.

"Mom, how do you always know how to make me feel better? Good thing that I am not at all stubborn like Dad." Claire snorted and gave her daughter's arm a squeeze.

"I will make you an appointment for as soon as they have available. Let's try not to worry about it in the meantime. Maybe see that boy Joe to take your mind off of things?"

"I never figured you for a matchmaker, Mom."

"Well, I am just saying that if I were thirty years younger and of course not married to your wonderful father, I may just go after that boy myself!"

"Mom!" Piper laughed and shook her head. Her mom always made her smile and knew how to make her feel better. "Let's go look at your flowers that I planted." Piper linked her arm in her mom's and led her outside.

The next few days moved passed in a blur. Her mornings were spent either helping her dad with the sod or watching Charlie at the restaurant while Anna got the new menu items perfected. It was one of those quiet mornings that she was sitting in the restaurant watching Charlie build up a tall tower of blocks just to crash them over and do it again when she brought up her health to Anna.

"Do you think that there is something really wrong with me?"

"I'm sure. I mean all of your symptoms on WebMD probably pointed to numerous fatal illnesses."

Piper smiled. "I am that easy to figure out, huh? And yes, I think that I diagnosed myself with about five very rare diseases."

"Is that all? Good, I was thinking it would be more. Don't worry about it just yet. When is your appointment?"

A clap of thunder sounded, and the lights flickered. A storm was moving in making the sky a dark shade of purple. Piper walked over and flipped on a few more lights. She had always liked storms when she could be warm and dry inside and just listen to the rain. She walked over to the window and looked out at the droplets that were hitting the sidewalk. The intensity of the storm was beginning to increase. Another clap of thunder boomed, and a lightning bolt slashed through the sky.

"Boom! Boom!" Charlie clapped his hands and seemed to be enjoying the storm and all of its noises.

"My appointment is this afternoon at three. I am meeting with Dr. Brown. I guess his office is off of Court and Tenth Street. It is right up the street from your restaurant. I think I will just jump on the bus and leave my car here so I don't have to worry about parking. I will just be glad after he can answer some of my questions."

"I am sure you will. Do you want to try some of my baked potato soup? It is a new recipe that I tried. It has been simmering on the stove for the last hour. I think it will warm us all up. There seems to be a bit of a nip in the air."

Piper looked out the window at the now fully dark sky. The clouds had opened up, and the rain was pelting the windows. The streetlights had turned on thinking it was dusk. Some soup may be just what she needed to take her mind off of her appointment.

At promptly three o'clock, Piper walked into Dr. Brown's office and shook off her umbrella as best she could. She checked in for her appointment and took a seat in the corner. She didn't have to wait long before a redheaded nurse named Lindy called her back.

"Go ahead and go around the corner to the scales, dear."

Piper followed and kicked off her shoes, and then removed her jacket and handed it to the nurse.

"Every bit helps, right?" Piper joked to the nurse. Lindy wrote down the number and mumbled, "Uh, huh. This way. Go ahead and put on the gown with the opening in the front. You can leave your pants on but remove your bra." She laid the gown on the table and turned and walked out the door, closing it behind her.

Piper wondered who designed these paper gowns as she slipped it on trying to pull it a few different ways to get comfortable. She ripped it a little on one side. She sat with her legs hanging over the table, and she began to swing them back and forth while she waited.

There was a knock at the door, and it clicked open. Dr. Brown walked into the room and introduced himself. He was a man in his midfifties with stark white hair and glasses. He had an easygoing smile and large hands. He shook Piper's hand, and then took a seat on the stool opposite the table that Piper was sitting on.

"Piper, why don't you tell me about what you have been experiencing lately, and we can see what we can do?"

Piper began to explain what she had felt and how her heart had raced. She said it felt like her heart skipped a beat. She had a habit of talking more with her hands when she was nervous, and her hands seem to be flapping around as she was describing the incident. She did not share with the doctor the part where she jumped to another parallel timeline. She was starting to believe that maybe her mind had conjured that up.

The doctor ordered a blood test to be done. He also said that he wanted her to wear a Holter monitor for twenty-four hours and see if they could catch her heart in action having one of these episodes. He said that a nurse would come in and fit one to her. He said he would be in touch once the blood tests came back.

Piper felt a little like a robot as she left the office being hooked up to the Holter monitor. Her arm tinged a little from where the nurse had drawn the blood. She sighed as she walked down the building steps and heard a few rumblings of thunder. It was still raining, and now she would have to wait for the bus at a soggy bus stop. It probably wasn't her best idea yet.

She opened up her umbrella and stepped out onto the sidewalk. She stepped lightly and tried to avoid the puddles that had formed on the sidewalk where it wasn't draining properly. She was nearly to the bus stop when a gust of wind blew and caught the umbrella in its grasp.

Piper let out a squeal and chased after it, becoming more drenched with each second. She grabbed a hold of the umbrella and was standing in the middle of the sidewalk wondering if she had just gotten the monitor wet.

A blue truck pulled up, and the passenger-side window rolled down halfway.

"Get in!" Piper looked over and saw an amused Joe in the driver seat. She took about one second to think about it and jumped over the puddle and yanked open the door. She slid into the truck grateful for the dry cab and heat that was already warming her up.

"As much as I thoroughly enjoyed that Mary Poppins moment with your umbrella, I thought you might be in need of assistance."

"Ha ha. Thanks. I am pretty well soaked." She looked down at her wet jacket and quickly took it off to examine her shirt underneath to see if it had gotten wet.

"Hey, I am trying to drive, and you undressing is kind of a distraction, not that I mind. I think that your other shirt is wet. Maybe you should take that one off too?"

Piper reached over and slapped him on the shoulder. "Touchy! It was just a suggestion." He laughed as Piper rolled her eyes. "Where are you coming from?"

Piper explained how she had been feeling and about her appointment. Joe listened intently and did his best to tell her that he was sure she would be fine.

"I haven't seen you in a few days. I thought maybe I had scared you off after our date." Piper chewed on her lip waiting for a response.

"I know. I was worried that you might be thinking that. I have been caught up in trying to get paperwork done and ready for my new job. I start in two weeks. Do you want to go to dinner and catch up?"

Four

O ver the next week, Joe spent all of his free time with Piper. She was on his mind when he went to sleep at night, and she haunted his dreams. She was his first thought in the morning. He looked forward to the sound of her voice, the scent of her skin, and the taste of her mouth. It had never been this way with any of the other women he had dated. He had been in love before, but not like this. She captivated him and just, when he thought he had her figured out, she would do something completely different and throw him off. He was falling in love with this woman that he had only known a short time. He found himself thinking about their future together and about having children with her. He found he wanted to protect her, love her, and grow old with her.

After those few weeks with her, he knew that he needed to have a place of his own and move out of his uncle's house. He had always worked since he was a teenager and had a nice little nest egg saved up. He had worked for a financial planner while he was in college, and that is where he not only learned about the business, but also found he liked being able to help people with their money. He was savvy about investing and had already made quite a profit on his investments.

His first few years in the business had proved to him that he could be successful. He had been approached by a headhunter to try out a new firm in a different city an hour away from where he had been working for the past five years. He was always up for the challenge and decided it was as good of a time as any to make a move.

He thought that it was time for him to buy a house. He would have Piper help him find one. She may not know it yet, but it would be a home that they would raise their family in.

His uncle recommended a friend of his that was a realtor and who could help him get started. Joe made contact with her that afternoon and told her what his criteria were for a home. She agreed to line up a few houses to see for the following day. They would meet at ten at her office.

Joe was excited and dialed up Piper. "Hello?" It always sounded like Piper was smiling when she answered the phone.

"Hi! Are you busy tomorrow morning to help me go shopping?"

"I don't have any definite plans. I have to spend a few hours working in my classroom but can do that in the afternoon. Why? What do you have something planned?"

"I want you to help me find a house."

"A house? That is kind of a big purchase!" she giggled. "I thought you were going to ask me to help you buy some new clothes or shoes. I would love to help you find a house though. What time?"

"We are meeting at Joan's office at ten. It is Brownstone Realty. I will pick you up around nine, and we can get a quick breakfast."

"That works for me. I am babysitting Charlie tonight, so I won't be able to meet you for dinner. I will miss you."

"That is okay. I will miss you too. I have some paperwork that I need to get collected before we meet the realtor tomorrow. Have fun spoiling your nephew. I will see you in the morning."

"Sounds good. Good night!"

"Night, Piper."

She hung up the phone and glanced at her watch. She had a few hours before she had to be at her brother's house and thought she had time to get a few errands done before she headed over. She was in midmotion of grabbing her purse and keys when the phone rang again. She thought maybe Joe had forgotten to tell her something and smiled when she picked up the phone.

"Hello?"

"Hello. May I please speak with Piper Samson?"

"This is she."

"Hi, Ms. Samson. This is Lindy calling from Dr. Brown's office. We have the tests results back from your blood work. You have hypothyroidism. It is a hereditary condition where in your case your thyroid is underproducing the hormone needed to regulate some of your systems. Whenever patients come in with heart palpitations or racing pulses, we always check the thyroid. You will need to be on medicine for the rest of your life. It is a pill that you will take in the morning on an empty stomach. It should help with your heart symptoms within a month or so. Do you have any questions?"

"I don't think so right now."

"I will send over a prescription to your pharmacy, and it should be ready for you to pick up within the hour. Please call our office if you come up with any questions."

"I will. Thank you for calling. Bye."

She had a thyroid problem? She felt like walking. She opened up the kitchen door and headed out to walk around the pond for a bit. The grass got a little longer as she got closer to the pond. It brushed on her ankles and made a swooshing noise as her shoes slid through it.

If the thyroid condition could explain why her heart raced and felt like it was skipping a beat and could be treated with medication, how could the hallucinations be explained? Maybe when she saw the woman that looked like her twin it had been her mind playing tricks on her. How else could it be explained? She had even walked into her parents' house, the house she had grown up in; and although the house looked the same on the outside, it was somehow different on the inside. The pictures were new, and things that had been in the same spot for years were no longer there.

She had been tired that day. Had she fallen asleep and dreamt the whole scene? She had awaken outside on the grass and wasn't in the kitchen like in the dream. That had to be the explanation. She had always had very vivid dreams in color and could always remember them. Her brothers had always teased her when she told them about her dreams saying that they were so detailed and far-fetched.

She started to feel better about the whole episode. That had to be what had happened. A duck quacked in the pond to her left and startled her from her thoughts. She felt as though someone was watching her.

She looked up and standing about seventy-five feet from Piper, she was standing, the woman from her dream. The sunlight was behind her, and her golden hair seemed to shine. She had a blank expression on her face and appeared to be just as confused as Piper was.

Piper seemed to come out of her fog and snapped into focus.

"Hey, you! I want to talk to you!" Piper began to run toward the woman. The woman seeing Piper start to race toward her turned and ran. Both women were athletic by nature. Piper was closing the gap between them. In an instant her flip-flop got caught under some weeds and tripped her. Piper fell down in a heap. Crying out and yelling for the woman to stop, Piper tried to hoist herself up with her arms and looked up sharply. As her eyes were trained on the fleeing woman, all at once the woman was gone. She had just disappeared in broad daylight. One minute she was here, and the next second she was gone.

Piper pulled herself up and slowly walked over to the area where she had last seen the woman. She looked down at the ground and saw that the grass had been depressed where the woman had been running. Something glittered on the ground and was caught in the sunlight. Piper stooped down and picked up the small silver charm that was lying there. It was a simple tiny heart. The loop that would have attached it to the bracelet was slightly open at the top. She realized at that moment the woman was not a dream or a figment of her imagination; she was real and alive just as much as Piper was. Where had she come from, and most importantly why had she come, and what did she want from Piper?

*   *   *

Pip was out of breath and panting. She put her hands on her thighs and leaned down and tried to slow down her breathing. What the hell had just happened? Who was that woman, and why did she look just like her, but with long brown hair?

She glanced down at her right wrist and noticed that her oldest charm that had been a gift from her grandma was missing. She was still inspecting her bracelet when she heard her name being called.

"Pip!" Joe had gone back to the car to get a drink of water for his dog, Toby. They had only been at the dog park for one hour, but his eight-month-old Bassett Hound puppy was full of energy and had been running full steam around the pond and playing with the other dogs. He was walking back toward the pond with Toby when he saw her and smiled. The sunlight seemed to create a halo of light around her head, and her blonde hair was blowing slightly around her face. She looked flushed and concerned. As he got closer to her, he noticed that she was panting and breathing heavily.

"What's wrong? Are you ill?"

"I don't know. I think I might be, or else I am going crazy." They walked over to a nearby picnic table and sat down.

"Here. Have a drink of water and take it easy. Just breathe. When you are ready, tell me what happened."

Pip took a long swig from the green water bottle and then sighed. How could she explain this to Joe without sounding crazy?

*   *   *

When Piper walked into Anna's house, she seemed preoccupied. She snatched up Charlie and held him close to her chest and kissed him all over his chubby cheeks. He was squirming and giggling and demanded to be put down. He was just what she needed after her experience today by the pond. Piper told herself to snap out of it and enjoy the distraction that came fully bundled in a two-year-old's body.

"We are just going to dinner tonight so we won't be late. Thank you so much for doing this. Charlie has been talking about you coming over all day. How are you doing? How is Joe?"

"I guess I am helping him look at houses tomorrow. I really like him." Piper blushed and smiled.

"I think he is a great guy, much better than some of the other men you have dated. Just be sure he continues to treat you well. Otherwise he will have to deal with me." Anna laughed and picked up her purse. Greg walked into the family room from the bedroom.

"Hey, sis. Thanks for watching the little man for us tonight." He bent over and scooped up Charlie into his arms. "Be good for your aunt. I love you, buddy."

"Have fun!" Piper waved from the door as they walked out hand in hand. She turned and looked at Charlie. "Okay, what should we build first?"

Five

Piper tossed and turned that night. The sheets wrapped around her legs, and she woke up a few times in a cold sweat. She felt like she was chasing the woman the whole night, but just when she was within reach, she would disappear. She woke up in the morning feeling like she hadn't slept and was exhausted. She decided that she wanted to tell Joe about the two incidents, but she wasn't ready just yet. She wanted to try and wrap her mind around it more before trying to explain it to him.

She hoped a shower and a piping hot cup of coffee would wake her up. She showered leisurely and climbed out of the tub into the steamy room. She flipped her head over and wrapped her hair in a towel. She did feel slightly better already. She took her hand and wiped away a circle on the mirror that had gotten steamed up. She peered into the mirror and studied her face. It was so much like the other woman's that she had seen twice now and haunted her dreams. She was determined to find answers. She pushed that out of her mind and slipped into a cotton emerald green tank dress. She put some mascara on her eyes and finished off the look with a light pink lip gloss.

She walked into the quiet kitchen and got a cup of coffee. Joe would be here in five minutes to pick her up. She wrapped her hands around the cup of coffee as though trying to warm up her entire body with just that small mug. She took a deep breath and took a long gulp of coffee then washed out the cup and put it in the dishwasher.

Piper thought she would wait outside for Joe. It was a beautiful morning. Her mom had planted lily of the valley on the walkway up to the front porch, and she inhaled deeply their sweet smell. There were just a few wispy clouds in the sky and a slight breeze. A mother bird called to her mate a few trees over.

Joe pulled up in his truck and almost leapt out of it and ran over and picked her up in a giant hug. He took her lips to his and slowly, warmly fitted his mouth to hers, moving slowly, taking his time. The kiss deepened, and her need for him grew more intense. She wanted him and could feel it with every part of her body. She still wasn't used to the flutters that she felt in her stomach after just a kiss.

When he pulled away, Joe said, "Good morning, beautiful. I needed a kiss from you to start my morning off right. Should we grab a quick breakfast?"

Flushed and tingly, Piper responded, "It's my favorite meal of the day. I'm starving."

It felt so good to be this close to him and smell the soap on his skin from his recent shower. She poured warm maple syrup on her mound of French toast and savored each bite as she listened to him talk about his work starting next week and his plans for his business. He was so motivated and secure in his plans. He wasn't afraid to go after what he wanted. His confidence made him that much more attractive to her. She was looking forward to today and finding him a house.

Joe paid the breakfast bill and took one last sip of his coffee. "Are you ready?"

"Let me just run to the restroom, and then I will be good to go. I can meet you out at the truck."

"Sounds good." He stood and took her hand to help pull her out of the booth. He watched her walk away and thought to himself that he never got tired of looking at how that woman moved. He dug his keys out of his pocket and swung open the door. He stepped out into the sunshine and put his sunglasses on, smiling and thinking what an exciting day it would be.

They pulled up to Joan's office a few minutes before ten. Joe was a very punctual person and prided himself that he was always on time. They walked into the real estate office that was already buzzing with activity. Phones were ringing, and the secretary was on the phone at the front desk. She motioned that she would be just a minute. A few agents were running copies on the copy machine. Another agent was struggling with a stack of legal-sized documents to get them to her desk before they all scattered.

"I am sorry for the wait. Good morning, and how can I help you?" the young dark-haired woman behind the front desk asked.

"We have an appointment this morning with Joan Stark. I'm Joe Reynolds."

The woman picked up her phone and buzzed Joan. "Joan, your clients are here to see you. Thank you." She hung up the phone. "She will be right out. Can I get you a coffee, soda, or water?"

"Piper, what would you like? I think I would like a water please."

"I will take a water too, please."

The woman left her post and headed for the back kitchen area. She returned with the two waters just as Joan was coming out to meet Joe and Piper. She was a spunky woman in her midsixties. She had pure white hair that she wore in a bob. She was not very tall and moved with definite propose. She had a beautiful smile and was dressed sharply with a deep plum shirt beneath the dark gray suit.

Joan strode up to Joe, and Piper and extended her hand. "It's nice to meet you in person. I have some lovely homes set us for us to view today per your criteria that we discussed on the phone. I can drive my car so we can all go together."

Joe introduced Piper and explained that he may need her womanly advice to help him today.

Joan laughed and said, "It wouldn't be the first time I have heard that, dear!"

She led them out to her black SUV. Joe climbed in the front passenger seat, and Piper slid into the back. Piper glanced around at the tan leather interior and noticed how spotless the vehicle was. There was a blue cooler behind the driver seat.

"I see that Sophie already got you some waters. I have more in that cooler along with some cheese and crackers if we need a little snack later in the day. Feel free to help yourself."

Joan got all of her paperwork situated and pulled away from her parking spot.

"The first home that we will view is a quaint three-bedroom ranch with an unfinished basement. The kitchen was recently renovated. The home is about fifteen years old."

The three talked easily while they drove to the house. It was a short drive from Joan's office. They pulled up in front of a brown ranch with green shutters. The yard was well tended, and there were a few green bushes in the front of the house under the windows.

"Let's go have a look."

They got out of the car, and Piper and Joe walked up to the front door hand in hand. They stepped out of the way while Joan punched in her code on her SUPRA key to release the house key from the lockbox that hung on the front door. The key popped out, and she used it to unlock the deadbolt and pushed open the door.

The front door opened up into a modest foyer, and the walkway followed around to the galley kitchen. It had an eat-in kitchen and overlooked into the family room. The bedrooms made up the right hand side of the house while the two-car attached garage claimed the left.

The kitchen had been recently renovated and had black appliances with a brown and black granite kitchen counter. It was set up nicely, but Piper really couldn't see herself making meals in this kitchen. She didn't want to push her ideas on Joe and decided to let him tell her what he thought of the house first.

Joe came up from behind her and brushed his hand up her right arm and squeezed her shoulder. He bent down and placed a kiss on her neck.

"What do you think?"

"I think that the kitchen has been nicely redone. What do you think?" she asked him.

"I agree that it has been well done, but I don't know. The house just doesn't feel like the one. Do you know what I mean? I like how the kitchen overlooks the family room, but it just doesn't flow for me."

"I know exactly what you mean. Should we move on to the next one?"

They found Joan waiting for them in the next room. They explained to her how they were feeling and decided to move on to the next house. They piled back into the SUV.

They continued to look at homes for the next few hours. All of them were nice and had different components that Joe and Piper liked about each of them, but none had that perfect fit just yet.

Joan suggested that they stop for a sandwich for a few minutes and recharge. They pulled into the little sandwich shop on the corner. After they placed their orders, they took their sandwiches outside to eat on the patio.

"I hope you aren't getting frustrated yet, Joe. We still have a few more houses to look at. If we don't find the one that you are looking for today, there is always tomorrow. We will find it, don't worry."

"Oh, I am not worried. I know that I will know the right house when I see it."

They finished their sandwiches, and Joan filled them in on the houses that they had yet to see.

They went to two more houses, and still Joe still didn't find the one. Piper was beginning to think that they would have to continue their search tomorrow. She was staying positive as she spoke to Joe and reassured him that the right house was out there. She used a few of her own words to reassure herself. She sighed in the backseat and glanced out her window.

They were making a left turn onto Pinecrest Court and heading up into the cul-de-sac.

"Here's our next house, 8585 Pinecrest Court," Joan explained as she maneuvered the steering wheel to pull into the driveway.

A small gasp escaped Piper in the backseat. Piper gazed at the house and knew that this was the house they had been looking for. She just hoped that the inside looked as perfect as the exterior.

It sat nestled back on the lot surrounded by pine trees that flanked the sides of the house. It was a two-storey house that was a mixture of light gray hardi-plank siding and stone. It had white shutters that matched the white front porch that wrapped along the side of the house. There was a porch swing that had a thick cushion complete with pillows that Piper could imagine swinging on at the end of a long day. The front door was a deep burgundy color that was framed by side light windows. There were two comfy-cushioned white wicker chairs that held a table in between them. Piper could see herself having her morning coffee enjoying the comfort of those chairs.

The emerald color grass had been freshly mowed at a diagonal. Beautiful shades of purple and pink tulips surrounded the oak tree in the front yard. The walkway up to the front porch was lined with more tulips and flowering plants. The flower boxes that hung on the white railing of the front porch were overflowing with trailing ivy and vibrant yellow sunflowers that were a stunning contrast to the white porch.

It was although Joe could read her thoughts and could feel her excitement. They climbed out of the SUV and excitedly rushed up to the front porch. Joan unlocked the front door and stepped inside, pushing the door open as she went.

Natural light poured into the two-storey foyer and shined off of the cherry-colored hardwood floors. The large window above the front door had been left uncovered and allowed the sunlight to light up the entire foyer, including the staircase that swept to the second storey to the right. On the right hand side was a formal dining room with a chair rail and trayed ceiling. Walking through that was the butler's pantry and wet bar.

Beautiful open glass cabinets were set above the wine bar, and a small wine refrigerator was below the granite countertop.

Joe continued into the gourmet kitchen. The kitchen cabinets were an antique white color that looked slightly distressed. They were a bold contrast from the deep cherry floors. The appliances were all top of the line and stainless steel. The one wall held most of the cabinets and a small desk. The other curved wall housed the extra deep farmhouse kitchen sink below the oversized window that overlooked the private backyard. The ten acres behind the house were slated as a forest preserve and held hundreds of trees. The natural green canopy of the trees provided shade to the back part of the lot line.

The kitchen overlooked a great room. It had vaulted ceilings with exposed wooden beams that created a homey feel in the large room. The stone gas fireplace that reached as high as the ceiling was the focal point of the room, drawing Joe's eyes to the crackling fire that had been started to stage the house. The floor-to-ceiling windows hung on either side of the fireplace.

"I will take it," Joe stated to Joan.

"We haven't even seen upstairs yet!" Piper laughed as she grabbed Joe's hand and pulled him with her toward the grand staircase.

The staircase had been left open without carpeting and showcased the beautiful wood along with the smooth hardy railing that ran the length of the stairs.

At the top of the stairs on the right was the master bedroom. It had French doors that opened into the huge room. It had been tastefully decorated in a light cucumber color that was just the right shade to be calming. It had a large sitting area straight ahead and the adjacent area for a bed and night stands on the right. Joe could easily picture of four-poster bed piled high with a thick comforter and pillows. He could imagine waking up next to Piper or spending lazy Sunday mornings in bed.

In one corner of the room sat a makeup table and stool. There was no other furniture in the house, and this piece surprised and delighted

Joe. It reminded him of his grandmother's. He remembered that she would sit at her dressing table and get ready when he stayed with her. She had all of her little powders and brushes laid out neatly in a row. He used to watch her getting ready for the day when he was a boy while he was playing on her floor. She would tell him stories of when she was a girl and would laugh as she told tales of long ago and powder her nose.

"Joan, what is the story with that table?"

"This house was bought about a year ago from an older couple by an investor. They sold the house to move closer to their children and grandchildren. The investors renovated the house completely, redoing the kitchen and bathrooms in the house and refinishing the floors. The seller told me about the dressing table and said that he needed to remove it but just hadn't had a chance to get it out of the house yet."

"I want him to leave it, and I will buy it along with the house as long as we like the rest of it." He took Piper's hand and continued down the hallway to inspect the guest bathroom and the other two bedrooms. They were nicely set up with ample closet space.

Joe stopped Piper in the last bedroom and turned her toward him. "Piper, I love this house. What do you think?"

"I think it is perfect! If you don't buy it, I may have to," Piper joked. "It has everything that I can think of that is important in a house. It feels homey and inviting along with a ton of natural light. The setting is just gorgeous. All of those trees in the back!" Piper didn't want to add that she could see herself living here in this house with him. She didn't want to get ahead of herself just yet. He may not feel the same way as she was starting to feel about him.

"I think so too. Let's go find Joan and have her write an offer up for me," Joe confidently nodded his head and took off in search of Joan.

They headed back to Joan's office and wrote up a fair offer. They gave the seller twenty-four hours to respond; however Joan was confident that they would hear back before then. She promised to call them with an answer once she heard back from the seller.

"It's a beautiful evening. Do you want to pick up some fried chicken from Jasmine's, and then have a picnic by the pond behind my parent's house?"

"That sounds like a great plan. Then we can eat, and it will help me keep my mind off of the house while we are waiting to hear back from the sellers."

"Good. I will call Anna and place our order."

Forty-five minutes later, they were set up on a blanket, and Piper was pulling out the food that Anna had prepared for them.

"Wow! She knows how to do it up right. We have fried chicken, mashed potatoes, gravy, biscuits, and grapes. Complete with cheese cake for dessert."

Joe was pouring the white wine into plastic glasses and smiled at how easily Piper got excited about the food.

"You are such a foodie," he teased her. "How do you look like you do and eat like you do?"

"Just lucky I guess," she said with her mouth stuffed full of a biscuit.

Joe looked at her and laughed. He leaned over so he was resting on his side with his legs stretched out in front of him and propped himself up with his right arm.

The night was mild, and it was a full moon. The moonlight reflected off of the water and seemed to illuminate the area around them. The locusts were humming, and an occasional toad was making a throaty croaking. There was a slight breeze that set Piper's hair in motion, and she had to tuck it behind her ear.

"So how did you know that you wanted to be a teacher?"

"My mom was a teacher. and I have always liked children. I want to have a few of my own one day." She smiled sweetly and continued, "I worked in a daycare when I was in high school, and I guess it was never really a question for me on what I wanted to be when I grew up. I was excited at the chance to go away to school, but when it came down to it, I knew that I wanted to come home to teach and be near my family.

I mean who else could keep my brothers in line and spoil my nephew like I do?"

Piper continued to talk on about her passions and about her childhood. Joe was entranced as he sat and watched her eyes light up and heard the passion in her voice as she talked about her family and her love for them. He wanted to feel that way about his experiences and have that with her. He loved his brother and his parents but hadn't experienced the love that Piper had known. He envied how easily she spoke about how much she loved her parents and her brothers. He wondered if she would ever feel that passionate about him.

"Let me do the dishes tonight," Joe picked up her paper plate and his and threw it in the sack with the other trash. "All done." He smiled at her. "I can't believe how clear it is out tonight. Look at all of the stars we can see." He lay back down on the blanket and stretched out with his hands behind his head. "Did I ever tell you that I studied astronomy in college as a minor? So I am good with stars."

"Astronomy, huh? Don't you mean astrology?"

"Oh, sure. That too. Look up there. It is King Arthur's Belt."

"I think you mean Orion's Belt. You are lousy at reading the stars. You should stick with your day job," Piper joked in and leaned over to peck him on the lips. She began to pull away.

"Where are you going?" he whispered.

"Nowhere. There is nowhere else I would rather be than with you right here."

She lowered her head to take his warm lips on hers. His hands were soft and gentle and not at all demanding as he caressed her back and ran his fingers up her spine. She shuddered at his touch.

"Are you cold?"

Piper shook her head no and, keeping her eyes on his, slowly began to unzip her dress. She stood and let it skim down her body until it fell in a puddle at her feet. She was still wearing the crème-colored wedge sandals and had on a white bra and white lace panties. She looked like a painting as she stood in front of him silhouetted in the moonlight.

He moved up to a sitting position with his legs still out in front of him. She straddled him and slowly began kissing his neck while she was unbuttoning his shirt. When she got his shirt unbuttoned, she slid it off of his shoulders. She used her tongue to lick a trail down the side of his neck and onto his belly. She kissed and licked all the way down to his belly button, and then stopped to undo his pants.

Joe wanted her more than he had ever wanted anyone. He didn't trust himself to let go fully, afraid that he would hurt her. He allowed her to take the lead and had to admit that he was enjoying watching her.

She motioned for him to lift up his hips so she could take off his pants. Then she stood and slowly hooked her thumbs in her panties and slid them down her shapely thighs until she kicked them off. She unhooked her bra and stood completely naked and beautiful in front of him. Her breasts were full and round, and her nipples were taunt and erect.

Joe stood and pulled her close to him; a million little sparks flew just from the sensation of their bodies pressed together. He took his thumb and let it trail down the side of her breast. He raked his teeth down her neck and sucked and kissed his way from her ear down to her breasts. He teased her taunt nipple with his tongue until she moaned in pure pleasure.

Piper had to fight for control as the sensations were driving her to the edge. Joe kneeled in front of her and pulled off her shoes one by one. His clever, soft hands skimmed up her leg and traced the interior of her thigh. His long fingers gently stroked and teased her center. She shivered as he cupped her and moved his fingers in a circular motion and slowly plunged them in and out of her.

She began to go limp and moldable in his hands. He laid her down carefully on the blanket, searching her face. Her eyes opened and looked at him clouded with desire. She arched her back and sighed, lost in her own world of pleasure. His hands were skilled. He was gentle but knew how to apply the perfect amount of pressure. She was reeling from the sensation. She moaned and tilted her head back with pure pleasure and felt herself release.

Even as she was still sighing softly and shuddering, Joe eased himself into her. A soft moan escaped her lips. As her warmth and wetness took him deeper inside of her, he hovered over her and watched her face as he slowly drove deeper into her. She was so warm and wet that he was worried that he wouldn't last long in this position. He rolled over onto his back, pulling her on top of him as he moved.

She was straddling him and gripped his shoulders and pulled him until he was in a sitting position with his legs stretched out in front of him. He bent his head and began sucking and licking her nipples. He cupped her breasts in his hands. Her hands roamed through his hair, and she tangled her fingers in it. She leaned in to take his mouth on hers. He parted his lips for hers as she took him in a kiss that was both demanding and desperate.

He used the pads of his fingers to tease and pinch her tight nipples. She moaned in pleasure. He watched as her chest rose and fell in quick breaths. He was having a hard time keeping his breathing even. He wanted more. He leaned back slightly and raised his hips. He needed to be deeper inside her.

Piper had never lost all control as quickly as she was with him. He felt so good and so right beneath her, and she began to rock faster taking him deeper into her with each motion. Her body ached with desire for him, and she needed more. She arched her back and could feel her pulse racing, keeping time with his ragged breathing. He reached up and took a hold of her face with both hands. She crushed her lips unto his, breathing desire and wanting into every flavor of their kiss.

He moved his hands down her back, lightly caressing her hips with his fingertips. He left his hands closed around her tiny hips, helping her to ride him with more force and speed. She tipped back her head, and her hair tumbled over her shoulders. She gripped his shoulders tightly and allowed the pleasure to spread through her whole body until she was quivering with every inch of her being.

She couldn't hold on to the sensation much longer and opened her eyes to find him watching her. She caught his gaze, and holding onto him, she took them both over the edge together.

Piper rolled off of Joe and was panting but smiling.

"Whew! I think I need to work out more," she teased, and then laid her head down on his chest and wrapped her leg and arm across his body.

Joe was full of many different emotions right now. He hadn't planned on this happening tonight. As he lay here with this beautiful woman draped over him and his hand softly stroking her hair, he felt relaxed and wonderful.

"Stay with me tonight. Sleep with me here under the stars, Piper."

Piper nodded and whispered, "Okay." She closed her eyes and fell into a peaceful, dreamless sleep tucked into the warm body of the man she loved.

Six

Piper stretched and slowly opened her eyes. She found Joe was staring at her.

"Morning. What are you doing?"

"Just watching you sleep. Do you know that you talk and make little noises in your sleep?"

"I know. Was I talking about anything that made any sense?"

"I could only make out a few words, but it sounded like you were having quite the discussion with someone."

"My mom always said that if I did something that I wasn't supposed to do when I was little, I would come clean in my sleep."

"A very good thing to know. I will have to remember that. What are you doing today?"

"I thought that I would go into my classroom and," Piper paused and peered over Joe's shoulder. She saw some movement and a flash of red. She quickly stood and wrapped the blanket around her. She squinted her eyes and strained to see past the small clump of trees off to their left.

Joe started to stand up, and as he was straightening, Piper saw her. She was standing not even twenty feet away wearing a red jacket and khaki shorts. She was so close that Piper could make out the darker flecks of green in the eyes that were staring back at her. Piper gasped.

Joe reached out and grabbed a hold of Piper's shoulders with his back turned to the woman.

"What's wrong?"

"Right there! Turn around!" Piper shouted at Joe, desperate for him to see the woman too.

Piper followed Joe's eyes as he scanned the clearing and the small patch of trees seeing no one or nothing. Where had she gone?

"I thought I saw something." *Or someone*, thought Piper.

"It could've been a deer or another animal. Are you okay? You are shaking," Joe asked her concerned as he rubbed his hands up and down her arms.

No, she wasn't okay, but how could she explain to Joe what she had just seen? Why was this woman appearing in her life and more frequently? She needed to get answers, but how?

"I'm fine. I just startled myself. It must have been a deer or something. I always see them out in the morning."

Joe began pulling on his pants and tugged his shirt on over his head. He slipped his shoes on and held out the dress for Piper to put on.

"I would rather be taking this dress off than helping you put it on," Joe teased as Piper snatched the dress from him and quickly slipped it over her head.

"Don't tempt me." Piper smiled as she slipped on her sandals and started to fold the blanket into a neat square.

"I have to work in my classroom for a good chunk of the day. I need to get my bulletin boards up and ready for class. School starts in a week. Teachers have to go back before the students, but they will be starting soon enough. Could we meet up later in the day and grab dinner?"

"Sure. I would like that. I will keep you posted on what I hear from Joan on the house. Maybe we will have some celebrating to do."

They walked back up to the house, and Joe opened the door to his truck. He pulled Piper in close and took her lips against his. He lazily and softly kissed her. He laid his right hand against the side of her face.

"Have a good day. I hope you get lots done. I will check in with you later."

"Sounds good. Call me if you hear from Joan." Joe climbed into his truck and backed out of the driveway. He returned the wave that Piper gave him and headed down the road.

Joe had almost made it back to his uncle's house when his cell phone rang.

"Hi, Joe. It's Joan. I just heard back from the sellers. They apologized for taking so long to get back to you. He was on a business trip and just returned into town late last night. He has a counteroffer for you. Do you have time to meet me at the office so we can go over it?"

"I sure can. How about I come to your office in forty-five minutes. Does that work?" That would give him enough time to shower and change his clothes.

"That works just fine. See you then."

In precisely forty-three minutes, Joe rolled up to Joan's office and strolled inside. The secretary greeted him and told him that Joan was waiting for him in the conference room. She led him down the hall to where Joan was waiting with a cup of coffee and a stack of papers.

"Good morning, Joe. How are you? Would you like a cup of coffee?"

"Sure. Thank you. I am fine. How did the offer turn out?"

"I think you are going to be pleased for the most part. He agreed to closing and possession in one month. All of the items we asked to stay at the house will stay including the makeup table. The only thing that was changed was the price. He countered at ten thousand dollars, higher than your offer. We can counter again. We also have ten days to do an inspection."

"Let's meet him halfway on price and come up another five thousand dollars. Everything else is acceptable to me."

"Why don't I go see if I can get a hold of him now? His agent said that he was free this morning. I will be right back." Joan walked out the door and headed back to her office.

Joe was nervous, but an excited nervous. It would be nice to be in his own place. He had some ideas for the house and how he could make it feel more like his. \ First things first, he needed to own it.

Joan walked through the doorway with a big smile on her face. "Excellent news. The seller has agreed to your terms. Congratulations! Now we will schedule the inspection, and as long as that goes well, the house will be yours and close in a month."

Joe stood up and shook Joan's hand. "Thank you so much for your hard work. I am really excited."

"I will call and set up the inspection this afternoon. What day this week or next works for your schedule?"

"I start work on Monday, so this week would work the best."

"I will call and see what is available and get back to you this afternoon."

"Thanks. Have a good rest of your day. Talk to you later this afternoon." Joe slid back his chair and put his hands on the table to push him up. He couldn't wait to tell Piper the news.

Piper worked in her classroom most of the day. A few of the other teachers she would be working with were there too. She made plans to go to lunch tomorrow with Stacy, a fellow teacher, who promised that she would help Piper with her first week of lesson plans.

Piper worked on making name tags for the students' desks. She made a job chart and clipped their names on their mailboxes. She began labeling the chapter books that she had bought for her classroom library. Her morning and afternoon flew by. Her stomach grumbled, and she realized that she hadn't eaten anything all afternoon except for a Snickers candy bar. She glanced at her watch and saw that it was close to three thirty. She decided that she should start wrapping things up since she was meeting Joe for dinner.

She knelt down to pick up a piece of paper off of the floor, and when she stood up, her head was swimming. Her heart pushed against her chest and began to race. She grimaced and instinctively reached her right hand up and rubbed her chest. She coughed hard a few times hoping to get her heartbeat regulated. She began to get dizzy, and then everything went black.

When Piper woke up, she was crouched on the floor on her knees. She reached out and ran her hand through the beige shag rug that she was sitting on. he glanced around and noticed that she recognized this place. It was the house that Joe had made an offer on, except this house was decorated, and the furniture had been strategically placed. The décor was modern with a sleek white couch and a glass coffee table. Nothing was on the end tables or the coffee table. The walls were painted a light gray, and all of the furniture had clean lines. Nothing was out of place. Not a speck of dust was to be found. She looked over to the rug where she had been sitting. It used to have very neat vacuum lines in it, and now she could see where her footprints were that had crushed and matted down the rug.

There weren't any personal effects to give her a clue to whose house she was in. She decided to trudge upstairs to see if she could find answers there. She reached the top of the stairs and started into the master bedroom on the right. The king-sized bed was neatly made with a white comforter, and the bed was anchored by an upholstered headboard.

She gasped when she turned her head and saw the same makeup table that had been left in the house that Joe was buying. She walked over to it and fingered the makeup brushes and powders that were neatly lined up. Her hand reached over and picked up the small silver frame. Her hand went to her mouth in disbelief as she stared down at the people in the picture. She was looking at herself in a wedding dress, yet the woman in the picture had blonde hair. It was pulled back away from her face and covered with a veil, but Piper could still see that the hair hidden beneath the veil was definitely blonde. The woman appeared to be laughing with her head tilted back and was holding onto a man that looked identical to Joe. He was neatly dressed in a black tuxedo and was smiling down at the laughing woman. Piper quickly returned the picture to the makeup table. She had to get out of this house.

She began to run down the stairs and was heading for the back door when she heard a whimpering noise coming from the laundry room. She cautiously made her way toward the sound. She was relieved to find a puppy behind a baby gate lying on an oversized dog bed.

"Hi, little fella." He moved over to her wagging his tail so hard that it shook his whole rear end. He placed his front legs on the gate and began to lick her hand. He looked to be less than a year old and was a Bassett Hound.

"Let's see what your collar says your name is. Toby Reynolds," Piper said out loud, and then stopped herself. Reynolds? Like Joe Reynolds?

Piper felt herself slipping away from the house and the unfamiliar furniture. When she woke, she was sitting on the floor in her classroom. She leaned her head back against the cupboard and tried to make sense of where she had just been. She looked up at the clock that hung over her classroom door. It read 4:30. She had been gone for nearly an hour. The first time she had jumped, that is what she decided to call it, the episode lasted a few mere minutes. This time she had been gone for close to an hour. She needed to tell someone about what was happening to her. In that instant she knew whom she needed to tell. She needed to tell Joe, and she needed to tell him soon.

She got in her car headed toward home. When Piper pulled into the driveway, she realized that she wasn't entirely sure how she had gotten home. She had driven home automatically and hadn't even thought about the turns because her mind was so preoccupied on this other woman and her life and how closely it paralleled her own life.

She shut off the car and pulled her keys from the ignition. She climbed out of the small white Mazda Miata and shut the door. She used the keypad to let herself into the garage noticing that her mom's car was already in the garage.

She found her mom in the kitchen making dinner. "Hi, stranger. I haven't seen much of you lately. Are you going to be staying for dinner? I am making tacos."

"Hi, Mom. I am going to dinner with Joe. I hope he has found out about his house. He made an offer on one yesterday and is hoping that he would get an answer today. How have you been?"

"I am good. I have been keeping busy with my book and gardening club. I am hosting the book club here next week, so I will have to get everything set up for that. How is the working in your classroom going?" Claire asked.

"It is going. A few of the veteran teachers have been helping me. I really like my mentor too. I found out today that I have twenty-three students in my class. I can't believe that school starts next week."

Piper's cell phone rang. She pulled it from her pocket and noticed it was Joe.

"Hello?" she answered.

"Hi. Are we still on for dinner tonight?"

"I'm planning on it. What time are you thinking?" Piper answered.

"I am starving. I missed lunch, so I can go anytime."

"Me too. I only had a candy bar, so I am hungry too." Thinking back to the candy bar brought her thoughts back to the jump that she had done only about an hour before. She became distracted and realized that she had stopped listening to what Joe was saying.

"Hello? Are you still there?" Joe asked.

"Oh, sorry. I was thinking about something. Do you want to pick me up in about twenty minutes? We can go to dinner at Jasmine's if that sounds good."

"That works for me. See you soon."

"Bye." Piper hung up the phone and returned it to her pocket. She smiled at her mom who was doing her best to look busy, like she hadn't just eavesdropped on the entire conversation.

"You have been seeing a lot of Joe. How are things going with him?" she asked casually while she began chopping up the lettuce for the tacos.

"Things are going well. I really like him, Mom. I have to run and get freshened up. He will be here soon to pick me up."

"Enjoy your dinner, dear. See you later."

"Thanks! We will talk more later," Piper called over her shoulder as she was already making her way up the stairs.

Piper decided on some jean Capri's with brown sandals. She pulled the light blue halter-top over her head and ran a brush through her hair. She powdered her nose and brushed her teeth. She added a fresh coat of lipstick and took once last look in the mirror before grabbing her purse and heading downstairs.

They were settled into a cozy corner booth when Joe said, "I have news. I got the house! I close in a month. Everything was pretty easy to agree upon in the contract."

"That is wonderful news. I bet you are so excited. Congratulations!" Piper reached over and squeezed his hand. She smiled at him and admired how relaxed and happy he looked. His dark hair had fallen across his eye. She watched him as he brushed his hand through his hair putting it back in place. His eyes had a sparkle in them as he told her about the negotiation process and how the counteroffer had gone.

The waitress came over and took their drink orders. "I will have a Blue Moon please," said Piper.

"I think I will have the same." Joe was looking over the menu at the new food items that Anna had just added. "I may try the special tonight. It looks good. I haven't had steak for a while."

The waitress brought the beers over and placed a basket of bread on the table. "Be careful with the bread. It just came out of the oven. What can I get you to eat?" She looked over at Piper first.

"I will have the small filet please. Can I have it medium well? Also can I get a side salad with ranch please?"

"Sure, that is just a little bit of pink in the center. Does that work? Do you want any French fries or a baked potato?" the waitress asked.

"That is great. I will have a baked potato with just cheese and bacon please."

The waitress turned to Joe. "What can I get for you?"

"I am going to have the special tonight. Can I get my steak medium rare please? I will have a salad with blue cheese and well done French fries, so they are crispy."

"That also comes with broccoli or asparagus spears. Which do you prefer?" she asked Joe.

"I will have the asparagus please."

"Coming right up." The waitress closed her pad with their orders and walked away.

"I'm really excited for you, Joe. I am so glad that you got the house. I can tell you are happy. I need to tell you something, and I am not sure how you are going to react. I have thought about how I would tell you this in my mind all day, and am worried what you are going to say." Piper was uneasy as she wondered how Joe would react to her jumps.

Joe leaned in toward her. He had a nervous feeling in the pit of his stomach.

"What is it? You know you can tell me anything, Piper," Joe added cautiously.

Piper knew that the next few moments would tell a lot about Joe and how he felt about her. She thought about how crazy it was going to sound when she told him about what she had seen and experienced.

"I don't even know where to start," Piper began. "The first time I experienced this, I was in the backyard planting flowers for my mom. I started to feel kind of funny. I got a little dizzy, and my heart started beating really fast. I think I blacked out. When I woke, I went into the house to get a glass of water. But the house wasn't my parents' house. It looked the same from the outside, but the inside was not the same."

The server brought the salads to the table and asked if they needed anything else. She moved away from the table, and Piper continued with her story. Joe was listening so intently that he didn't pick up his silverware to eat his salad. He just sat with his eyes on her and hanging on every word, trying to absorb the information.

When Piper got to the part where she saw the other woman that looks just like her, Joe's eyes got a little bigger, and his mouth opened slightly. He wasn't commenting on anything yet. He was just letting her tell her story.

When she finished with the part about how the glass had shattered on the kitchen floor and how she woke up outside at her parent's house, Piper stopped talking and waited patiently for his reaction.

Joe took a pull on his beer. He set the bottle down but didn't let go of it. He hung on to it and moved the bottle, making the beer swish around in circles. Piper could see that he was wrestling with the story she had just told him.

Finally Joe spoke, "That is unbelievable, Piper. I mean really unbelievable. I do believe you and what happened to you. I can't explain why I do, but I believe you. It sounds crazy. Has it only happened once?"

"That's just it. It has happened three times now." Piper dug into her purse and pulled out her wallet. Tucked inside the back zipper she pulled out a tiny heart charm. She handed it over to Joe.

It looked so miniature in the palm of his large hands. He examined it closely, and then looked up with surprise at Piper.

"What is this?" Joe asked turning the charm over in his hand.

"That is what I found after my second jump. I was down by my parents' pond and when she appeared and I tried to chase her. It must have dropped off of her bracelet. I found it tucked in some matted grass that had been pushed down from where she was running."

Joe's head was spinning. "You said that you have "jumped" three times. What happened the third time?"

Piper explained what had happened this afternoon. She told Joe about his house, although it wasn't his house precisely.

Joe picked at his salad and pulled off a chunk of bread and dipped it in the olive oil. He placed a piece of bread in his mouth and silently sat chewing his bread while he was trying to wrap his mind around what Piper had just told him.

"It really isn't even worth it trying to figure out how it happens or why?" Piper quietly stated. "I have been trying to understand it all since it started happening, and the only thing I could come up with was I am crazy or it was a dream. But when I found the charm, it all became real for me. Concrete. She is real and as alive as you or me."

The server came to the table and delivered the meals to each of them. She asked if they needed anything else. Joe thanked her saying that they were fine.

"I am sorry that you have been struggling with all of this on your own. How can I help?" Joe asked concerned.

"I don't really know how you can help. I guess just be here for me and not think I am crazy."

"Well, any crazier than you already are," Joe tried to make light of the situation to take some of the tension out of the air.

"Of course. It does feel really good to be able to share this with you." Piper leaned in and gave him a quick squeeze of the hand. She put her lips on his and sweetly kissed him for a few seconds before pulling away with a smile. "Thanks for being here for me."

The rest of the meal hurried by with talk of what Piper was going to do the next time it happened. Joe tried to change the topic a few different times with talk of the house, but Piper was distracted. He tried to reassure her that it was all going to be okay even though he felt like he was trying to assure himself the same thing.

They finished the meal, and Joe paid the bill. They walked out into the steamy night. The humidity was high today, and it felt like he was drinking the air. He opened the truck door for Piper. She slid in, and then leaned over to open his door. They drove back to her parents' house mostly in silence, both of them having a lot on their minds.

As the truck rolled into the driveway, a few rocks crunched underneath the tires as it slowed to a stop. Piper asked Joe if he wanted to come in.

"Do you mind if I take a rain check? I have a lot on my mind now. I am going to try and figure this out for us, Piper. Please try not to worry. Let me know if it happens again. In the meantime, why don't you get some rest, and we can talk more tomorrow?" He took a hold of her face with both hands and looked into her big green eyes that were gazing back at them full of worry and concern.

She nodded and somehow did feel slightly comforted in the fact that she had told him, and he hadn't just blown her off or thought she was crazy. She leaned her head on his shoulder and sighed. She glanced up at him and managed a smile. He bent his head and slowly took her lips on his. He took his time and was surprised at how her warm lips could set his body off in little fireworks. He responded to her touch, and she seemed to melt into him.

She pulled away from him and could smell his aftershave on her skin. She walked to the door and raised her hand up in a small wave. She watched him pull out of the driveway and felt a sense of relief that she had told him. Hopefully he would be able to come up with some answers as to what was happening to her.

Seven

*   *   *

"It's a great day at Reynolds's Realty. How may I direct your call?" Rose answered cheerfully. "Sure. Just a moment please." Rose punched a button on the phone and hung it up. She glanced up and smiled as she saw the trim blonde woman tucked arm and arm with the tall gorgeous man come around the corner.

The sunlight caught hold of Pip's golden spun hair, and it seemed to illuminate her face. She reached up and tucked her hair behind one ear to keep it from blowing in her eyes. Joe stopped to pull open the door for her, and as she slid passed him, he thought about how lucky he was to have met her five years ago.

"Good morning, newlyweds! How are you, boss? I put all of your messages on your desk. Pip, I just sent a call to your voicemail too."

"Thank you, Rose," Joe said, and then turned to Pip. "I will catch up with you later." He gave her a quick peck on the cheek and walked briefcase in hand into his office.

Pip stopped at the mailboxes and gathered her mail before heading to her office.

She smiled as she walked in and glanced at the nameplate on her desk that read Pip Reynolds. She still wasn't used to her new name even though she had been married for six months. She sighed happily as she thought about her life and how happy she was.

She had gone to college to become a teacher but on a whim decided that she would go to a real estate seminar that one of the local brokers was having on how to become a real estate agent. She thought, what the hell? She didn't have anything to lose and went to see what it was all about.

There were nine other people that had the same idea that night. When she strolled in and took a seat in the front, she had no idea how her life was about to change.

In walked the most handsome man she had ever seen. He was dressed sharply in a crisp white shirt with silver cuff links. He had on an ice blue paisley tie that matched his eyes. His hair was slightly longer and was so dark brown that it was almost black and had just enough waves in it to appear tousled and damn sexy. He was tall, probably standing around six feet five inches and commanded attention. He had structured cheekbones and beautiful white teeth. When he smiled, his eyes lit up and had just the right amount of smile lines around his eyes and mouth. Pip imagined kissing that mouth, and her body responded just from thinking about the warmth of his lips.

That night as she listened to him speak about the opportunities in real estate, she found that she was fascinated. It would be a definite perk to work closely with him, but the real estate business intrigued her as well. When he finished talking and explaining how to get a real estate license, she decided to go and introduce herself.

Joe had noticed her as soon as she had walked into the room and took a seat in the front. He found that he had a hard time concentrating on what he was talking about. He found himself getting distracted by her pale gray green eyes. They seemed to take him in and fascinated him. Her lips had been painted a dark, plum color and were glossy and found that he couldn't take his eyes off of her pouty mouth as she laughed at something the person next to her said. He imagined what it would be like to take her lips onto his. Her hair was the color of spun gold and was sleek and shiny, as it swung just under her shoulders in a styled bob. She was athletic and toned, and her shapely long legs seem to go on for miles from what he could see of them in her dress skirt.

Pip strolled causally over to Joe and gave him an easy smile as she walked up to him extending her hand. "Hi, Joe. I am Pip Samson. I really enjoyed your talk about the real estate business. You definitely have my curiosity piqued. I would like more information on how I can get started. How long have you been in this business?"

"Hi, Pip. It is my pleasure to meet you. I am glad that you found my talk interesting. I would be glad to help you get started in the business. To answer your question, my dad has been in this business for thirty-five years. I have grown up with talk of real estate constantly around me. When I finished high school, I decided that I would go into business with him. I got my license that year and was a salesperson for a few years. I got my broker's license after I was in the business for about six years. My dad recently retired, and I took over as the managing broker of this office. I currently have sixty-seven agents under me."

"Wow. That sounds interesting. Could you be talked into grabbing dinner with me tonight? I would like to pick your brain a little more about this if you don't have plans?"

Joe smiled easily. He would gladly clear his plans to go to dinner with this beautiful woman. "I actually don't have plans. I cleared my schedule for tonight's seminar."

"Great! Do you want to go up to the new Italian place on the corner of Dobson and Grant? I can meet you there after you finished up here." Pip glanced back at the causal line that had formed behind her, all wanting a moment of Joe's time.

"Sure. I will get there as soon as I can finish up here." He smiled at her and shook her hand.

Joe watched her easy stride as she moved away from him. He turned to the man that had been patiently waiting behind her. "Hello. What questions can I answer for you?"

Pip smiled to herself thinking back to that evening when she met her future husband. She had gone on to get her real estate license and had been Rookie of the Year her first year in the business. She found her knack for the business and related well to her clients. They seem to like her soft-sell approach but understood that she would fight hard to protect their interests. About 65 percent of her business now was repeat clients who were looking to make a move up. Another 25 percent were referrals from her past clients. She had made a name for herself in the real estate community and was proud of herself for her accomplishments.

Her husband joked with her and said one day soon she would probably get her broker's license and try and take away the managing position from him. She didn't have any interest in that right now. She was happy helping people find their dream homes and teaching real estate classes at night and weekends. She felt like she used her education a little when she taught the classes. She found that she really liked sharing her real estate experiences and related them to the classes that she taught.

Pip's office phone rang, and it snapped her out of her daydream. "Good morning, this is Pip Reynolds. Oh, hi, Tammy. Just calm down. I will be right over and bring some new property disclosures with me. Don't worry, we will get it taken care of. Okay, sure. See you soon."

Joe had been standing in the doorway watching her. As she hung up her phone, she began to nibble on her lip, a nervous habit that she had been doing ever since he knew her.

"What's up? Was that Tammy over on Crestview Drive?" Joe asked Pip curiously.

"It was. After that big storm last night, she got water in her basement. I am taking over new property disclosures for her to fill out. I will also help her get someone in to get the water mess cleaned up. I am going to head over there now before my appointment with my new clients at two. Should I just meet you at home tonight for dinner?"

"That sounds good. I have a closing in the morning and just need to check with loan officer that everything is set. I hope your appointment

goes well. I will be anxious to hear about it. I will have the wine ready."
He winked at her and headed out of her office and down to his.

She pulled a stack of paper from her left desk drawer and clipped
them together. She stuffed them into her briefcase and grabbed her keys
and purse. She called good-bye to Rose as she pushed open the door and
headed to her car.

She depressed the unlock button on her remote key. Her white
BMW X5 lights flashed and beeped as the door unlocked. She threw her
purse onto the passenger seat and started up the car. Her music came on
blaring. She was glad that she was the only one in the car. She laughed to
herself and could hear Joe saying that she was jamming out again. She
couldn't help it and always listened to music and sang at the top of her
lungs to every song on the radio.

She swung her car into the driveway of the cute brick bungalow that
she had just listed two weeks ago. The property had already had a lot of
interest in it, and she hoped that they would get an offer soon. Tammy
and her husband, Frank, were selling and moving into a retirement
community. Tammy was a sweet older woman that reminded Pip of her
aunt. She strode up the sidewalk and found Tammy was waiting at the
door holding onto her toy poodle, Bear.

Pip fondly scratched the small dog between the ears and gave a warm
hello to Tammy. She stepped inside the bright, cheerful home and said to
Tammy, "Let's go have a look at the basement."

Pip quickly assessed the damage in the basement and pulled out a business
card of a local cleaner that specialized in water damage and cleanup.

"Here is Flynn's number. Please tell him that I sent you to him, and he
will give you 15 percent off. He gives my clients a deal on his services,"
Pip handed Tammy the card. She gave her the property disclosure forms
for her to fix, and once they were initialed and signed, Piper placed them
in her briefcase.

"That should do it. I will bring over the new disclosures to leave at
the house tomorrow. Have a good afternoon, Tammy. Bye, Bear." She
patted the dog's head and slipped through the front door.

Pip headed back to her office and had a few minutes to spare before she was meeting with her new clients. They had found her off of her webpage and were driving in from out of town. Over the next couple of days, Pip hoped that she would be able to help them find a suitable house.

She ran into the restroom quickly and had just returned to her office when she was paged. "Angie and Tate Highstrom are here to see you, Pip," Rose said over her intercom. She glanced down at her watch. They were right on time.

Pip pulled into the driveway of her light gray two-storey house and saw that Joe had all of the front lights burning. She still was amazed that they had found this perfect house. It was so welcoming with the white front porch that wrapped around the side of the house. They had spent so much time out on the porch swing having a glass of wine and discussing their days. She loved all of the natural light that poured into the house on sunny days. On the chilly fall days, she liked warming herself up in front of the large stone fireplace that was really the centerpiece of the great room.

She sighed happily to herself and smiled when she walked into the kitchen. Joe had his back to her and was busy slicing up some tomatoes for the salad. He had an open bottle of red wine on the counter and had already poured himself a glass. He was quietly humming along to the country music he had playing in the background. Joe liked all different types of music, but tonight he must've been in the mood for a little Kenny Chesney.

Pip came up behind Joe and slid her arms around his chest and gave him a quick squeeze. She rested her cheek on his back shoulder. He felt so warm and could feel his muscular back through his dress shirt that he still was wearing.

"Hi, babe. Sorry I'm a little later than I thought I would be. I just finished up with Angie and Tate," Pip told him while he began pouring her a glass of wine.

He handed her the glass and asked, "How did it go with them? Did you see some good houses?"

Pip took a sip of her wine, and then leaned back against the counter, cupping her wine glass in her right hand. "Well, we just got started. We saw some of their house picks this afternoon. She had found a bunch on the Internet that she wanted to see. I had already seen most of them. Do you remember that one over on Vine Street?"

"How could I forget? It was a disaster and smelled really badly," Joe replied and shook his head remembering the house that they had toured a few months back and took a sip of his wine.

"Right, that's the one. The one that needed a fresh coat of fire," Pip teased and snapped a bite off of a carrot that Joe was cutting up for the salad. "Tomorrow we are looking at my choices of houses. I think that they will be pleased at what I have found for them to look at. What are we having for dinner? It smells amazing."

Joe turned on the oven light, and Pip peered into the oven and smiled when she saw the bubbling lasagna made courtesy of Stouffer's.

"They really do make a mean lasagna. I made garlic bread with lots of garlic." Pip laughed, and as the sound of her laugh traveled over the music, Joe found that the sound still made his insides jump. He looked at Pip, and then at the timer on the oven that was counting down from twenty-two minutes.

Joe smiled devilishly, and Pip could feel his eyes on her as she looked up, still with a carrot in one hand and her wine in the other. He just had to look at her with those eyes, and she would feel a tingling feeling in her belly and begin to get warm. She put her glass and carrot down and reached up to pull her clip out of her hair that held the sides up and away from her face. Joe watched the strands of silky blonde hair fall loosely around her face.

Joe usually let Pip take the lead on how they made love. Sometimes she wanted it in a quieter, slow pace where they would lazily make love and take their time. Other times Pip wanted it fast and hard. This was one of those times. He was happy to oblige.

He reached up and ran his fingers through her hair, and then stopped with his hands on each side of her face. She reached up and wrapped her hands around his wrists, and stretching up on her tiptoes, she angled her head so she could hungrily crush her lips on his. The reaction in her body was the same as it was the first time they had kissed. His lips sparked a million little sensations that rocketed through her body, threatening to explode all at once.

She began to quickly untie his tie, and whipping it off, she tossed it aside. She was struggling with unbuttoning his shirt while he was trying to get her jacket off. She kept working on the buttons with her right hand and reached up and grabbed his head with her left. She yanked his head down so she could plunder his lips and softly moaned. He closed his mouth on hers, breathing in her soft noises.

She quickly became impatient with how long he was taking to get her jacket and shirt off. Pip peeled her shirt off and unhooked her black lace bra. She unzipped her skirt and stepped out of it revealing a black thong underneath.

She was beautiful standing there. Her face had gotten slightly flushed, and she stood staring at him with her green eyes ablaze with desire.

She pressed herself against him and slightly began moving her hips against his, until he was throbbing with desire. "I want you," she murmured as she ran her hands up his bare chest, her eyes pleading with him to take her.

Joe reached down and cupped her rear end in both hands and pulled her up until she was straddling him with her legs wrapped around his back. He slipped into her easily. He continued to stand with her wrapped around him, and he backed her up to lean against the cupboards.

She arched her back and tilted her head back. She softly sighed his name. "I need more. Faster," she commanded.

He was plunging deep inside of her and knew that she was close to the edge. He was too. They continued to move as one until her eyes snapped open. Her eyes locked with his as they came over the wave together.

They sat down on the floor, spent, and then heard the oven timer going off. They looked at each other and laughed.

Pip jumped up and shut off the timer. "Thank goodness! I am starving. Can you go grab our robes while I pull this out of the oven please?"

"Sure thing." He strode out of the kitchen and headed toward the stairs.

"Nice ass!" Pip catcalled to him as he was leaving.

"I know, you can never get enough," he taunted her as he turned the corner to head upstairs.

They ate their dinner that night with the wax slowly melting the candles as Pip filled Joe in on her day and about her appointment with her new clients. Pip cleared their plates and told Joe to go and relax while she did the dishes.

"I can do them," Joe stated.

"It's the least I can do since you made dinner." Joe ended up sitting at the counter and talked to her while she loaded the dishes into the dishwasher. Pip loved evenings like these. She felt so relaxed and happy.

"I'm going to take Toby on a walk around the block. Do you want to come with me?" Joe asked leaning down to snap the leash on Toby's collar.

"No, I think I will just relax and read a book for a little bit," she kissed him good-bye, and then sat down on the white couch and tucked her legs up under her. She reached down to get her book, and when she sat back up, she started to feel dizzy.

Pip's heart began to race and thud. She could hear the thumping beating in her ears. Everything went black.

*   *   *

When Pip woke, she was still in her house, but it wasn't her house. There were boxes stacked all around the room. Some of the tops of the boxes were opened. As she looked closer at the boxes, she noticed that they were moving boxes labeled with what room the boxes went in.

She heard a clattering noise in the kitchen and began to walk toward the noise. She had a sinking feeling that she already knew who she would find there. She rounded the corner and standing in a pink tank top and cut-off jean shorts stood the woman that looked like her with the dark, chestnut hair. She was reaching up putting coffee mugs into the cupboard. She was quietly singing under her breath.

Pip stood and watched her. When she finished placing the mugs up on the top shelf, she turned and let out a shriek.

"It's you! Who are you, and where do you keep coming from?" Piper asked from the kitchen.

Stuffing her hands in her robe pocket, Pip replied, "I was just about to ask you the same thing. My name is Pip Reynolds. Who are you, and why do you look just like me?"

"Pip Reynolds? I'm Piper Samson. Are you married to Joe Reynolds?" Piper's hands began to shake. This was surreal.

"How do you know my husband? Does he know you?" Pip had just gotten her question out of her mouth when the image of Piper Samson began to fade, and then turned black.

*   *   *

Pip woke on the couch in a cold sweat and shivered. She wrapped her arms around herself in an attempt to settle herself. It wasn't helping. She heard the garage door creak open, and she ran into the mudroom where Joe was just walking in with the dog. She threw herself into his arms and buried her face in his chest.

"Baby, what's wrong? You're shaking. Look at me." Joe pulled her away from him so he could look at her. She looked up at him with a startled expression on her pale, white face, and her eyes had a look of desperation in them.

Eight

*   *   *

"Joe! Joe!" Piper hollered as she ran from the kitchen. She tripped over the edge of a box and quickly resumed her balance as she took the stairs two at a time.

"In here," Joe called from the master bedroom. She found him in the midst of a stack of boxes. He was collapsing the ones that he had already unpacked and was piling them in a corner. "What is it, Piper?"

"She was here—in the kitchen. I talked to her," Piper was out of breath.

"Who was here in the kitchen?" Joe asked as he moved toward her.

"The woman that looks like me. I talked to her and found out her name. It's Pip Reynolds," Piper explained. "She is married to Joe Reynolds." She watched Joe's expression as he figured out what that meant.

"You mean that she is married to another version of me? This is totally bizarre. What exactly did she say?"

"We just exchanged names, and when she told me hers, I asked if she was married to Joe Reynolds. She asked me how I knew her husband and if her husband knew me. Then she vanished as quickly as she appeared. She was wearing a white bathrobe. She looks just like me with the exception of her blonde hair. It makes me wonder if her life is like mine, except now I know that she is married."

"She obviously has extremely good taste in men," Joe joked trying to lighten the mood. Piper smiled slightly.

"I don't know why our lives are interconnected. It seems as though we are drawn to one another. I haven't figured out any more than that, but I really don't feel like she is a threat to me. I felt this time that she was as uneasy as I am about the whole thing. I wish the experience had lasted longer."

"Let's take a break from unpacking for a little while. Let's go and have a drink and sit out on the front porch. All of this stuff will still be here tomorrow. Thank you so much for agreeing to help me unpack. It would've taken me days to do all of this." Joe took Piper's hand and led her down to the kitchen.

The nights were starting to get chilly. "Piper, why don't you go and grab a blanket out of that box cleverly marked 'blankets,' and I will whip us up a drink that will warm us up." He strode into the kitchen and went to work on whipping up a mixture of hot chocolate laced with Bailey's Irish Crème and melted two Andes mints into the mug. He was just finishing up stirring the drinks when Piper came in with a red and black plaid blanket in her hands.

Joe grabbed one mug in each hand and headed outside to sit on the front porch with Piper. They sat down on the porch swing, and Piper spread the blanket out so it covered both of them. She took a sip of her drink.

"This is really good. Perfect for a night like this," she said as she leaned her head on Joe's shoulder and listened to the creaking of the swing as she slowly pushed it back and forth with her toes.

"Do you know what is perfect?" Piper looked up at Joe and waited for him to continue. "You are, Piper. These last few months with you have been really special to me. You are really special to me, Piper. I hope that I am not scaring you off by telling you this, but I love you. I have been falling in love you with for some time now." Joe looked down and cleared his throat. He hoped that Piper felt the same way about him but needed her to know how he felt.

"I love you too." She reached up and stroked her fingers through his hair and let her right hand fall and rest against his face. She brought her lips to his and slowly savored the moist and warmth of his mouth. She found comfort there and in him. She felt loved and protected.

"Will you stay tonight with me? This house doesn't feel complete without you in it," Joe asked Piper, his eyes almost pleading with her.

"Okay. You twisted my arm," Piper laughed and stood up and grabbed his hand and pulled him up with her. "I'm cold. Come inside and warm me up."

She led him into the great room and started to move some of the boxes away from the fireplace. Joe flipped the switch and turned the fireplace on. It roared to life, and the flames seem to lick and devour the logs. The fire crackled and snapped and put out a warm glow.

Piper stood in front of the fireplace and held her hands out in front of her to warm herself up. Joe looked down at this beautiful woman, and then wrapped his arms around her torso from behind. They rocked in place, and Piper leaned her head back against Joe's chest. She let out a contented sigh.

Joe reached down and softly moved Piper's hair so that it fell onto one shoulder exposing her neck. He slowly began to trail kisses down starting from her ear to her shoulder blade. She reached up with her left arm and ran her hand through his hair, anchoring his head on her neck. He continued to suck and lick his way around, exploring all of her arched neck.

Piper got goose bumps just from his touch and began to tremble with anticipation. It felt so good to be pressed up against him with her back molded into his muscular chest. His mouth seemed to know all of the right spots that made her insides get tingly and raw with desire.

Joe picked her up swiftly and cradled her in his arms. He walked over to the soft red rug and carefully laid her down. His sometimes rough and demanding hands were gentle and slow, taking his time with each caress and stroke as he touched her.

He wanted to see and taste every inch of her and savor each moment. He carefully pulled her jean shorts over her small hips, inching them down until they were completely off. She lifted her arms above her head allowing him to pull the tank top off and shaking loose her hair in the process. Her shiny hair of loose curls tumbled down around her shoulders. She sat wearing just her panties in the light of the fire and looked up at him through her eyelashes.

"You are wearing too many clothes," she told Joe, her voice husky with desire. Her breath caught as she watched him pull off his clothes and place them aside. She peeled off her panties and lay back, pulling him with her.

He slid into her slowly, and she shuddered at the pure pleasure of it. As his hips slowly started to move, she matched his motion while keeping her eyes on his. His mouth closed on hers and possessively held her lips in a deep and sultry kiss.

She slowly ran her fingertips over his back and began to move her hips, urging him to go faster. "No. I want to take my time. Enjoy each moment," he whispered to her. She nodded and closed her eyes for a minute, taking in the feeling of moving as one.

Love seemed to pour through every inch of his being and filled her. She savored each movement. When she couldn't hang on any longer, she moaned his name. As she was still shuddering in a moment of pure pleasure, he joined her and rode the wave until it washed over both of them.

Piper woke in the morning with the sunlight streaming in through the windows. She reached over to the other side of the bed, her hand searching for him. The sheets were still warm, but he was gone. She sat up and ran a hand lightly through her hair.

"Good morning, beautiful. I made us some breakfast," Joe said, and he strode in carrying a tray of scrambled eggs, fruit, and toast. He placed it on the bed next to her and leaned down to quickly kiss her before climbing back into bed.

She stabbed a fork through one of the strawberries and popped it in her mouth. "What are your plans for the day, babe?"

"Actually this may sound crazy to you, but I think I need a dog. I couldn't have one at my old place because I lived in the city in an apartment. I have a fence here now and plenty of room. I want to go to the animal shelter and see what dogs are up for adoption. Do you want to come with me?" Joe asked her.

"Are you kidding? I love dogs. I would like to come," Piper got excited to see all of the fuzz balls of puppies that would be wandering around. "My mom never let us have a dog when we were kids. She said that she didn't want the mess. Did you have a dog when you were little?" She asked between bites of toast.

Joe set down his orange juice, and then replied, "We always had dogs. We rescued each of them though and never bought them from a pet store. I thought now would be a good time to get a puppy before the weather gets cold. It isn't any fun to house-train a dog in the winter."

"Let me just hop in the shower and we can go," Piper told Joe as she was already moving toward the bathroom.

"I will clean up the breakfast dishes and will unpack more boxes while I am waiting for you to get ready." Joe took the tray and whistled as he walked down the stairs and into the kitchen, happy and feeling grateful that he had met Piper.

When they arrived at the shelter, there were so many different puppies to choose from. A woman at the front desk led them back to a visitation room and asked which puppy they wanted to see first.

"Could you just bring in a few different kinds please? I am not sure what kind I want yet," Joe asked the woman.

"We just got in a new litter of Bassett Hounds. A woman found them in a ditch on the side of the road. There are three females and a male. I will bring them in," the rescue worker told Joe.

The pups came tumbling into the room tripping over each other and stepping on each other's ears, which drooped down covered with velvety fur. They were brown and white in coloring, and the male had a stripe of white down his face. His eyes looked sad, and he came over and plopped down at Joe's feet and whined, looking up at him with those big eyes and big ears. Joe reached down and scooped him up. His little body wiggled with delight as he put his front paws up on Joe's chest and began licking his face.

"Aren't you just the sweetest little fella? What do you think of him, Piper?"

Piper's heart had already melted at the first sight of the puppy. "He is perfect."

Joe told the woman that he would take the male puppy. He was busy picking out a collar for him and getting the necessary paperwork filled out. He filled the counter with toys, food, dishes, and a dog bed. Piper laughed as she watched him roam around the store looking for more things that his new puppy might need.

Once everything was paid for and everything was in order, they walked out of the store with the puppy cradled sleepily in Piper's arms. He snuggled into her lap as Joe pulled the truck away from the shelter and headed toward home.

"What do you think you will name him?" Piper asked Joe looking down at the warm little body that was curled up contently in her lap.

"I am going to name him Toby, I think," Joe explained. Even from the driver seat, Joe could see the shocked expression on Piper's face. "What's wrong? You don't like that name?"

"Joe, didn't I tell you that blonde Pip had a bassett hound puppy too? His name is Toby. So far I haven't found many things where she and I are alike, except for now this dog, and she also has the same makeup table that you have," Piper explained as she was stroking Toby's soft ear.

"I don't have to call him that. It was just a thought."

"Actually I think that the name is perfect for him. You know I believe that everything happens in life for a reason. There is a reason that the other Pip and my life are interconnected. I may not know what it is just yet, but there is a definite reason—a reason for everything," Piper spoke those words out loud as she watched the countryside pass by outside her window. She didn't know if she was trying to make Joe understand why Pip had come into her life or make herself understand. Either way she hoped that the reason would become clear soon.

Piper became quiet as she glanced out the window and bumped along on the road. She was lost in thought but did seem comforted holding onto Toby that slept, softly snoring nestled in her legs.

The days were getting shorter as the winter months came on with a vengeance. There was already so much snow on the ground, and winter had officially just started. Piper sighed as she looked out of the window. She hated the cold but had to admit watching the snowflakes fall silently was very peaceful. She stood at the kitchen window in her parent's house cradling a cup of hot tea in her hands. She looked out at the swirling snow and looked down to the frozen lake. Everything was blanketed in pure white snow.

She smiled as she thought of what her students were probably doing today since school had been cancelled, giving an early start to the weekend. She had actually enjoyed sleeping in this morning too with no place to go. Her mom was out helping her dad clear some snow at the airport. He had a new snowblower that he was so excited to use that he was clearing everyone's driveways and helping out complete strangers just to get a chance to use it.

It was nearly ten in the morning, and Piper was thinking ahead to the weekend. Joe had called her last night to ask her if she would go to a Bed and Breakfast about a half an hour away tonight to celebrate school conferences being over. He had also just wrapped up a large case at work and said that they needed to celebrate.

Piper trudged up the stairs to start packing for the weekend. Her sister-in-law had stayed at the Bed and Breakfast and raved about the food. She said that it was a lovely home run by a couple that had moved to the area fourteen years ago from New Jersey.

Piper began carefully folding her sweaters and placing them in her duffel bag. She took out her makeup bag and unfolded it. She saw something spill out of it, and it dropped to the floor, making a slight jingle noise. She glanced down and stooped to put up the small object. It was Pip's heart charm. It sat glittering in her hand, so delicate and tiny. She wondered what the story was with the charm. She tucked it into her pocket and made a mental note to get the clasp fixed on it.

She was folding her jeans neatly and was just about to place them in her bag when she heard a loud crash downstairs. Alarmed, she grabbed a hold of a bat out of her brother's room and quietly snuck down the stairs. She tiptoed around the wall that led to the kitchen with the baseball bat propped on her shoulder and ready to use.

"Damn it! Ouch!" Piper heard a woman's voice cussing in the kitchen and realized that it wasn't any woman's voice but her own. Blonde Pip was back and was standing at her parent's sink holding her bleeding finger.

Piper saw the wound and rushing over to her said, "What happened? Here, wrap this towel around it and apply some pressure." she handed Pip a dishtowel and wrapped it around her finger.

"Thanks," Pip responded tucking a blonde strand of hair behind her ear. "I don't know what happened. I was at my house cutting up an apple. My knife was dull and ended up cutting my finger instead. I remember looking down and seeing the blood, and the next thing I know, I'm here in your kitchen. Is this your house or your parent's house? It looks similar to my parent's house."

Piper studied the blonde woman that was standing in front of her talking to her like they were friends. She didn't even seem bothered by the fact that they looked identical, except for the color of their hair and that she dressed slightly differently with a bright blue silk dress shirt and black slacks. Piper was used to more casual clothes since she dealt with children all day and their messes.

"It's my parent's house. I moved back in with them when I got a new teaching job and moved back home. You seem like you're not bothered at all by our jumps. Does that mean that you have figured out why we have been popping into each other's lives?"

Pip chewed nervously on her bottom lip and glimpsed down at her hand that was still wrapped tightly in the yellow dishtowel. "No, I don't think that I have it all figured out yet why this is happening. I don't feel like you are a threat to me though. I feel as though I know you already. It sounds strange for me to say it out loud, but I feel like you are an extension of me. Our lives are a little bit different and maybe our personalities too, but I still think I know you."

This was the longest amount of time that they had ever had in the presence of one another. Piper thought about what she had said and replied, "I feel like you have been put in my life for a reason. I'm not sure I know yet why. I have something of yours." Piper reached into her pocket and pulled out the heart charm. She held it out for Pip.

Pip's green eyes lit up, and she replied excitedly, "You found it! I thought I lost it that day." She reached out to take the small charm from Piper's hand. When their hands met, Pip said, "I kind of was expecting a lightning bolt or something to happen when we touched."

Piper laughed and confessed, "Me too! What is the significance of the charm?"

"I got this charm bracelet from my gram. She started it with the little heart charm and would add to it when she went on trips. She would bring me home little trinkets from her travels. She meant the world to me. I just lost her this year. It was heartbreaking for me. I miss her every day." Pip sadly looked down and wiped away a single tear that had rolled down her face. "What about you Piper? Tell me about yourself."

"Well, I moved home to live with my folks until I can get a place of my own. I teach fourth grade at Silver Oaks Elementary School. I am dating an amazing man named Joe Reynolds. He bought the same house that you live in. I have to confess, I have been in your house before."

"What? Was anyone home?" Pip asked.

"No, I didn't see anyone, but I met your dog Toby. He was quite the watchdog and almost licked me to death," Piper explained.

"That would be my fearless dog. As you may have guessed, I am married to Joe Reynolds. We got married about ten months ago. We dated for quite a while before that. He is amazing as you say," Pip smiled, and her eyes lit up as she talked about Joe. "We met and are both real estate agents. He is the managing broker in my office."

"Why do you think that you are staying here for so long this time? Every time I have jumped it has only been for a few minutes, an hour at the most."

"I have never hurt myself before. I always jumped before when I was doing everyday things. Maybe being hurt or fear elongates it."

"How's your finger doing? Has it stopped bleeding?" Piper reached over and loosened the towel to look underneath it.

"It feels better. I can't feel my heart beating in it as much anymore. Uh, oh. I think I'm leav—" She didn't even finish her sentence before she vanished and left Piper standing, holding the yellow blood-stained dishtowel in her hand.

"Well, at least this time I found out more about her," Piper said out loud to no one. She looked down at the dishtowel and had proof that what she just experienced was real.

The snow had finished coming down only about two hours before. Everything was clean and white. The sunshine reflected off of the snow making it shimmer like diamonds. They pulled into the driveway of the inviting Bed and Breakfast. It had a large brick front porch and had dark green shutters. They walked up the wide front steps and were instantly greeted by a Siberian husky with bright blue eyes. He sauntered over and immediately wagged his tail and began licking Piper's hand.

She leaned down and stroked his soft fur and crooned to him, "Hi, good boy. What's your name?"

"Reggie, you leave those nice folks alone. Go lay down. Go on now." A plump older woman wearing a white apron came out and greeted them on the porch. "I hope he didn't bother you too much. He loves people. You must be the Reynolds. Please come in."

Piper just smiled at Joe. She wasn't a Reynolds yet but liked the sound of that. "Nice to meet you. I'm Piper, and this is Joe," she said extending her hand.

"Let me show you to your room. Are you celebrating anything special?" Marta asked as she climbed up the grand staircase.

"We are just celebrating being together and a few accomplishments at work," Joe explained.

"That is always a reason to celebrate in my opinion. Here we are. This is your room on the left." She swung open the door. "Dinner is served in the main dining room at six this evening. You can preorder breakfast by filling out the card on the bed, and then hanging it on your door tonight. Be sure to specify the time you want breakfast delivered. Will you be needing anything else?"

"This is lovely. Thank you," Piper told the woman. Marta left them to their privacy. Piper stepped inside the quaint room. It had a four-poster bed with a canopy. The comforter and the canopy were both made out of the same fabric. It had a cream background with burnt red images swirled throughout. The bed was covered in pillows and looked like the perfect place to spend a snowy evening cuddled under the warm, fluffy down comforter.

There was a fireplace with a mantel made out of cool marble. Piper ran her hand over the smooth stone and looked at the perfect little decorative touches that had been placed all over the room.

Joe called to her from the bathroom. "Piper, come check out this bathroom. Look at the tub." Piper went, and her eyes settled on a large clawed-footed bathtub. There was an assortment of bath bubbles and candles resting on the vanity. She thought she would definitely like to try those out after dinner tonight.

She moved over to Joe and wrapped her arms around him. "This is perfect. Thanks for arranging all of this." She reached up and slowly kissed his lips. Joe encircled her in his arms and deepened the kiss until she pulled away breathless.

"I thought maybe we could walk around to a few of the little shops before dinner. Does that sound okay to you?" Joe asked.

"It sounds fun. I haven't been to this town since I was a little girl. I used to come with my mom when she would go to the fabric store on the corner. I am excited to see if much has changed. Let me just change my shoes first." Piper slipped off her shoes and bent down to zip up her boots.

"Ready. Let's go," she said as she wrapped her scarf around her neck and pulled on her mittens. She grasped Joe's hand, and they walked down the stairs and out into the snow. It was peacefully still and quiet, and much of the snow was left undisturbed from where it had fallen a few hours before.

It was one of those cold days that froze the nose hairs when breathing. There was no wind today, which was rare and made being outside bearable. It was only four forty-five, but the sun was already starting to set as it gave off a reddish, orangey glow.

The snow crunched under their feet as they made their way around the small town, window-shopping and stopping into some of the stores on the main street. They strolled into a dog bakery and picked up a dog bone for Toby, decorated pretty enough to eat.

"Where is Toby tonight?" Piper asked Joe concerned.

"I took him over to my uncle's house for the night. He didn't seem to mind all of the extra attention he was getting when I dropped him off. Do you want to head back so we can be on time for dinner at six?"

"Sure. I am getting hungry anyway, not to mention that I am freezing." Piper grabbed Joe's hand and pulled him along at a quicker pace.

Marta set them at a cozy corner table that was close to the fireplace. Its warm glow seemed to fill up the small room and made the dining room inviting. They both ordered a wedge salad with ranch dressing and filet medallions for their entrée.

Piper absentmindedly stirred the cinnamon stick in her spiced apple cider with a splash of rum. She looked across the table at Joe whose cheeks were still rosy from the coldness of outside. He looked so vibrant and happy sitting across from her.

"I'm so lucky to have met you. Thank you for planning all of this. It has been a really nice evening." Piper reached across the table and gave his hand a squeeze.

"I'm the lucky one, babe. You have brought so much happiness into my life. I guess that I didn't really realize before how much was missing from my life before I met you." His thumb traced a small circle on her hand.

The waiter brought over their salads, and they were about halfway through when Piper brought up what had happened to her earlier in the day.

"I saw Pip again today. She showed up in my parent's kitchen and had cut her finger. She stayed longer today, and we were able to talk," she explained between bites of her salad.

"You waited until now to bring this up? Did you feel threatened at all by her? What did she say? Are you okay?"

Piper laughed. "Okay, one question at a time. I am fine. I didn't feel threatened by her at all. In fact I felt somehow relieved that I was able to talk to her and learn some things about her. She and her husband are real estate agents. Which strikes me as a little bit funny because I honestly considered doing that before I went into teaching. It is like she is another part of my personality. I think she is a lot like me but has some parts that are very different. Her visit was more lengthy, and we think that fear or being hurt enables us to stay longer in each other's world."

"It is all so interesting to me. Has either of you figured out why it is happening?"

"No, not yet. It felt like she was kind of like my sister in some ways. We felt really comfortable with each other."

They finished up their meal, and their conversation switched to lighter topics. He laughed as she told stories of things her students had done. She was so vivid when she spoke that he could imagine what she was saying clearly. She spoke with her hands, and her eyes smiled when she laughed.

The waiter came over to ask about dessert. "I have dessert waiting up in the room," Joe explained quickly to Piper knowing that she always had to have her dessert right after her meal. "Are you all finished?"

They headed up to their room, and as Joe was fidgeting with the key in the door lock, he seemed to be nervous all of a sudden. Piper leaned against the door jam and smiled. She had never seen him like this. He was usually so confident in all he did.

When she finally heard the doorknob click, Joe pushed open the door. Piper gasped with surprise and looked at Joe. "Come on in, beautiful." Joe took her hand and led her into the darkened room. It was lit only by candlelight, and there were pink roses that made a pathway to the bed that was covered in rose petals. Soft piano music crooned in the background, and the candlelight seemed to dance and sway, casting shadows on the walls and ceiling. Next to the sitting area, a bucket with champagne rested chilling, and chocolate-covered strawberries waited on a silver platter. A bath had been drawn in the tub, and more rose petals were floating on the water.

When Piper turned back around, Joe was down on one knee and was holding out a ring. "Piper, I love you. I love how you can make me laugh even when I am having a bad day. You are always so full of light and see the positives in everything including me. Will you do me the honor of marrying me?"

"Yes, Joe! I love you—yes. A thousand times yes." She kneeled down so she was level with him, and her eyes welled up with happy tears as he slipped the ring on her finger. It fit perfectly.

"How did you know my ring size?" she asked curiously.

"I had some help from your mom. I asked both of your parents for their blessing," Joe explained as he wiped away her tear from her cheek.

She cupped both sides of his face and passionately pulled him into a kiss that he could feel with every inch of his being. Her kisses still made his insides tickle. and a warm feeling instantly spread through him.

When he pulled away from her, she could feel her legs were shaky and weak. "Whew! I hope that I still have that feeling when we are ninety," she teased him.

He chuckled and poured her a glass of champagne. She reached down and plucked a strawberry off of the tray. She wrapped her mouth around it and moaned softly when she bit into the chocolate sweetness.

"Now this is a good dessert." She slowly began to slip out of her sweater and dropped it to the floor while making her way to the bathroom. "We wouldn't want the bath to get cold." She paused in the doorway and motioned to him with her finger to come join her.

He watched her standing in the doorway, illuminated only by candlelight. Her pale skin was smooth and taunt, and her hair fell loosely covering one of her breasts. He was filled with desire looking at him with love in her eyes. He crossed the room to her and scooped her up. Placing her carefully in the tub, he said in a low whisper, "Let's see if we can warm this water back up." She looked up at him and nodded while he shut the door quietly behind him.

Nine

*   *   *

She was late. She had been late before, but she didn't think her period had ever been this late before. She and Joe wanted children and had been married a little over a year, so it would be okay in the timing. They hadn't been trying to get pregnant, but if it happened it would mean that it was meant to be.

Pip needed to go grocery shopping tonight after she met with her last client and could pick up a pregnancy test then. Kirsten was dropping off an earnest money check, and it wouldn't take too long. When she finished with Kirsten, she popped her head into Joe's office.

"Hey, I am going to run to the grocery store on my way home. Do you want anything in particular for dinner this week or need anything else?"

"I think I am good. Oh, maybe pick me up some Red Vines please?" Joe asked sweetly.

"Sure. Catch you at home then." She pulled on her jacket and headed out to her car. There was a light dusting of snow on the windshield. She hated to scrape the windows, so she used her windshield wipers, and it pushed the light fluffy stuff off.

"Nice." She clicked on her radio and pulled out of the parking lot and headed to the store.

Pip thought that she would get the pregnancy test first so she could hide it under the food items. She shook her head and chided herself for feeling like she needed to hide it. She was married for goodness sake, and it was her own business.

Next she filled her cart with loads of different fruits. She passed the cheese section and grabbed some string cheese and threw it into her cart. She headed to the meat department. There was a young dad with his son in the cart standing in the aisle.

"Do you want hamburger or steak tonight, Grant?"

"I want pasta," the young boy responded from the back of the cart.

Pip smiled as she thought to herself that the dad was losing the battle. She needed to get some chicken but didn't want to interfere with the meat discussion going on. The plastic bags were standing in front of the man and his son. She thought that she could just grab one on her way by as not to hold up the man.

While continuing to push her cart, she reached up with her right hand and grabbed the clear plastic bag. It didn't release like she had hoped, and she stopped, holding the now three bags in her hand.

"That didn't work out as smoothly as I had hoped!" she grinned and told the man.

"I was kind of hoping that you were going to pull it a little harder, and the whole roll was going to go with you. That would've been awesome."

Pip threw back her head and laughed. Her throaty laugh sailed over and caught the attention of the man that was standing in the bread aisle watching the whole scene unfold.

He rubbed his chin and felt the three days of stubble. "Interesting," he whispered to himself. Pip had moved on down the aisle and didn't seem to notice the six-foot-tall man with sandy blonde hair that was following her. He kept just enough distance that to the casual observer he looked like any of the other grocery shoppers.

His mind wasn't on the groceries at all as he began pulling random things off the shelves and piling them in his cart. He could catch a faint whiff of her vanilla scent. He watched her walk in front of him, and he could feel himself getting hard as he imagined grabbing on to her little hips.

She pulled her cart into checkout lane seven, and he veered into the self-check-out lane so he could keep an eye on her. He heard her heels clicking as she walked by him. He shoved the bags into his cart and followed her out of the building.

Pip loaded her groceries in the back of her SUV. She felt as though eyes were on her and glanced over her shoulder. She quickly pushed the button on the tailgate so it would close. She climbed in the driver's seat and locked the door. She pulled out onto Creek Road and glimpsed in her rearview mirror. She didn't notice anything out of ordinary. She shook off the feeling and decided it would be good to just get home.

Three cars behind Pip followed a midnight blue Honda Civic with tinted windows. She may be unaware of him, but he was certainly aware of her.

Pip pulled into the garage and smiled when she saw Joe's car already parked in the garage. She punched the garage door button to close the door and grabbed two bags of groceries. She carried them in and set them on the counter.

"Hi, love. I have a few more bags in the car. Do you mind helping me bring them in?"

"Of course." He walked passed her and gave her a quick kiss on the lips and swatted her rear end.

She was pulling out the groceries and putting them on the counter when he walked in with the rest of the bags. "Did you have a good day? How did your meeting go with the Simpsons?"

Pip continued to unload the groceries while he began pulling the fruit out and loading it into the refrigerator. "My meeting went well. The Simpsons are a nice couple. They have a home over on Clemson that they want listed in the next week. How is your load right now? Would you consider colisting it with me?" he asked her.

"I have three of my listings closing on Friday, so I would be fine to help with yours." She stopped talking and realized that Joe was staring at the pregnancy test that she had just pulled out of the bag and was holding in her hand.

"Are you pregnant?" He rushed over and picked her up and swung her around.

Pip squealed, "Put me down. I don't know if I am or not. I am late and thought that I should take a test. If you will put the rest of the groceries away, I will go and take the test. Give me three minutes." She rushed out of the room.

She read the directions on the box. "Looks easy enough," she said aloud and ripped open the foil wrapper that held the stick. She followed the directions, put the lid on, and set it on the counter. She glanced at her watch and noted the time. Three minutes seemed like an eternity when she was waiting on a little positive or negative sign. She waited for four minutes just to be sure and was reaching for the stick when she heard a knock on the bathroom door.

"I'm sorry. I couldn't wait. So are you—pregnant?"

"I was just about to check. Come in, and we can look together." They peered down at the little purple stick and in the window that read a negative sign. Pip was surprised at the disappointment she felt. She definitely wanted children but hadn't planned on them yet. She was more than a little surprised that she was sad that it wasn't positive.

"Oh, well. We weren't even trying. We can start trying to get pregnant if you are ready." She looked up at him with her bright green eyes.

"I think that I would like that. I think that I am also really going to enjoy the trying part. They say practice makes perfect," he added with a sly grin.

Pip laughed easily and took his hand. "Let's go and make dinner, and you can fill me in more on the Simpson's house."

Pip stepped outside into the sunshine. It was one of those rare sunny days that felt actually a little warm in the middle of the winter. She took a deep breath and tilted her face up to take in the sunshine. She loved the feel of the warmth on her face. She sighed and could almost imagine lying on the beach and feeling the sand between her toes. A car honked its horn, and it broke her out of her daydream.

She needed to go and put a "for sale" sign in the Simpson's yard, and today was perfect since some of the snow had melted in the warm sun. She pushed the button on her remote and opened her trunk. She placed the sign in the trunk and smoothed down the sign rider sticker with her name and number on it. Joe's info was on the other side of the sign. The house was about twenty minutes across town, and Pip was planning on making a quick follow-up call on her way over to their house.

Pip got her phone call made and pulled up to the house. She thought that it probably wouldn't take too long to get the house sold. She was planning on having an agent tour next week. She pulled the sign and her hammer out of the trunk and trudged up the now clear sidewalk and into the yard. She put her sign in the snowy grass and started hammering away at the top of the sign, hoping to get it pushed into the ground. She got it in only a few inches. The ground was frozen solid. She needed to put more weight into it. Glancing around to see if anyone was looking, Pip climbed onto the little T that the bottom of the sign made. The only car on the street was a midnight blue Honda Civic, but she didn't think anyone was in it. She proceeded to hop up and down on the sign until it stubbornly anchored into the ground.

"Clever girl," he said as he watched her hopping up and down on the sign. "This may be more fun than I originally thought." He tightened his grip on the steering wheel and started to hum.

Pip decided that she was done for the day. She headed home, and since it was only around four, she knew that she would beat Joe home. She pulled into the garage, and when she opened the door to the house, she was immediately met by Toby. He barked a quick hello to her and licked her hand.

"Hi, buddy. I missed you today too," she said and crouched down and gave him a rub all over his neck and ran her hands down his silky ears. "Do you want to go for a run?"

She put her purse down in the kitchen and hung up her jacket. She kicked off her heels and carried them upstairs. She quickly changed into her running gear and slipped on her shoes. She pulled the laces tight and sat down on the floor to do her stretches. Toby was getting antsy and was whining at the door to go.

Pip headed downstairs and scribbled a quick note to Joe. "I went on a run. Be back soon. Love you." She taped it to the garage door so he would be sure to see it when he came in.

"Come on, boy." Pip grabbed his leash and hooked it onto Toby's collar. He immediately started pulling toward the park with his nose to the ground. It was getting close to dusk, and the streetlights were just beginning to flicker on. She breathed the brisk air into her lungs and thought how good this felt.

Pip began to make her way around the small park up the street from her house. She could smell people grilling dinner. She smiled as she thought about how everyone likes to grill when an unusually warm day happens in the middle of winter. Her stomach growled as she breathed in the different aromas.

She noticed that her shoelace had become untied. She stopped and bent down to tie it. Toby started to growl and barked twice. "What is it, boy? What do you see?" Pip scanned the trees and the area around her. "No one is there, Toby."

He pressed himself against the tree. His warm breath came out in smoky puffs. "Oh, but you are mistaken, dear Pip," he whispered keeping an eye on the blonde woman that was only about fifty feet from him.

Toby was really becoming rattled. She pulled on his collar. "Stop, Toby. That's enough!" And then Pip saw her. She appeared twenty feet up on the path in front of her. A ski hat covered up Piper's dark hair with only the ends of her ponytail jetting out from under the cap.

Piper walked over to where Pip and Toby were standing. "Looks like we had the same idea. How are you, Pip?"

"Hi. No wonder why my dog was going nuts. He probably couldn't figure out why he was smelling two of us." Pip reached down and stroked Toby's head. "Good boy."

Piper reached up and pushed a strand of dark hair back under her cap. The light caught her engagement ring, and it sparkled. "Looks like you have some news to share, huh?" Pip exclaimed as she took Piper's hand to examine the ring. "It is beautiful. Congratulations."

"Thanks. We got engaged about a month ago, but I still smile each time I look down and see the ring on my finger. I guess it never gets old. I have been feeling pretty tired lately and kind of sluggish, so I thought maybe a run would wake me up. It really isn't helping much. How have you been, Pip?"

From where he was standing, he couldn't see the other woman that Pip was talking to. Damn it! She had ruined his plans. He knew that Pip would turn and run home before too long because she never stayed out long after dark. He quietly returned to his car thinking that their face-to-face meeting would have to wait until another time. That bitch better not ruin things for him again. He ground his teeth together and punched the car door.

Joe was showing some out-of-town clients quite a few houses that afternoon, so he was late when he got home. Pip was curled up on the couch under a blanket, Toby lying at her feet snoring. She was watching her soap opera that she taped daily. She carefully sipped the hot chocolate with Bailey's in it, and then set it down on the table.

She heard the door creak open at the same time as Toby. He barked and growled, never leaving her side. "Hey, babe. I'm home. Where are you?"

Pip paused her show and called, "I'm in here. How did the showings go?" Joe walked into the room carrying the mail and reached up to loosen his tie.

"Good. I think that we found a couple of acceptable houses that they liked. I am showing them a few more in the morning. They have to make a decision by the afternoon. They are driving home tomorrow evening. Have you eaten? I'm starving."

"I did eat already, but I left you a plate in the refrigerator. You just need to warm it up. Why don't you go ahead and get your shower and get changed, and I will heat up your food," Pip told him throwing the blanket off of her and standing up.

"Thanks. I will be back in a second." He leaned down and quickly grazed his lips on hers. "You're the best. Have I told you that today?"

"Not today, but it never gets old hearing it," she said and smiled as she walked by him and veered toward the kitchen. She pulled out the plate of beef stroganoff and set it on the counter. She reached in and grabbed the bowl of fresh fruit she had cut up. She removed the crescent rolls off of the plate so they wouldn't get too heated up and placed the plate in the microwave with a paper towel over it.

While the food was heating up, she filled a glass with ice and water and squeezed a lemon into it. She put all of the food on the table and was just lighting the candles when Joe strolled into the dining area.

"This looks amazing. Thank you." He quickly sat down and didn't waste any time digging into the beef stroganoff. Pip sat down in the chair closest to him and pulled up one of her legs underneath her. She filled him in on her day and told him about her new clients as he ate dinner.

Across the street he could see her easily through the window. The warm cozy kitchen was lit up in the dark night. He watched her as she tilted her head back and laughed. Enjoy her while you can, for soon she will be mine.

Ten

*   *   *

Piper woke with a start and was sweating. She was so sick to her stomach. She moaned and rolled over and looked at the clock. The numbers 4:19 AM was blaring back at her. She still had a few hours before she would have to leave for school. Hopefully she would feel better by then. She took a few deep breaths and tried to go back to sleep. Her stomach felt like she had a rock in it. She sat up, and as soon as her feet hit the floor, she took off running for the bathroom. She barely made it. She lay down on the cool tile and felt better, but was clammy and damp with sweat.

Maybe she would feel better if she showered. She turned on the faucet to let the water warm up. She caught a glimpse of her face in the mirror. Her face was thin and pale, and she had dark circles under her eyes. She pressed a hand to her belly. She swayed and leaned down quickly to vomit into the toilet. She felt her hair being lifted off her neck and held back.

"I'm sorry that you are sick, Piper." Her mom stroked her hair and held it back.

"I woke you up. I'm sorry, Mom. I don't feel well at all. I am wondering if I need to call sick into school today. I don't think I can teach."

"Why don't you go get back in bed? I will be back in a little while to check on you."

Piper walked back weakly to her room and picked up her cell phone off of her nightstand. She punched the number in for the subcaller and left her information on the recording.

She fell back asleep and slept until nine that morning. She still felt queasy, but at least she hadn't vomited again. She went downstairs and made herself some toast. She felt tired and weak, and her body was sore. Her breasts even ached. This was some bug, she thought.

She felt better by the afternoon and decided that it must have been a short-lived illness. She still felt extremely tired but was able to function again without feeling like she was going to vomit.

Piper went up to the school after the students had gone home for the day and worked on getting caught up. She had plenty of papers to grade and needed to work on lesson plans for next week.

She switched on her radio and started to plug away at the stack of papers on her desk. She didn't realize how long she had been working until her cell phone rang, and she saw the time. It was already eight o'clock.

She picked up the phone and answered it with a smile curving on her lips. "Hi, babe. How was your day?"

"My day was good—busy. I am trying to get this one case done and didn't realize it was so late already. I wanted to call and check to see how my beautiful bride to be was?"

"I am still at school working too. I called in sick today. I was up early this morning vomiting. I am feeling better now. Are you healthy?"

"I feel fine. I am sorry to hear that you were sick. Are you feeling better now?" Joe asked with concern in his voice.

"I am feeling much better, thanks. I was wondering if we could take a look at some of the reception places this weekend? They usually book up pretty fast, and I want to get our first pick."

"Absolutely. I don't have much going on this weekend. Do you think that your mom would like to join us to help us look?"

Piper smiled. "You know that's why I love you. You always know what makes me happy. That would be great. I am sure that my mom would love to go and give us her opinion. I will ask her when I get home tonight."

"This all sounds good. I haven't had dinner yet, so I am going to let you go. I will hopefully see you tomorrow. I love you."

"I love you too. Good night, babe," Piper sighed as she hung up the phone. She loved that man.

When Piper woke up in the morning, she felt queasy again. She was able to keep from vomiting, but the thought of food made her sick to her stomach. What was going on with her lately? She pushed herself to get up and ready. She couldn't afford to miss another day of school. Her students were in the middle of a big project that was due at the end of the week. She needed to be there to help with the editing and to answer questions.

She made her way downstairs slowly and was sitting at the kitchen table staring at her orange juice when her mom came in the room.

"Are you sick again, Piper? You know, when my stomach was upset when I was pregnant with you and your brothers, I used to eat saltines. They seemed to help. Do you want to try a handful of those and see if it settles your stomach?"

"Sure, Mom. I don't know why I have been feeling so crummy lately. Maybe I am not getting enough rest." She took the plate of crackers that her mom was holding out to her.

"I hope you feel better, dear. I am off to get my haircut. See you tonight."

Something her mom had said made Piper stop and think. Her mom had said that she was sick when she was pregnant. Piper glanced up at the calendar hanging on the wall and mentally started doing the math of when her last period had been. Could she be pregnant? She was on the pill, so how would that be possible? She thought that she would stop and get a test on the way home from school today just to be sure.

The day seemed to drag by as the minutes felt like hours until the final bell rang. She would usually stay much longer than she had to and work in her room, but today she darted out right at four o'clock when the teachers could leave.

She pulled into a Walgreens parking lot and ran in to get a pregnancy test. There was so many different kinds that she finally settled on one that had two tests in the box.

She was thankful that neither her mom nor dad was home when she pulled into the house. She immediately ran up the stairs to her room and dumped her coat and purse on her bed. She pulled the pregnancy box out of the brown bag and took it into the bathroom. She washed her hands thoroughly, and then read the directions on the box.

She would have her answer in three minutes. She sat patiently on the edge of the tub and waited. She couldn't help her knee that bounced up and down nervously. She watched the second hand slowly tick away. When three minutes were up, she blew out her breath and slowly stood up, wiping her palms on the front of her slacks.

Piper picked up the purple stick and stared down at the little result window. It had a positive sign. Was she reading it correctly? She took the other test just to be sure. The results were the same. She was pregnant.

She picked up the phone and immediately dialed her OB-GYN's office and asked the receptionist about getting an appointment. Piper was told that she wouldn't be seen until she was ten weeks pregnant. The nurse estimated that she was about six weeks along based on the date of her last period. She set up an appointment for the following month. The word "pregnant" still sounded foreign to her ears. How was she going to tell Joe? She decided that she would tell him tonight.

Piper let herself into Joe's house and stooped down to soothe an excited Toby. She clipped on his leash and walked him around the block. He lifted his leg on all of his usual spots, and when they turned the corner and headed back to Joe's house, Toby seemed satisfied to be going home.

She was just getting the leash put away and pulling her boots off when Joe walked in. She greeted him in the kitchen and went in for a long, deep kiss.

"What a nice surprise. I didn't know that you were coming over. How are you feeling?" Joe asked her as he shook off his coat and hung it in the closet.

"I'm feeling okay. I missed you and thought we could have dinner tonight." She walked over to his refrigerator and pulled it open inspecting the choices for dinner. "You don't have a whole lot of options in here."

"I know. I need to go grocery shopping, but haven't had time with this big case. It is eating up all of my free time. Let's just do carryout."

Piper was fidgety and was having trouble sitting still. She paced around the kitchen while Joe was digging in his drawer for his carryout menus. He stopped and started to laugh when she passed by him for the third time.

"What has you all revved up? You are going to wear a hole in my floor with your pacing. Come and sit down and tell me what's wrong. Is it one of your students again causing trouble?" Joe took her by the hand and led her into the family room.

Piper plopped down on the chair and sighed. She looked into his beautiful blue eyes and saw that he was looking at her with such love that she calmed down just a little.

"I don't know how to tell you this, so I am just going to come out and say it. I'm pregnant." She searched his face and tried to get a reading on his expression.

He sat still and silent for a moment. "I am going to be a father?" Joe asked, his voice slightly cracking.

"Yes," her voice came out in a whisper as she wrung her hands together in her lap. She still couldn't tell what Joe thought about having a baby.

He took a hold of her hands and held them in his own. "I'm so happy, Piper. It is obviously not how I had planned it, but what the heck? We are going to have a baby!" He grabbed her and crushed his lips to hers possessively, and then squeezed her in a hug.

"Okay. Stop. You are crushing us!" Piper let out a laugh. "So I take it you are okay with the timing?"

"How did this happen? I thought you are on the pill?" he asked her curiously.

"I am, but the nurse told me today that any antibiotics will make the pill less effective. Do you remember last month when I took Augumentin for that ear infection? I guess that is when it happened."

"Well, this changes a lot. I want you to move in here with me. I don't want to miss a moment of this pregnancy. Also, I think that we should move up the wedding to this summer."

"This summer? But that is only a few months away. How can I possibly get everything done in time?"

"I will help, and so will your mom. We can do it. And as far as you moving in here, you will just have to bring your clothes." Joe looked around at his scarcely decorated family room. "I could use some help buying some furniture for this space. I don't really know how to decorate."

Piper choked back a laugh, "You think that you need more furniture than a few card table chairs?"

"Listen to you. It is a hard day for me to admit that I need help. All joking aside, I love you so much, and am really excited to be adding to our family. You mentioned that you spoke to a nurse today. What did she say?"

"She said that I can't come in for my first appointment until I am ten weeks along. I am about six weeks pregnant now. She estimated that I would be due in mid-November. Do you want to come to my first appointment with me?" Piper thought that she already knew the answer based on the way his face lit up as she was talking about the baby.

"Of course I do! I am not going to miss anything with this baby. Now let me run out and get you some food. I know it is a school night, and I want you to get some rest. Does Chinese food sound okay to you? I thought I would just run up to the restaurant up the block."

"That sounds great! I will take chicken lo mein with rice please," she replied, and then leaned in for a sweet, soft kiss.

"All right. Sit tight. I will be right back." He grabbed his coat out of the closet and snatched his keys off the counter. He winked at her and headed out the door.

*   *   *

It was early on a Saturday morning, and Pip was sitting at the kitchen table looking out the back window watching the daybreak. She closed her eyes and smiled as she listened to the birds starting to chirp and sing their love songs to one another. It was springtime, and she loved the way the trees were starting to get new buds on them.

She slowly sipped her coffee and reached down to stroke Toby as he lay asleep at her feet. She hated to leave Joe in bed this morning and get up so early, but her stomach hurt and had awakened her. She couldn't figure out why it was hurting in the morning for the last few weeks. She had taken another pregnancy test and ended up getting her period later that day. She knew she wasn't pregnant.

She got up from the table and was pouring herself another cup of coffee when she suddenly felt a presence in the room. She turned around sharply, and standing in her bathrobe was Piper.

"Hi. You couldn't sleep either huh?" She tucked her brown hair behind her ear.

"Hi yourself. I have this awful stomachache that woke me up. Do you want some coffee?"

"Is it decaf? I think I know why your stomach hurts. I'm pregnant, Pip." Her brown hair swung down over her shoulder as she dropped her head and placed a hand on her belly.

"Oh my gosh! Congratulations! How far along are you?"

"I am just about nine weeks. I have an appointment next week to see my doctor."

"The coffee is leaded. Do you want some orange juice instead? I was just going to take my coffee outside on the back porch. I know it is still chilly, but when the sun pours onto the porch at this time of the morning, it will warm us up. Let's take our drinks and go and sit outside. You can fill me in on everything that has happened since I saw you last." Pip grabbed a blanket out of the cupboard in the family room and opened the door for her guest.

Pip was right about the sunshine. It streamed onto the porch and seemed to take the chill out of the air. They each sat in the chaise lounge chairs, and Piper threw the blanket over her legs and tucked it in around her. She took a sip of her orange juice and placed it on the small table next to her.

She smiled at her newly found friend and thought how easy it was to talk to her. She was becoming more like a sister to her. She felt safe with her and knew that she could tell her anything.

"We were surprised when I found out that I was pregnant. It wasn't planned, but I really believe that everything happens for a reason. Joe is ecstatic about this baby. He hovers over me and won't let me lift a finger. I didn't know he had it in him—I usually wait on him."

"Amen, sister! I do the same for my Joe!" Both of the women shared a laugh and knew how the other one felt.

Joe rolled over and felt Pip's side of the bed. It was still warm, but she was gone. He was alone, and even his own dog had abandoned him. He sleepily rubbed his head and ran a hand through his hair and peered outside. It had just started to get light. What was Pip doing up this early on a Saturday? He intended to find her and drag her back to bed.

He pulled on a shirt and tugged on a pair of sweats. He slipped his feet into his slippers and yawned as he made his way downstairs. He smelled coffee as he was about halfway to the kitchen. He poured himself a cup and looked out on the back porch. He could see his blonde-capped bride laying back on the chaise lounge. He decided to join her.

He pushed open the door and said, "Good morning, babe. I've come to drag you back to bed—"

In that instant, Joe saw her. She was sitting opposite Pip on the other chair with chestnut hair that was tousled from sleep. She had the same pale green eyes as Pip and looked enough like her to be her twin. The two women were both staring at him.

Joe dropped his coffee, and it shattered onto the deck spilling the hot liquid onto his leg. "Shit! Ouch! What is going on here?" Joe looked from his wife to the other dark-haired woman.

Immediately Pip got up and went to his side. "Are you okay? Are you burned?"

"I'm fine," he growled. "Tell me what is going on. Who is this woman that looks like you, and why are you talking like you are best friends? You have never even mentioned her to me before."

"Joe, this is Piper. Piper, this is my Joe. Piper comes from another place that is like our world but is slightly different. She is engaged to Joe Reynolds and just found out she is pregnant. She is a fourth-grade teacher and lives in our house on her side. We started jumping into each other's lives a little while ago. It happens at odd times, sometimes when we are hurt or scared or just because. We have been able to stay longer each time, and then go back to our own world. I'm sorry I haven't told you about her. I didn't want you to think I was crazy. I was planning on telling you soon. Please don't be mad," Pip pleaded with Joe and laid her hand on his arm.

Joe shook her hand off his arm. Both Pipers looked at one another. Piper was glad that when she told her Joe, it had gone better than this. She began to feel her heart race.

"Umm, Pip? I think I am leaving. Nice to have met—" and with that she was gone.

"What the hell? What just happened?" Joe turned to Pip and stared at her.

"Shush! Your yelling is scaring the birds. Let's go back inside." She hooked her finger in the handle of the coffee mug and took the orange juice glass in the other hand and waited for Joe to open the door for her.

Joe shook his head and, seeing that she intended to continue this conversation inside, hesitantly opened the door for her. He followed her into the kitchen.

"Look, Joe. I didn't mean to upset you by not telling you about this. The first few times, the jumps literally lasted mere seconds. This one today was the longest we have ever had. I thought you were asleep, and she just appeared while I was pouring my coffee. Please don't be mad." She went to him and could tell that he was beginning to soften up.

"I would have told you earlier if I had felt like I was in danger. Our lives are somehow interconnected, and we still need to figure out why this is happening to us. I love you. I'm sorry, babe." She rubbed her hands up his arms and locked them around his neck.

"Let me make it up to you." She took his hand and started to lead him upstairs.

"You are trying to make me forgive you with sex? I guess I will let you make it up to me just this once—or maybe twice." He slapped her butt as she climbed the stairs in front of him.

She let out a laugh and challenged, "Race ya!"

Eleven

*   *   *

Piper woke up to a bright, sunny spring day. She could hear the birds chirping outside her window. She rolled over onto her side and softly placed a hand on her belly. She smiled and already felt so much love for the baby growing inside of her. Joe was still asleep next to her, softly snoring. Between Joe and Toby, it was hard to say who was snoring louder. It was a wonder she could get any sleep between the two of them making all of that noise.

She carefully slid out of the bed and slipped her feet into her slippers. She gathered the clothes that she had carefully laid out the night before and took them with her into the bathroom. She quietly closed the door behind her and turned on the faucet for the water to heat up in the shower. Today is the day that she would get to see her baby on the ultrasound. She was already dreading going through a whole school day before her appointment. She hoped that the day would go by quickly.

She went to the bathroom, and then pulled her nightgown off over her head. She felt the water and climbed in, letting the hot water pelt her back. She tilted her head back and let the water wash down her hair and neck. Her back hurt, and the hot water felt so good. She began singing to herself and realized how happy she was.

She stepped out of the shower and flipped her head over and wrapped her wet hair up in a white towel and piled it on top of her head. She rubbed lotion all over her body and especially on her belly. Her stomach was usually so flat and now had a slight bump to it. She had just gotten on her panties and bra when Joe opened the door and peeked in.

"Am I too late for the show?" he inquired.

"Ha ha," Piper said sarcastically. "Come in and shut the door. I'm freezing."

"Today is the big day. Your appointment is at four fifteen? My last client is at two thirty, and I should finish up a little before four. I will just meet you there."

"That will work. It is Suite 102. Dr. Waters. I will wait for you in the lobby, and we can go in together."

The day seemed to be passing in slow motion as Piper checked her watch for the hundredth time. The three thirty bell rang finally, and she dismissed her students telling them to have a good weekend.

"Don't forget to read for twenty minutes a day. And fill out your reading log!" Piper called as the kids were pushing their way out the door.

Piper packed up her stuff and cleaned up her room for the next thirty minutes. She took to the parking lot at a cross between a jog and a skip. She piled into her Miata and headed toward the doctor's office.

She saw Joe's tall muscular back first as she pulled open the door and walked into Suite 102. She grinned when he turned and saw her. She walked over to the receptionist and checked in.

"Hi, I'm Piper Samson here to see Dr. Waters."

The friendly receptionist with short spiky black hair with glasses on the tip of her nose smiled and said, "The nurse will be right with you. Do you have your insurance card, dear? I also need you to fill out this paperwork." She handed Piper a clipboard with some forms.

Piper took them and sat down and began to fill the forms, while Joe went over and started rifling through all of the different brochures on hospitals, midwives, baby diseases, and breastfeeding. He looked to be fascinated by each of them, and Piper softly chuckled as she watched him take one of each of them. He plopped down next to her and began reading the first one in his stack on breastfeeding.

"How's that working out for you?" Piper teased him but secretly enjoying how excited he was about the baby and how supportive he was being.

"Hmmm? Did you know that your nipples will get cracked and may bleed when you start breastfeeding? Amazing."

"Yeah, I can think of another word for that. Dreadful. That sounds absolutely dreadful! I am still going to try breastfeeding but will have to ask the doctor how to avoid bleeding, cracked nipples. That isn't my idea of fun."

A nurse came to the doorway wearing light pink scrubs and, looking down at her clipboard, said, "Piper Samson?"

"That's me." Piper and Joe stood up at the same time and made their way over to the nurse. Piper handed her the clipboard with her paperwork on it. Joe had the brochures gripped in his hand.

"Good afternoon. Let's step over to the scales please, and I will get your weight." Piper glanced down at the nurse's name tag that read "Monica."

Piper leaned over and placed a hand on Joe's shoulder and struggled out of her shoes. Joe looked at her and shook his head, his lips curved up.

"What? I think my shoes weigh a good two pounds." Piper stepped on the scale, and Monica pushed the weight until it balanced at 133 pounds. She wrote that number down in Piper's chart.

"Please follow me to room number four on the right. Go on in and sit up on the table please." Monica took her temperature and blood pressure. She asked about the first day of her last period and used a wheel contraption to estimate that the baby's due date was November 13th.

"The doctor will be able to give you a better due date once he does the ultrasound and takes some measurements. Go ahead and put on the paper gown. You can leave your bra on. The doctor will be in shortly."

Piper pressed a hand to her belly. "Why am I so nervous? I feel like I am waiting on a guy to ask me to prom or something."

"It's a big day to get to see our baby. Relax. Besides, this brochure says that ultrasounds don't hurt one bit." Piper punched him lightly on the arm and grinned at him.

There was a soft knock at the door. It opened slowly. and in walked Dr. Waters. He was a shorter man in stature and was nearly bald. He had dark rimmed glasses on and green scrubs. He immediately walked over to Piper and shook her hand, and then turned to Joe and did the same.

"Nice to meet you both. I'm Dan Waters. Do you mind if I ask a few questions first about your pregnancy, and then we can do the ultrasound?"

The doctor went through a series of questions relating to Piper's overall health and her family's medical history. He also asked Joe some questions about his family's medical history.

"Before we do the ultrasound, I would like to hear the baby's heartbeat." He took out a bottle of gel that had been warming and squeezed it out on Piper's stomach. He held the Doppler on her belly and moved it around. A fast swooshing sound filled the small examining room. Piper had never heard such a sweet sound. Her heart filled to the brim with love, and she squeezed Joe's hand.

"You can tell this is the baby's heartbeat because it is faster than yours," Dr. Waters explained. He moved the Doppler to her groin area, and the sound slowed down to a steady rhythm. "That is your heartbeat. Can you hear the difference?"

Piper nodded. He moved the Doppler back to the baby's heartbeat, and the sound sped up again. This time the sound was slightly different.

"Hmmm. Interesting," Dr. Waters mumbled and raised his eyebrows slightly.

"What is interesting?" Joe asked alarmed.

"Let's go ahead and do the ultrasound. I want to check something. I am going to try and do an ultrasound on your belly, but if we are having trouble seeing the baby, I will switch to a vaginal ultrasound. Sometimes you have to do that when the fetus is so small." He switched on the machine and spread more gel on Piper's stomach.

He positioned the monitor so Piper and Joe had a clear view of what he was seeing. He moved the ultrasound wand across her belly slowly and then stated, "There." He pointed to the screen. "That is the head and its body. Its arms are really like little nubs right now." The fetus moved on the screen.

"That's our baby, Piper." Joe looked at the screen, amazed and a little overwhelmed.

Piper looked up at Joe with tears in her eyes. This wasn't like anything she had ever experienced.

"Correction. Those are your babies. Plural." Dr. Waters moved the wand and pointed to the screen. "I thought I heard a second heartbeat on the Doppler but wanted to be sure before I said anything."

"Babies? I am having twins?" Piper was shocked. Joe's eyes got big as he crouched close to the monitor.

"Yes. It looks they are fraternal. This means that two eggs were released and fertilized at the same time. See? They each have their own placentas."

Everything that the doctor was saying was falling on deaf ears for Joe. Holy shit! Two babies. He immediately started worrying how they would be able to take care of two babies when he didn't really know how to take care of one.

Piper on the other hand was talking all at once, firing questions off left and right. Joe's head started to spin. He needed to sit down.

Piper looked over at Joe's pale face and instantly saw the worry there. She was nervous too, but so excited. She knew that she needed to say something to Joe to soothe him.

"Babe, look at it this way, now your hair can turn all gray in one year because we will have not one, but two drivers getting their licenses."

"Not helping, Piper."

She chuckled, and Joe couldn't help but laugh. She sighed. Twins. I am in love.

*   *   *

Pip was sitting at her desk staring at the computer screen. She had been working on a Broker's Market Analysis for the past few hours. She pinched her eyes closed and then opened them and blinked a few times. Her eyes were tired. She was tired. She needed to get some more sleep.

She needed to take a break and move around a bit. She got up from her desk and ventured back toward the vending machines. A few Hot Tamales and a Diet Cherry Pepsi might just wake her up enough to help her finish her report. She swung by the mailboxes on the way back to her office.

The secretary was stuffing everyone's box with a memo. Rose handed her the piece of paper. "Have you seen this yet, Pip? Another one has been reported. Please be careful."

"I always am. Thanks, Rose." She glanced down at the memo in her hand. Corporate had put out a warning about a man that has been assaulting real estate agents at their open houses. His description was a six-foot white male with sandy blonde hair approximately 185 pounds. They didn't have a license plate number for him but listed him as driving a blue Honda Civic. The president of the company reminded every agent not to take chances and be safe.

She read the memo as she walked back to her office. It always worried her when she got memos like that. When she first started in the business, she didn't have to worry about things like this. She believed in the good in people and sometimes wasn't cautious enough. It helped to be reminded of the need to be on guard occasionally.

She plopped down at her computer chair again and woke up her sleeping computer. "Okay, let's knock this thing out," she spoke out loud.

"Talking to yourself again, babe? You know that I already think you are crazy." Joe's lips twitched at the corners. "How is your day going? Are you about done here? It is getting close to five o'clock."

"I know, but I want to finish up this BMA before I call it quits for the day. I'm almost done. Why don't you head home and start dinner? I will be home shortly."

"Are you sure? I hate leaving you in an empty building alone," he said slightly worried.

"The door automatically locks at five. I will be fine. I am parked out front and will carry my pepper spray on the way to my car."

"Did you see the memo about the man that is targeting agents? You can never be too careful, Pip."

"I know. I will be. Now scoot. I need to get this finished up before I can leave."

The office was quick to clear out that evening. Pip completed the BMA just before six and was ready to get home. She packed up her briefcase and shut down her computer.

He had been sitting in the parking lot for the last hour, waiting. He knew that she was alone, as he had watched that idiot husband of hers leave an hour before. All of the main lights were off in the office except for a faint glow that must be coming from her office. He liked the dark. He did some of his best work in the blackness. It had been too long since he had smelled her. He needed to be close enough to hear her voice or her laugh. He was growing impatient. How dare she keep him waiting like this?

He could pretend that he was interested in a house. Then she would have to talk to him—give him the attention that he deserved. He looked around him and walked to the front of the office building. His finger extended to reach for the doorbell when he heard a man's voice.

"Can I help you with something?" He turned and looked sideways at the older man that was looking him square in the eye. He recognized the man as an agent in Pip's office.

"Oh, sure. I'm from out of town and have my addresses mixed up. Can you tell me how to get to the Grand Hotel?" As the agent was telling him directions, he wasn't listening at all. He was seething inside and kept having to squeeze and flex his hands to keep from wrapping them around the agent's neck. No, he wouldn't lose control—again. Not just yet. He turned and stepped off the curb and moved toward his car. He could hear Pip's voice as she greeted the older man until the door swung closed. Patience, I must have patience. She will be mine soon enough.

Twelve

*　　*　　*

The past few months had flown by in a blur. Piper couldn't believe that the school year was ending this week, and her wedding was in a few weeks. She had mixed emotions about school finishing. After much discussion with Joe, Piper decided that she would not return to teaching in the fall. The price of daycare for the twins would be more than her salary. It didn't seem worth it. She was also excited to be at home with the babies. She didn't want to miss a single moment.

Each afternoon after school let out, she would stay in her room and pack a few boxes. She couldn't believe how much stuff she had accumulated over the years. She did throw out some things but wanted to keep a majority of the stuff in case she ever went back to teaching after her kids were in school.

She smiled as she looked down at some of the pictures of her students over the years. She had so many fond memories of the children and had met a lot of parents, some of whom were still good friends.

Piper needed to rest for a minute. She arched her back and pushed her hand into her lower back. She was starting to show just a little, but the students hadn't noticed. She could still squeeze into her slacks but just didn't button the top button. She had laughed when Joe was lying on the couch one night having stuffed himself with French silk pie and had unbuttoned his pants. He had told her that he didn't want her to feel left out.

She grinned thinking about how wonderful Joe was and how wonderful their lives were. She gingerly rubbed her belly and began to sing, "You are my sunshine" to the babies.

She felt a small flutter against her hand and was shocked. She tried to determine if she had just felt one of the babies move. She sat down and was still—waiting. She realized that she was holding her breath. She took a deep breath and blew it out, thinking maybe she had imagined it. Just when she had given up and was standing up to continue packing, she felt the same flutter again, like minibubbles. She laughed out loud. What an amazing feeling.

She figured that she could be done for the night and packed her things into her purse. She turned off the lights and locked her door. She headed down the hallway to the doors. Pushing them open, she paused and smiled as she saw Joe leaning against her car, his arms crossed in front of him.

She felt her breath catch as his smile started at his mouth and worked all the way up to his eyes. The flutters that she felt now were not from the babies but from the way that he looked at her. She never felt so desired or loved.

"What are you doing here?" She walked over to him and wrapped her arms around his neck. She stretched up on her tiptoes and lightly pressed her lips to his.

"Hi, gorgeous," he whispered in her ear as he nudged her hair out of the way so he could kiss her neck. "I just finished up a meeting on the corner two streets over and thought I would stop by and see how the packing was going. Are you done for the day?"

"I am. You have perfect timing as usual. Guess what? I just felt the babies move. It felt like butterfly wings, tiny little flutters."

"That is amazing. Do you think that I can feel them too?"

"I don't think so, not yet. I am sure in a few more months when they get bigger you will be able to. Are you done for the day?"

"I am. Should we go home and eat dinner? Do I need to stop and pick up something on the way home?"

"You are so thoughtful," she grinned at him. "I put a chicken in the Crock-Pot this morning before I left for school. I am going to make some rice and rolls with it. Does that sound okay?"

"That sounds great. I will meet you at home."

Joe threw his napkin up on the table and pushed back his chair. "That was a good dinner. Thank you. I will clean up the dishes. Why don't you go relax in the other room?"

"Thanks, honey. I may just do that. I am tired tonight."

"It's no wonder. You have been going like crazy trying to get school finished up and get the wedding plans done. What do you have left to do with the wedding stuff? How can I help?"

Piper rose and picked up her glass and plate and set them next to the sink. She began wiping down the table. "I think that we are actually in good shape. Mom has been so good to get most of everything arranged. I'm glad that we decided to do a small wedding at my folk's house by the pond. I think it is really going to be nice. We will probably have some things to work on this weekend."

"All right. Well, just tell me what I need to do. Make me a list. You know I work better off of a list. And you're so good at making them too, boss," he said and winked at her.

"You would be lost without all of my sticky note lists. Admit it, you secretly like them."

"They are something all right." Joe smiled to himself remembering the time that he opened up his medicine cabinet to see one of the sticky notes. Piper had told him not to forget to pick up his dry cleaning after work. He had shaken his head at the randomness of the note in the medicine cabinet, but he didn't forget his shirts. She was damn good.

He watched her walk into the great room, her hair loose and swaying across her back. She had on comfy pants and a tight Henley shirt. He could just make out her baby bump and thought she had never looked sexier. He turned back to the dishes and hurriedly loaded the dishwasher and washed the Crock-pot. He wanted to go in and sit with her.

She plopped down on the brown leather ottoman and yelled over her shoulder, "Don't forget to put the Crock-pot away after you wash it. It doesn't like it when you leave it on the counter."

He threw the wet dishrag at her. She squealed with delight, and then blew him a kiss.

*   *   *

Pip was putting on the last touch of her mascara and looked over at Joe who was just finishing up tying his tie. "Where is your open house today?" she asked him before pouting her lips to apply her lipstick.

"I'm at the house on Station Street. Where are you today?"

"I am at the new construction house on Cody Drive. I will be done at four. Do we want to meet somewhere for dinner or just come home?"

"I will just pick up something on the way home from my open house. It is close by Frank's. I could pick us up some wings and pizza. Does that sound okay?" he asked.

"Perfect. Love you. Hope you get some new clients." She kissed him quickly on her way out the door.

She steered into the driveway and opened her trunk. She pulled out the open house sign and stuck it in the ground. It was a nice day so she hoped that she would get a lot of traffic. She could see kids out playing on the street and riding their bikes. One of the neighbors was out mowing their lawn.

She unlocked the door and stepped inside. She began flipping on all of the lights. She inhaled through her nose and thought that she would never get tired of that new house smell. The house had been well built and was a large ranch that sat on a pie-shaped lot. She ran her hand along the smooth granite countertops in the kitchen. She carefully arranged the flyers with her name and number on them and stacked them on the island.

The house was empty except for a lawn chair that the builder had left for her. She positioned the chair by the front window and sat down to read her book. She had a steady stream of visitors through the house along with some nosy neighbors. Joe had called around three to see how her afternoon was going. His open house was pretty dead. All in all, she had about eight visitors, and a few of them may be serious buyers. She talked to three of them who weren't working with an agent and said she would follow up the next day and answer any questions. It was three fifty-eight, and she began walking through the house turning off the lights.

She was in the kitchen when she heard the front door swing open. There was always one that came at the last minute. She put a smile on her face and walked around the wall to greet him.

He watched her walk toward him. Her blonde hair had grown longer and was hanging in shiny curls just below her shoulders. Her lips were glossy and had been painted a deep red. He had been waiting for this moment for a while and could feel himself getting hard just looking at her.

"Hi. Welcome. This home was recently finished and is offered at $427,000. There are many great features about this home. Please have a look around, and I will answer any questions that you may have after you finish the tour."

His voice was deep and raspy as he began to speak, "Pip, I would like you to show me around if you don't mind."

Her eyes narrowed when she heard her name. She was wearing her name tag, but it still sounded odd when strangers used her name so freely. She pushed that thought aside and smiled, "Of course."

"We can start with the left wing of the house. There are three bedrooms situated away from the master allowing for optimum privacy." She walked ahead of him about three feet. He could smell her vanilla perfume. It was light and airy and immediately stirred him in his groin.

She continued to talk about the house, and then stopped abruptly in front of the adjoining bathroom. He ran into her and trailed his fingers down her arm.

"Excuse me. I don't feel comfortable with you touching me. Kindly back off." She turned sharply and tried to move away.

He reached out and grabbed her arm and spun her around so she was staring directly at him. He was taller than she was by about three inches, and she noticed that his hair was sandy blonde and tousled away from his face. The force of his hand on her arm suddenly made her insides start to get queasy.

"I have been watching you for a long time. Don't turn away from me." He gripped her face in his hand and reached up with the other hand and twirled her hair around it. He brought his nose to her hair and inhaled. She could feel his warm breath on her neck. She tried to yank her head back and have him release her, but he only tightened his grip on her making her cry out.

"See what you made me do. You made me hurt you. Now just be quiet." He pressed himself against her, and she could feel that he was hard as he shoved himself onto her thigh.

She began to tremble, and reaching up with her hand, she tried to grab his hand and move it off her face. He yanked her head back with his hand and clasped a hold of her wrist with the other hand. He didn't have a good grip on her wrist because she was wearing a chunky silver bracelet and had wrapped his hand around that first. He readjusted his hand further down on her arm and jammed it above her head. He positioned her head to the side so her neck was exposed. He ran his scratchy tongue down the side of her neck, and then nipped at the skin just below her collarbone.

Keeping her one arm above her head, he reached around and removed a knife from his pocket. He expertly flipped it open so the blade was exposed. Pip squeezed her eyes closed and held her breath.

"I didn't want to have to hurt you, Pip. You were made to be with me and not with that stupid husband of yours." He lifted the knife up to her throat and pushed the tip lightly into her neck. She froze in fear but couldn't help the trembling that was taking over her body. She felt a small trail of blood running down her neck.

He brought the knife up to her head and sliced off a chunk of her hair that had been hanging across her face. "Just a little something to remember you by when you are gone," he whispered into her ear.

She was getting light-headed from the fear that was bubbling up inside of her. Her heart began to beat rapidly as she could feel his hands roaming her body. She closed her eyes and felt herself starting to slip away into blackness.

*　　*　　*

Joe heaved out an exaggerated sigh and plopped down on the couch next to Piper. "I finished all of the dishes and even put away the Crock-pot. I never knew you had such strong feelings about dishes and items being on the counter," he teased her and wrapped his arm around her shoulder.

"Sorry, I just like to have everything in its place." She rested her head against his shoulder and closed her eyes for a second. She had her legs tucked up underneath her and was wrapped in a soft chenille blanket. Toby had taken up the edge of the blanket and kept a sleepy eye on her and Joe.

"Are you tired tonight, babe? Do you want to skip our walk?" Joe asked as he rubbed his fingers slowly down her arm.

"No, I think I will still be up for going. I just want to rest for a few minutes." Toby's head perked up, and he softly began to growl sensing something.

"What is it, Toby?" Joe reached across Piper and began to stroke his fur. No sooner had Joe spoken those words than suddenly lying in a crumpled heap on the floor was Pip.

"Holy shit!" Joe let out a gasp and quickly stood up, not believing what was right in front of him.

"Joe, it's Pip. Something is wrong. Help me with her." Piper quickly moved to her side and crouched down to her.

Pip's eyes were squeezed shut, and she was as pale as a ghost. She was trembling and didn't seem aware that she had jumped. She was weeping softly.

"Pip, it's me and Joe. You're safe. Open your eyes and look at me. You're safe. Shhh, now. It is going to be okay," Piper softly crooned to the shaken woman that shared her looks and was still dazed on the floor.

"Piper? Is that you?" she tentatively whispered, tears welling up in her eyes and falling silently down on her cheeks. She wrapped her arms around Piper and hung onto her as though her life depended on it.

"What happened? You were obviously scared or hurt to have jumped here. Come sit down on the couch. You have some blood on your neck. Joe, can you go get her some hot tea please and a rag to wipe up the blood?"

Joe was still standing in the same position as when Pip entered their great room. When Piper addressed him, his eyes seemed to snap back to focus. He was still trying to comprehend what was happening. Piper had told him about the other woman with blonde hair that looked like her, but it was something entirely different when he witnessed it with his own eyes.

He slowly retreated into the kitchen to get the tea, half scared to leave the shaken woman and half worried that his Piper would somehow vanish. He quickly made the tea and carefully carried it into the great room and set in on the coffee table. Piper had moved the woman to the couch and had wrapped her in the blanket. It was amazing how much the two women looked identical. The only distinguishing feature was the other woman had gold spun hair, and his Piper had a slight baby bump. Their mannerisms were the same. Joe studied the blonde as she tucked her hair behind her ear and wiped away a tear from her cheek.

Piper held out the tea to her, and she carefully held it to her lips and took a warming sip. "Pip, when you are ready, please tell us what happened. I'm worried about you."

Pip took a deep breath and began, "I was just finishing up at my open house. I was turning out the lights and heard someone come through the door a few minutes before four. He seemed to know me although I have never seen him in my life. He called me by name. When we got back to the bedroom area of the house, he—" she paused and tried to collect herself. Her lips began trembling again. Piper reached over and held her hand.

"Take your time. You are away from him now. You are safe," Piper continued holding her hand and waited patiently for her to continue.

"He grabbed me by the hair and yanked my head back." Her hand went absently up to her head, and she rubbed the back of her scalp gingerly. When she did that, Joe noticed that she already had bruises welling up on her wrists. He was becoming so agitated watching this woman tell about this horrible experience. He couldn't help but feel protective of her.

"He also grabbed me by the wrists and held one of my arms over my head. He lost his grip at first when he grabbed a hold of my bracelet." She held out her arms and showed them to Piper. Piper gasped and put her hand to her mouth as she looked down at the already angry red finger marks that were imprinted on her wrists.

"Wait, did you say that he grabbed your bracelet first?" Joe asked Pip. She nodded. "Hold on and don't touch your bracelet." Joe jumped up and ran into the kitchen. He returned with a plastic bag. He turned it inside out and, covering his hand with the plastic bag, reached up and took the bracelet off. He flipped the bag over and carefully zipped it closed with the bracelet securely inside.

"The police may be able to get his fingerprints off of your bracelet. That could help find out who did this to you." He handed her the bag, and she hesitantly took it and placed it in her pocket.

"He had a knife. He pressed the tip of it into my neck." Her hand went up to her neck to the slight cut that was there. She took the rag that Joe had brought in and held it to her neck.

"He cut my hair and said he was keeping it to remember me by when I was gone." She fingered the strand of hair near the left hand side of her face that had been frayed off.

"I don't really want to think about this anymore. Luckily he wasn't able to do anything more before I jumped. I can still smell his breath and feel his teeth from where he bit me." She pulled down the front of her shirt and showed them the mark from where his teeth had punctured her delicate skin.

"I am so sorry." Piper leaned over and wrapped her arms around her friend. The two women clung to each other, both quietly sobbing. Joe felt helpless as he watched his Piper comforting her friend. If he felt this way about a woman he had just met, he wondered how the other Joe would react when he found out. He shuddered thinking about his Piper going through something like this.

He thought that they all could use a strong drink. He quietly backed out of the room and went to the kitchen. He made himself a whiskey and coke and poured some Bailey's straight up into a glass. He took a chance that Pip would like Bailey's too since his Piper liked it. Joe poured a glass of lemonade for his Piper and carefully balanced them as he walked into the other room.

The women were softly talking when he handed each of them their drinks. Pip had more color in her cheeks now and smiled up at him when he placed the drink in her hand.

She spoke directly to Joe and said, "You are a looker, aren't you? We have good taste in men, huh, Piper?" Joe seemed shocked that she could joke so easily after what she had experienced.

Piper laughed. "She is teasing you, Joe. Her husband looks the same as you." She smiled at her friend and was encouraged that the scum hadn't taken away her fiery side. She knew at that moment that Pip was going to be okay.

Joe asked if maybe Pip would feel better after a long hot shower. The women climbed the stairs together. Joe watched them head into the master bedroom, and then turned back and headed to the kitchen. He was going to make a dinner plate for Pip. He planned to take care of her as long as she was in his house.

Pip came down the stairs dressed in Piper's sweatpants and an oversized sweatshirt. Her blonde hair was wet and combed back away from her face. Her face had been washed clean of her makeup, and she just wore a little bit of lip gloss. She looked more relaxed and at ease as she walked into the kitchen.

"I want to thank you both for being so good to me. It's funny, Piper, we keep our toiletries in the same drawer. I am feeling better after the long shower. I am starving though."

Joe pulled a plate out of the microwave and set it on the table. "Good. Sit down. I made you a plate while you were in the shower. We just had chicken tonight and rice. What can I get you to drink?"

"I will have a glass of milk please, but I can get it. I think I have a good idea where you keep your glasses." She smiled over her shoulder as she open a cabinet door and reached up for a glass.

The three of them sat at the table, and Pip dug into the food. Toby sat at Pip's feet hoping to get a scrap of table food. Joe smiled to himself when he saw Pip sneak him a piece of chicken just like his Piper does when she thinks that he isn't looking.

Joe leaned forward and addressed the blonde Pip, "You are staying a long time. Is this how long your visits usually are?"

Pip was busy chewing her food and merely shook her head. She took a sip of her milk and then explained, "No, but lately we have been staying for a longer period of time when we jump. I am really worried about Joe. I am sure that he is going mad with worry when I didn't come home from the open house. Corporate had put out a memo about the man that attacked me. He was already concerned about me. I wish there was some way that I could get back to him or let him know that I am okay." She nervously chewed on her lip, and then blew out a deep breath.

Piper reached across the table and rested her hand on Pip's hand. "Try not to worry. I am sure that you will be going home soon. Joe is just going to be glad that you weren't hurt any more than you were. I have to say that I am relieved that we can jump so you were able to get out of that situation."

Pip laid her fork down and pushed her plate forward on the table. "I'm stuffed. Thank you so much for dinner. Do you mind if I go to bed? I am exhausted."

"Sure, I will take you up to the guest room and make sure that you are settled."

"Good night, Joe, and thanks again." She gave a small wave as she got up from the table and headed toward the stairs.

"Good night, Pip. I hope you sleep well." Joe called after her.

Piper tossed and turned that night and woke in the morning feeling like she hadn't slept. She had awakened a few times in the night and had tiptoed to the guest room to check on Pip. She was breathing deeply each time that Piper checked on her, and so she would creep back to her room as not to disturb her.

She rolled over and glanced at the clock. It read 6:41 AM. She peeled back the sheets and slipped out of her room to check on Pip. The bed was empty. Piper laid her hand down on the sheets and could still feel her body heat. Pip had been here not too long ago. She knew that Pip had gone home and hoped that Joe would take care of her.

Her eye caught Pip's neatly folded clothes stacked on the chair. She immediately went to them and felt the pocket. She pulled out the bracelet that was still in the plastic bag.

"Damn it! How am I going to get this to you?" she said out loud.

She padded back into her room and tried to be quiet as she got out her clothes so she could shower.

"I'm awake. She's gone, isn't she?" Joe asked groggily.

"She is. I checked on her in the night a few times, and she was still here. I think she must have just left because the sheets are still warm. I hope they find who did this to her and sooner than later. Look what she left behind." Piper held out the bracelet for Joe to see. "How will the police be able to identify him without it?" Piper hugged her arms to her chest and looked out the window at the sun as it was just starting to pop over the horizon.

"That bracelet could be the key in getting that sicko behind bars. Piper, I think you are going to have to carry it on you in hopes that you jump soon and can get it back to her. Although frankly I really don't want you to jump anymore. This is a serious situation with someone that is obviously obsessed with a woman whom you look identical to. And you are pregnant with the twins on top of it all." Joe's voice was starting to rise slightly as he was talking.

"Babe, I understand your concern. I really do, but I don't have any control over when I jump or how long I stay. I just have to tell you that I will be as careful as I can when I am over there. That is really all I can do."

She went to him and sat on the edge of the bed. She leaned down and kissed his forehead, and then pulled her head back slightly until she was looking him in the eye.

"I love you and these babies very much. You know that I will protect them as best as I can."

"I know, Piper, but I bet the other Joe thought he could protect Pip too, and look what happened." Joe sat up and pulled her into his chest. He hung onto her, and if he had his way, he would never let go of her.

Thirteen

*   *   *

Pip woke up in her bed and glanced over at Joe's side. It was still made and had not been slept in the night before. She looked down and was still wearing Pip's sweatpants and shirt. Damn it! She didn't have the bracelet. It was back in her pocket at Piper's house.

She needed to find Joe and let him know that she was all right. Toby found her first and was standing at the bottom of the stairs whining and wagging his tail. She quickly descended the steps and patted him on the head. He rolled over for her to rub his belly.

"Where's Daddy? Huh?" she asked him as she bent down and gave him a good rubdown.

Toby got up and trotted to the back door. Pip could see the top of Joe's head as he sat slowly rocking in the chair. She opened the door and stepped out onto the back porch.

He looked up and rushed over to her embracing her in a tight hug. She pulled back a little ways from him and looked at him. He hadn't slept, and his eyes were bloodshot, and he had dark circles beneath them. His face was covered with dark stubble. His hair was tousled and looked like he had run his fingers through it about a hundred times.

"Babe, if you aren't a sight for sore eyes. I have been so worried. What happened? I showed up at your open house when you didn't come home. Your car was still there, but I couldn't find you anywhere." He refused to allow her out of his sight and kept his arms locked around her.

"Let's go in and sit down. I am going to need you to listen to me without interrupting no matter how upset you are going to get. This is going to be difficult for me to talk about, and I won't be able to get through it if you stop me." She took him by the hand and led him into the great room. Her sleeve had inched up on her right arm, and the dark purple bruises were visible.

"Oh my god! Pip, what happened? Who did this to you?" Joe demanded. He caught himself and tried to keep a hold of his temper when he looked into her face that had gone pale and into her eyes that were beginning to brim with tears.

"Please sit," Pip whispered not trusting her own voice. She didn't want to relive all of that again but knew that she had to tell Joe what happened.

Joe sat quietly and wrung his hands in a constant motion as he listened to Pip tell about the horrible experience. He went through such a wide range of emotions from anger to worry to sadness that she had gone through all of this, and he wasn't there to protect her. He listened to her description of the man and thought it sounded a lot like the man that had been reported in other women's open houses. No one had been able to get an identity on him yet.

"I think that I have his fingerprints on my bracelet," Pip explained quietly.

Joe leaned toward her and said, "What? Where is your bracelet? We need to go and report this to the police immediately."

"It is in my pants pocket—at Piper's house." Pip looked down and plucked a piece of lint off of the couch absentmindedly.

"It's at Piper's house? So you are telling me that you jumped to Piper's house? That is what got you away from this creep?" He reached over and wrapped his arms around her protectively. She quietly sobbed into his neck and nodded her head. She tightened her grip on him and held on to him tightly. She never wanted to let go.

He reached up and stroked her hair and quietly soothed her. He continued to hold her and comfort her while she quietly cried. He pulled her head back so he could look into her eyes. He took his thumbs and wiped away the tears that had fallen onto her cheeks. Her eyes were a bright green color, and the edges were red from crying. He held her face in his hands and took a deep breath.

"I am so sorry that I wasn't there to protect you from this happening. We have to report this to the police so we can catch this bastard. That bracelet may be the key to finding out who he is. Is there any way that you can make yourself jump to Piper's world and get back the bracelet?" he asked her quietly.

"No, I have never been able to make myself do it. We will just have to give it to police when we get it. Didn't you help that one police officer buy his house on Cherry Street? Do you think that we could go and talk to him this afternoon?"

"Yes. I think that your bruises need to be documented, and we need to tell him your story. I don't think that we should tell him how you were able to get away from him. I am not sure that he would believe you. It was hard for me to comprehend until I met Piper and saw her with my own eyes."

"I agree. Joe, I need to show you something else." She slowly pulled the neck of the shirt down to just below her collarbone. The bite mark was an angry purplish red color.

"Oh, Pip." Joe's eyes filled with tears as he looked at his wife sitting there exposed and vulnerable. "I am going to make this right. You don't have to be scared anymore. I am going to see to it that you are protected." He softly brushed his lips to hers, and she rested her head on his shoulder. He thought how lucky she was to have escaped when she did.

Pip had freshly showered and had pulled her hair back into a sleek ponytail. She sat in the passenger seat, and they had driven to the police station without her saying a word. Even though the days were already getting warm, Pip wore a long-sleeved blue shirt. She kept pulling the sleeves down over her hands as though she was trying to make them longer. You couldn't tell from looking at her that underneath those long sleeves her arms were covered in finger marks and bruises, which had pinched the skin. She had put on a brave face and sat stoically without saying a word.

As Joe pulled his car into the parking lot to the police station, he rolled to a stop; and keeping his fingers on the keys, he turned and smiled at her. "You can do this, babe. We can do this. I am going to be with you the whole time. I am sorry that you have to go through this again."

Pip sighed and took a deep breath. Her hand was on the door handle. "I love you." She leaned over and pressed her lips to his for a brief moment before pushing open her door and climbing out onto the sidewalk.

"Lee knows that we are coming. I think you may have met him once when he came into the office to drop off some paperwork. He is very thorough at his job and will get right to work on finding the bastard who did this to you." He placed his hand on her lower back and steered her through the doors and back toward Lee's office.

Lee saw Joe and Pip standing at his door and motioned for them to come in and sit down. He held up his index finger indicating that he would be just a moment.

"Thanks, Riley. I will be in touch." He hung up the phone and quickly stood. He came around his desk and extended his hand first to Pip and then to Joe.

"It is nice to see you again, Pip. I am awfully sorry that it is in these circumstances. Please sit down. Can I get you something to drink before we get started?"

"Hi, Lee. I am fine for now. Thank you for agreeing to see us today on such short notice. I have never had to do anything like this before. How do we get started?" Pip questioned.

"Please just tell me what happened in as much detail as possible. Even the tiniest details that you remember may be helpful, so don't leave anything out. I am going to take notes on what you tell me. Later I will show you some pictures of some men that have been convicted of assault. Maybe our man is among the lineup.

Pip began to tell the story again to Lee. He didn't wince or make any facial expressions to give away what he was thinking. Although Joe had already heard the story, he couldn't help but have to gulp down the anger that was rising up in his throat.

Pip pushed up her sleeves and showed her bruises to Lee. He brought out a ruler from his desk drawer and began to measure the size of the marks. He told Pip that Sally would be taking pictures of them a little bit later. Pip carefully pulled down the neck of her shirt and exposed the bite mark and the cut on her neck from the knife. Lee marked the location down on a drawing of a human body that would go in Pip's chart.

"What else can you tell me about the man that did this? Besides his description, do you have anything else for me to go on?"

"I was wearing a bracelet that I think I may have his fingerprints on it."

"That would definitely help. It could mean a conviction for him. Where is the bracelet? You didn't bring it with you today?" Joe leaned in closing the big gap that separated them.

"No, I didn't bring it today. I accidentally left it at my friend's house after this happened. I took it off immediately and put it in a plastic bag hoping to preserve his prints. I left it at her house."

"You need to get that bracelet and get it to me today. If we can link his fingerprints and you can identify him from the lineup, well it would really help to get this guy behind bars for a long time."

Pip shared a glance with Joe. She needed to get that bracelet back. How in the world she was going to get it?

They stopped to get Pip's car on the way home. It was still parked in the driveway where she had the open house. She got into her car and waited until Joe backed out behind her. She took a moment and looked up at the house. She let the anger that had been welling inside of her out as she unleashed a stream of obscenities at the house, the situation, and the man that had attacked her. She banged her hand on the steering wheel. Feeling slightly better, she backed out of the driveway and slowly drove toward home.

He was following her a few cars behind without her noticing. She had been with that idiot husband of hers all day, and this was the first time that she had been alone. Now she was in the car, so there was no chance for him to be with her. He was becoming more and more obsessed with her after he had touched her body and had his fingers in her hair. He reached into his pocket and pulled out the lock of hair. He brought it to her nose and inhaled her sweet scent. She fit so perfectly against him. He had no idea where she had gone or how she had literally vanished into thin air when he had a hold of her. Next time she wouldn't get away from him so easily. The next time he was playing for keeps.

Pip pulled into the garage and quickly shut the garage door behind her. Joe was hovering in the kitchen waiting for her to come in.

"Hi, babe. Are you hungry? I could make us a sandwich," Joe asked her as he ran his hand down her back.

"I am actually just really tired. Would you mind if I go up and lay down for a few minutes?" Joe nodded, and she turned and climbed the stairs. She could feel him still watching her and felt like she was going to lose it right there on the steps. She gave him a smile at the top of the stairs and retreated into their bedroom and shut the door.

She loved Joe for being so protective of her, but she needed some time to figure out what happened and how to deal with it. She felt very lucky that she was able to get out before anything more had happened but at the same time felt like he had taken a part of her.

She felt violated and looked down at the bruises on her arms, which were a constant reminder. She knew that in a few days the marks would fade, but would she ever be able to get over what had happened to her? What about the internal marks? How could she deal with the sadness, the hurt, and anger that she felt?

She threw herself down on the bed and let the tears come. She started sobbing into the pillow, and her whole body trembled as the raw emotion poured out of her.

Pip felt a hand softly rub her back. She looked up quickly and wiped the tears from her eyes, and looking back at her was Piper.

"I'm so sorry that you had to see me like this," Pip sniffed and wiped the dark mascara trails away with the back of her hand.

"Don't be sorry. Pip, you are always so strong for everyone else's benefit. When are you going to learn that you have to allow yourself to heal how you need to without always worrying about other's feelings? You are what pulled me here today. I was making a sandwich, and then suddenly I am here. It looks like my timing was pretty good," she said and continued to rub Pip's back. "Look what I brought back with me." She dug into her pocket and pulled out the silver bracelet that was in her pocket.

"Oh! The policeman said that the bracelet was critical to my case. I didn't know how I was going to get it back. How did you get it here?"

Piper brushed a wisp of chestnut hair out of her face and responded, "I have had that bracelet with me ever since you left. I didn't know when I would jump next but knew it would be important to your case."

Piper hugged her friend. She wiped away a single tear that wept out of the corner of Pip's eye. "You are going to be all right. You are going to make it through this. This is not going to define who you are. You are still a smart, strong, funny, beautiful woman. He didn't take that away from you. You have to fight back and not let this change who you are. You were a victim in all of this. Are you listening to me?"

Pip nodded and looked down. "I didn't want Joe to see how I was really feeling. He is beating himself up that he wasn't there to stop this. I tried to make light of it and have joked, but inside I feel sick, and a part of me feels broken. Do you think that I will ever feel the same way again? Will I ever get back to not being scared or being able to feel his hands on my body?" Pip's voice cracked as she choked back a sob.

"You absolutely will feel back to your normal self again. This is all going to take time. Time heals a lot of wounds. In the meantime you have a lot of people that love you and will support you. Give yourself the time that you need. Why don't you close your eyes for a few minutes? I will sit with you until you fall asleep."

Pip strained to keep her heavy eyelids open. She gave up the fight and let herself drift into a dreamless state. When she woke up, the light had changed in the sky, and she wondered how long she had slept.

She sat up quickly, remembering Piper and wondering if it had all been a dream. She glanced around the room and saw that she was alone, except for the bracelet, which was sitting on the nightstand. Piper had been here, and she had brought two things with her that Piper had really needed—the encouraging words that she needed to hear, and most importantly, she had brought the bracelet.

She scooped up the silver bracelet and walked over to the mirror to check her makeup. She reapplied a fresh coat of lipstick and powdered her nose. She headed downstairs and found Joe at the kitchen table working on his laptop.

"Piper was just here, and she brought this," she held out the bracelet for Joe to see.

He turned it over in his hand and, jumping up from the table, slipped on his shoes and said, "Let's go. Lee said that they needed the bracelet there as soon as possible. I can drive."

They walked into the police station together and immediately searched for Lee. He was walking back to his office and had a mug of coffee in his hand. He seemed surprised to see them again so soon. His gaze shifted to the silver bracelet that Piper was holding in her hand.

"Hi. I was hoping that I would see you back again today. I see that you found the bracelet. Let me get that to the lab and dust for prints. We will then run the prints in our database and see if we have any matches." He handed the bracelet to another police officer and explained what he wanted done. "Come into my office, and if you have time, I would like you to look at some of the pictures I have of men who have been convicted of assault."

Pip and Joe took a seat and watched as Lee pulled out a large green three-ring binder down from the shelf and placed it on his desk in front of Pip. "Now take your time. Look through each picture carefully. Many of the men look similar."

Pip knew that she would be able to pick out the man that attacked her if she saw his picture. His image was etched on her mind. She began scanning the pages looking for the man with sandy blonde hair.

Joe watched her patiently as she combed through the pages and pages of pictures of different men. He wished that he could help her. He didn't know how he would feel if she actually found a picture of the man.

She had plowed through about twenty pages of pictures, using her fingers to run down the center of each one as though that would help clarify the man if she saw him. Joe was just about to excuse himself to get a cup of coffee when she stopped with her finger on one of the pictures.

"This is him! Officer Lee, this is the man. Right here." She was pointing to a picture of a man with tousled sandy blonde hair and blue eyes. He had a pale white complexion and was placed in front of the police lines that showed he stood at six feet twp inches tall.

"Are you sure, Pip? This is the guy?" Officer Lee turned the book toward him and slipped the picture out of the plastic sleeve. "Let's find out who this man is."

He tapped the number into his computer that the man was holding in front of him. It took just a moment to search, and then his name popped up. Chad Barns. He had been convicted of assault a number of times and had already served two different sentences of five years. The last sentence, he had been paroled early for good behavior. He had been released from prison ten months ago.

Pip was shocked that she wasn't his first victim. She wondered how long ago he had started following her.

"What happens next, Officer?" Pip asked and groped for Joe's hand. He quickly found her hand and gave it a quick squeeze.

"Well, first we will—"

"I'm very sorry to interrupt, Officer Lee, but I have a match on those prints that I just ran. The name that is linked to the prints is Chad Barns."

"Thank you, Russ." Lee took the paper from the officer and set the report down next to the picture that Pip had just identified.

"This changes things and certainly solidifies your case. I will put out a warrant for his arrest. Joe, in the meantime, don't leave her alone until we can catch this guy."

"Don't worry, I'm not taking my eyes off of her." Joe wrapped a protective arm around Pip. She was chewing on her bottom lip and looked up at him through her eyelashes. He leaned down and kissed her forehead.

Fourteen

*   *   *

Piper woke up to a rumble of thunder and moaned and rolled over and looked at her clock. It was blinking 12:00. Great. The power must have gone out in the night from the storm. Of course it has to rain on her wedding day. She reached over and tapped on the face of her cell phone to see what the time really was. It was 6:57 AM. She needed to go to the bathroom for the tenth time anyway, so she may as well just get up.

She swung her feet over the edge of the bed and looked down at her swollen belly. She was twenty-one weeks pregnant and already felt so huge. Her mom had picked out a very flattering Empire-style wedding dress that hid her belly the best that it could.

She smiled as she looked around at her childhood room. She wanted to keep a little bit of tradition and not sleep in the same bed with Joe the night before the wedding, so she had stayed at her parent's house. It was hard to believe that in a few short hours she would be married, and in just a few months she would be a mother. Her life had changed so much in the last year. She felt so blessed to be marrying such a wonderful man.

She threw on a pair of shorts and a T-shirt and smiled to herself as she headed downstairs. She could already hear her dad from the kitchen bossing her brothers around, telling them they were going to set up the chairs as soon as the rain stopped.

"Good morning. Greg, what are you doing over here so early?" she asked grabbing a piece of bacon off of the plate that her mom had just set down on the table.

"I was forced against my will. Anna told me that if I didn't get my butt over here first thing this morning, I would be sleeping on the couch for the next week. That was all the motivation I needed. So here I am."

Piper was glad that they had decided to do a simple family gathering at her parent's house. Her mom had done all of the arrangements and had ordered white chairs to be set up around the pond. They had only invited family and a few close friends. One of Joe's uncles would be officiating the service.

"How is my little ring bearer doing?" Piper asked Greg.

"Charlie is doing well. He won't let that pillow you made him out of his sight. I think he even slept on it last night."

"He is going to look so cute all dressed up. Joe's cousin is the flower girl. I thought she could help guide him where to go. She is five years old going on twenty. She has been practicing for today by throwing Kleenexes down the aisle. I have her rose petals in the fridge ready to go."

Claire took Piper by the hand and pulled her up. "Come on. I want to show you something." She led her out to the garage, and Piper gasped when she saw it. Standing in the center of the floor stood a beautiful white trellis covered in white stargazer lilies and roses that climbed and twisted around the trellis, covering it in a romantic spray of white flowers mixed with dark green foliage. The scent of the lilies traveled to Piper's nose, and she softly inhaled.

"Mom, this is amazing. When did you have time to do all of this?"

"Well, it isn't every day that my only daughter gets married." She smiled and looked at her beautiful daughter. "Dad built it for me, and I just finished putting the final touches on it this morning. I think that the rain is stopping. We will move it down to the pond once the grass dries out a little bit. You know, they say it is good luck for it to rain on your wedding day."

"That's what they say. Thank you, Mom. It is truly beautiful."

"Come on." Claire wrapped her arm around Piper's shoulder. "Let's go in and fatten up my grandbabies a little bit by getting you a proper breakfast. Plus, you know those boys are just sitting around waiting for us to tell them what to do." Piper chuckled and pushed open the door for her mom.

Piper looked down at the scene from her bedroom window. The chairs had been draped in white cloth with a thick deep purple ribbon tied around the back of the chairs. The beautiful trellis of flowers had been set in the middle, creating an aisle between the chairs. The grass seemed to be sparkling a dark emerald green color from the rain. The weeping willow that hung over the entire lower portion of the grass clung on the edge of the pond and was gently swaying in the breeze. Lanterns had been hung in the trees and would create a dim glow once darkness was upon them. They were starting their vows at sunset, and already the sky was starting to change to an orangey reddish glow.

People were starting to fill in, and Piper could see all of the people she loved sitting and talking. Joe's parents were there, and were talking to her grandpa. Joe's brother was his best man. Anna was Piper's matron of honor and had been fussing over her all afternoon.

There was a soft knock on the door. "Come in," Piper called softly. Her mother pushed open the door and gasped. Piper was standing in front of an oval full-length mirror. Her back was to her mom. The crème-colored dress fit perfectly and had dainty lace-capped sleeves and a sweetheart neckline. The front of the dress was plain and softly flowed down in an Empire style that concealed most of her belly. The back was cut down slightly and showed off her toned back and flowed into a modest train. She had worn her hair up and away from her face. She had curled her hair and pinned the curls up loosely, and a few of them fell out of the pins and softly framed the edges of her neck. She wore a plain crème veil that was held in place by a band of pearls. A strand of pearls draped on her neck, and she was just finishing placing pearl earrings in her ears.

"Do I look all right, Mom?" Piper asked, suddenly concerned when she heard her mom gasp. She ran her hand down her belly and tried to smooth out any of the wrinkles with her hand.

"Baby, you look beautiful." Claire's eyes began to fill with tears. "I wanted to give you something that is borrowed and blue. It was Gram's. She would have wanted you to wear it on your wedding day." She slipped the delicate diamond and sapphire bracelet onto Piper's wrist and hooked the clasp. It shimmered in the light as Piper turned her wrist to look at it.

"It's gorgeous. Thank you, Mom. Please don't cry. You are going make me mess up my makeup." She hugged Claire. "I love you so much, Mom. Thank you for always being there for me. I couldn't have done this wedding without you."

"Piper, you know how much I love you. I am so proud of you, and know that you are going to have a good life with Joe and these babies. Now should we go down and make your grand entrance? Your dad is waiting downstairs for you."

Henry was waiting by the banister and looked up when he heard the clicking of her heels. His breath caught as he looked up at his beautiful daughter as she practically was gliding down the stairs.

"Hi, Dad." Piper slipped her arm into his and smiled up at him.

"You are stunning. I am so proud of you. You know, you don't have to get married. You could always stay and live with Mom and me."

Piper laughed, "You aren't losing me, Dad. I will just be down the road a few miles. I love you."

"I love you too." He leaned down and kissed her cheek, and then took a deep breath. "How is it that you are more calm than I am?" he asked her as they began the walk outside and around to the aisle. The wedding march began to play, and Joe stood at the end of the aisle beaming at her.

"I am calm because I knew that Joe would be waiting for me at the end of the aisle just as I know he will always be there for me. I love him with all of my heart."

"Well, if you're happy, then I have to be. Let's go get you married." Henry grasped her hand that was slipped through his arm and led her down the aisle.

Piper reached the end of the aisle and gave her dad a kiss. He shook Joe's hand and Joe took Piper's hand.

"Hi, beautiful." He smiled down at her and noticed that she was glowing.

She grinned up at him and then caught some movement out of the corner of her eye. A flash of blonde hair was all she saw before she moved behind the tree. She smiled and knew that Pip was here.

Joe's uncle began the ceremony, and their vows were exchanged just as the last few moments of sunshine shined down on them. When it was said that Joe could kiss his bride, he snatched her up and twirled her around as he crushed his lips passionately to hers.

Piper laughed as he put her down, and then placed her hand lovingly on his head as he bent to kiss her belly.

"I now pronounce you Mr. and Mrs. Joe Reynolds." A cheer went up through the gathering of their family and friends. Piper and Joe walked down the aisle hand in hand and grinned at each other.

The live band began to play, and the music seemed to catch on the breeze that swirled Piper's hair slightly as she looked up at Joe. She felt like she was in paradise as she contently swayed in his arms to the music. She looked around at all of her family and friends and sighed happily. The lanterns were lit, and white candles burned all over the different tables that had been set up around the makeshift dance floor. The scent of the lilies rose up to her nostrils just as the sound of laughter caught her ears.

"This really has been the most perfect night, Mrs. Reynolds. You look so beautiful. I am so lucky." Joe leaned in to kiss her lips softly and gently.

"I feel like the lucky one. I love you so much." Piper caught some movement out of the corner of her eye. "It looks like we have a guest from very far away. I am going to go talk to Pip. I won't be long." She reached up and placed a hand on his cheek and smiled up at him.

Pip was waiting around the side of the house for her, having watched the whole scene. The wedding guests were all out front, and she hadn't been spotted by anyone. She stood with her hands on her hips and quickly brushed a tear away from her eyes. Watching Joe and Piper together and so in love reminded her of her wedding day.

"Hey, you," Piper called as she walked toward her pulling up her wedding dress slightly so it won't drag on the ground.

"You look absolutely beautiful. The wedding and this"—she spread her hand out with her palm up—"is amazing. So private and lovely. My wedding was a big affair in a church with hundreds of guests, half of whom I didn't even know. I loved being a part of your special day. How are you feeling?"

Piper reached down and rubbed her belly lovingly. "I am feeling great! I look as big as a house, and my feet are already swollen, but somehow Joe puts up with me. How are you doing, you know, since the last time we saw each other?" Her eyes filled with concern, and she placed her hand on Pip's arm.

"I am actually doing okay. Joe doesn't leave my side. I haven't been able to go back to work just yet. I am still scared about the thought of being in a house by myself. I don't know if or when I will go back to work. I have nightmares about the situation and wake up screaming. Joe has been so supportive of me. I know it is killing him inside." Pip tucked her hair behind her ears, but the shorter piece refused to stay tucked and fell freely over her cheek.

"The man's name was Chad Barns." Piper gasped and clasped a hand to her mouth. "What is it?"

"I know a Chad Barns. He is a high school teacher that was a few years ahead of me in school. He is a good friend of Greg's. He has a wife and two children. I can't imagine him doing this." She slowly shook her head and tried to absorb the information. They really did come from two different worlds.

"They arrested him, and he is in custody waiting for his trial. They are trying to work out a deal with him since he has other priors and has already served jail time. It sounds like the Chad Barns on your side is a stand-up guy. I am so glad that you don't appear to be in any danger. I have been worried that the Chad on this side may come after you."

"I think that I am fading. I am so glad that I was here to witness this. Give my love and congrats to Joe—" And with that she was gone.

Piper walked over to where Joe was standing talking to some friends. She excused him and pulled his arm and led him over where they could talk privately.

"You will never guess what Pip just told me. The man that assaulted her is Chad Barns. Do you remember when you met him at the hardware store, the friend of Greg's?"

Joe rubbed his forehead and thought for a moment. "Sure. Does he have blonde hair and is about six feet tall? He seemed like a good guy."

"I think that our Chad is. Strange how some things could be so similar between Pip's world and ours and how others can be so completely different." The conversation was interrupted when Claire came over to the couple.

"Dear, it is time to cut the cake." She ushered them over to the table that held a simple but elegant white three-tiered cake that was decorated with real lilies.

"Please don't smash the cake in my face, Joe," she warned him.

"Now would I do that?" He grinned devilishly at her as he picked up a slice of the cake that they had just cut. He placed it between his fingers and moved it quickly toward her mouth, and then gently placed it in her mouth.

She carefully took a piece of the cake and slid it into his mouth, and then licked the frosting off of her fingers. The frosting had a hint of almond in it, and Piper groaned with pleasure. "I do love cake."

Joe snorted and looked at the happy expression she wore all over her face.

"You are definitely a hard one to please." He grinned at her and took her hand. "Are you about ready to get out of here?" Piper nodded her head.

"Let's go and say our good-byes. You still haven't told me where we are going tonight."

"Ah. That is for me to know and you to find out." The edges of Joe's mouth curved up in a big smile as he pulled her toward her parents.

Marta opened the door for them and cheerfully added, "Welcome back, Mr. and Mrs. Reynolds." She handed Joe the room key. "You look beautiful, Mrs. Reynolds."

"Thank you, Marta. It is nice to see you again." Joe struggled slightly with the bags, and they headed upstairs.

"I see that you packed light," Joe teased her.

Piper laughed. "Get used to it, is all I can say."

Joe set the bags down and unlocked the door. Piper started to walk in the door, but Joe stopped her. He scooped her up and carried her like a baby into the room.

"I can't have my new bride walking over the threshold by herself." He set her down and pulled the bags in. "You do realize that we are only staying for one night, right?"

"I know, but really there is no telling what sort of things I may need, so I just bring it all just in case." She smiled at him as she unzipped her bag and began to unpack her toiletries.

"Babe, I'm really sorry that we can't go on a proper honeymoon. I promise that I will make it up to you once the babies are born."

"Joe, don't worry about it. This has been perfect. Besides, anywhere that you are and that I'm with you is good enough for me. Now shoo. Go in the bathroom or something. I want to change."

Joe heard a muffled "Ready!" through the bathroom door and opened the door. Piper had lit candles around the room and had dimmed the lights. She had sprinkled rose petals on the bed and turned it down. She stood next to the bed in a white silky gown that cut down low and exposed her full breasts. The material clung to her body and swept down nearly to the floor. She had let her hair down, and her dark mane of chestnut hair fell loosely around her shoulders in soft curls.

Her hands went immediately to her belly, and she became slightly self-conscious. "I'm sorry that I am so big. Probably not what you had imagined on your wedding night." Her eyes cast downward.

Joe moved toward her and placing his hand on the side of her face whispered, "I think you are absolutely beautiful." He reached his other hand up and ran it through her hair as he was kissing her earlobe and slowly moved down the side of her neck.

She shivered, and a small groan escaped her lips as she hungrily took his mouth on hers. He slipped the thin spaghetti strap off her shoulder exposing her breast. He flicked his tongue on her already taunt nipples and teased and sucked them until she was arching her head back and pulled him closer to her.

He put his thumb through the other strap and pulled it down her arm so the nightie slipped to the floor into a puddle.

Her fingers struggled with the buttons on his shirt, as she couldn't seem to get them opened quickly enough. He placed his hands on hers and stopped her. He picked her up and strode over to the bed, lying her down amongst the rose petals. He quickly unbuttoned his pants and slipped them off.

He lightly ran his fingers up her calf and onto her thigh, caressing them and kissing them as he went. He lingered on her inner thigh and slid his tongue around her lips, softly sucking on her clit until it hardened, and she arched her back in pure pleasure. His tongue slipped easily inside of her wetness as he stroked her with his fingers. Her hips were moving at a quicker pace until she called out his name as she came.

She pulled him to her, and he slowly entered her, moving slow and watching her face with each stroke. Her green eyes looked up at him clouded with desire as he continued to ride her, gradually increasing in speed.

She was already sensitive, and it didn't take much for her to be filled with desire and the need for him to be deep inside of her. She lifted her legs and wrapped them around his hips so he could penetrate her more deeply.

She watched his face as they moved as one, knowing that he was getting close to the edge. He closed his eyes and let out a moan as he came, long and hard. She was just a few strokes behind him and shuddered as she released for the second time.

He rolled over and pulled her into his arms. He kissed the top of her head and took a deep breath. "I love you, Piper."

"I love you too. I am so glad that we are a family now." She sighed and closed her eyes. She fell into a peaceful sleep on the chest of the man she loved.

Fifteen

*   *   *

Pip walked out on the front porch in her white bathrobe and retrieved the paper from the front porch. Joe had laughed when she started getting the paper and had teased her about this little thing called the Internet that she could read the news on. She had insisted that she still liked to drink her coffee and read the news on real paper.

She carried it into the kitchen, and Toby sleepily lifted his head up and wagged his tail at her. He didn't get up from his spot by the window where the sunshine was pouring in. He sighed heavily and put his head on his paws.

Pip had insisted that Joe go to the office today. He had grumbled and complained about leaving her, but he had already missed so much time away from the office being at home with her. She had convinced him to go only because Chad was still held in lockup awaiting his sentencing. She did feel safer with him behind bars.

She poured herself a cup of coffee and clicked on the TV to one of the early morning shows. She cut herself up some fruit and mixed it in with some yogurt and granola. She took her bowl and coffee over to the table and sat down, pulling one of her legs up underneath her.

She started to scan the headlines about different local events that were taking place in the community. Her mind drifted, and soon she was lost in thought. She blew out a deep breath. Her mind had wandered to that day, and she could still hear his voice whispering in her ear. She shuddered at the thought and wondered how long it would be before she would stop being reminded of him and what he had done to her.

The telephone rang and interrupted her thoughts. She got up from the table and reached for the cordless phone, checking the caller ID. Not recognizing the name or number, she hesitated before answering the phone.

"Hello?"

"Hello. Mrs. Reynolds? This is Stan Hurd. I am the prosecutor in Chad Barns's case. Do you have a few moments?"

"Yes. What is this about?"

"Mr. Barns has agreed to a plea so the case will not go to trial. He was being charged with aggravated assault with use of a weapon and also of kidnapping since the assault happened in a private residence. With his prior convictions, he was looking at a prison term of six to eight years. His fingerprints that were pulled off of your bracelet along with you identifying him out of the lineup solidified the case against him. He pleads guilty to a lesser charge in exchange for dropping the kidnapping charge. He will be sentenced to five years in prison with a chance for early parole. I wanted to let you know what had happened with his case. Please don't hesitate to contact me with any questions." He gave her his number, and she scribbled it down on a piece of paper, not really paying attention to what she was writing.

She hung up the phone and plopped down at the table. She was trying to clarify everything Stan had just told her. She was still processing the information when the phone rang again.

"Hi, babe. Just checking in to see how your morning is going?"

"It's going. I just received a call from the prosecutor in Chad's case. He plead guilty to aggravated assault. They gave him a deal since he plead guilty and dropped the kidnapping charge. His sentence is five years in prison with the chance for early parole."

"Oh my god. How do you feel about all of this? I should come home."

"No, you don't need to come home. I don't know how I feel. I would like that bastard locked up for the rest of his life, but I know that won't happen. I guess that I am glad that he will be behind bars for at least a few years. Maybe he can get the help he needs. He is obviously a really sick man."

"I will finish up early today and come home. I don't want you to be alone. Will you call me if you need me before I get there?" Joe asked concerned.

"Of course. Don't worry about me. I will be fine. I love you."

"I love you too. See you soon." She hung up the phone and decided that she needed to burn up some of the stress. She took the stairs two at a time and changed into her running gear.

"Come on, Toby. Let's go on a run," she called to the dog as she grabbed his collar from the hook in the mudroom.

*   *   *

Piper padded around the kitchen in her bare feet. Her back was aching, and she stood at the counter and rested one hand on her back and held onto the counter with the other.

She was thirty-seven weeks, and the doctor had told her that she could have the babies any day now, and they would be safe. He was estimating that they both weighed around six pounds. She was getting little sleep at night between trying to find a comfortable position and going to the bathroom every few minutes.

She was excited to see them and hold them in her arms. She knew that the babies weren't identical, but she didn't know if they were boys or girls or one of each. Joe was guessing that they were boys since he had mostly boys in his family. She couldn't decide what sex she thought they were. She just wanted them to be healthy.

She felt a big kick followed by a severe cramp. "Ouch!" She bent over and grasped her belly. Toby picked his head up and walked over to her, quietly whining.

The contractions were coming more steadily now, and with each one it was just a little more intense. She had Braxton Hicks her whole pregnancy, but these felt different. She started to time the distance in between them. When they got to seven minutes apart, she called Joe.

"Babe. I think you need to come home from work. I think I am in labor."

"What? Shit!" She could hear him pacing around the office and could tell that he was getting frantic.

"Calm down. We still have time. My water hasn't broken. Just come on home and drive carefully. And don't speed like you usually do. I want you to be safe."

Joe hung up the phone hurriedly and grabbed his suit coat. He slammed his door shut and yelled to no one in particular, "My wife is having the babies. I have to go!"

Piper began to pace around the kitchen. She tried to breathe through the contractions but felt more like she was hyperventilating. Toby kept looking up at her and whining, staying close by her side.

"I need to go and put the final things into my hospital bag," she said aloud as she began to climb the stairs. She had made it only halfway up the steps when another contraction hit. The pain took her breath away as she gripped the railing and put a hand under her belly.

"Are you in labor?" A familiar voice asked Piper. Smiling, Piper turned to see her blonde friend.

"Yes. I'm glad you're here. Joe isn't very good with blood, and I may need your help in the delivery room. My folks are out of town till tomorrow. Do you think that you will stay that long?"

"I'm not sure, but I sure hope so. Where were you going? Go sit down, and I will get whatever you need."

"I was going up to get my hospital bag. Could you pack my toiletries in it please, and then bring it down? Joe should be home any minute." Piper waddled back down the stairs keeping a hand underneath her belly for support.

She had just got settled on the couch when she heard the garage door slam.

"I'm in here!" she called to Joe. He rushed in and was like a mother hen checking over her.

"What do we do? Are you okay? You aren't going to have the babies right now, are you?"

Piper laughed easily. "I'm fine. Now go help Pip with my bag. She's here and upstairs in our bedroom."

"All right. I will be back in a second," he said and left the room running for the stairs.

Joe walked into his room as watched as the blonde-haired version of his wife was just finishing zipping up the suitcase.

"Thank goodness you're here! I have no idea what I am doing. Please do what you can to stay."

Pip chuckled. "I will see what I can do. Now let's go and get to the hospital and have those babies."

Both Pip and Joe were watching Piper as she was trying to breathe through the contractions. The nurse had just come in and told her that Dr. Waters would be in shortly to break her water. The monitors were quietly keeping track of the babies' heartbeat, and the steady beeping filled the room.

"Piper, I'm Amanda. I am going to be your labor and delivery nurse. So will it just be your husband and sister in the delivery room with you?"

Piper looked toward the blonde version of herself. She thought how easily someone could mistake her for her twin. It was a lot easier to explain Pip as her sister as not to sound crazy.

"Yes. My folks are out of town and will be home tomorrow. My husband's name is Joe and my sister's name is—Pip." From across the room, Piper glanced at her and raised one eyebrow while choking back a laugh.

The nurse was flipping through a chart. "I see that one of your babies is breech. Dr. Waters said that you still would like to try for a natural vaginal birth."

"Is that even possible?" Joe asked coming to stand next to the bed. He squeezed Piper's hand and watched the monitor that showed she was having another large contraction.

"Yes. I have seen a lot of twins born where one is breech. A lot of times, after the first baby is born, it frees up space for the second baby to get in the head-down position. Dr. Waters will be closely monitoring the babies and will take them via cesarean if need be."

Ten hours later and the babies still had not come. Piper was keeping on a brave face and smiled weakly at Joe. She tried to close her eyes in between the contractions, but they were coming right on top of one another.

Joe bent and kissed his wife's forehead and tucked a piece of hair behind her ear. He walked over to Pip and whispered faintly, "I am worried about her. Do you think this is normal? How long can she go on like this?"

Pip laid a warm hand on his arm. "This is totally normal. She's doing great, and pretty soon you will be holding your babies in your arms."

"I hope you're right," Joe sighed and folded his arms over his chest.

"Mom, I want to call and introduce you to your new grandbabies. Graham Sawyer Reynolds was born at 4:37 PM weighing in at six pounds eight ounces and twenty-one and a half inches long. His sister was only eight minutes behind. Arie Lillian Reynolds is six pounds two ounces and twenty-one inches long. They are beautiful and perfect, Mom. I can't wait for you to meet them. Okay, I will. I love you too. See you tomorrow."

"It is killing her to have missed this." Piper looked over at Joe holding their daughter in his arms. She looked so tiny all wrapped up in the blanket with the pink cap on her head. Pip was holding Graham and was lovingly stroking his cheek.

"Hi, Graham. It's your aunt Pip. We are so excited to meet you and your sister. You made your mom and dad so happy today."

Piper looked from her son to her daughter and thought how it didn't even seem real. She was a mother. She had a healthy little boy and girl that would now depend on her. She had so many emotions running through her that it was hard to think straight.

"Pip, I'm so glad that you stayed. I thought it was a little touch and go with Joe when Graham first came out. I thought that he was going to faint!"

Both women laughed. Joe rolled his eyes and said, "Real nice, ladies. It isn't fair that you both gang up on me."

"Joe, where is your camera? Let me get a picture of the four of you," Pip asked.

"The four of us? That sounds strange and delightful at the same time," Joe dug into the bag and pulled out his camera. Piper held each one of the babies in her arms, and Joe wrapped his arm protectively around her shoulders. A happy family smiled up at the camera lens. The babies continued to sleep all snuggled and wrapped tightly in their blankets.

"Hey, Pip. Why don't you get with Piper and the babies, and I will get your picture too? We couldn't have done this without you."

"I thought you would never ask." Pip moved carefully around the side of the bed and sat down next to Piper. The two women smiled at each other, and then turned and smiled for the camera. Joe clicked the picture and grinned at the image that he had captured on film.

"Nice. Piper, why don't I put the babies in their bassinets so you can get some rest? I want to call my folks and some family members and fill them in on the good news."

Pip took the sleeping Arie and placed her in the bassinet with the sign that had a pink hand on it with Arie's name. She looked down at the sleeping babe, and a little feeling of envy crept up. She didn't realize until now how much she wanted a baby.

Joe carefully laid Graham down in the bassinet next to Arie.

"I am going to just head outside of the room to make some calls. Why don't you try and get some rest? I am so proud of you, babe." He leaned over and brushed a gentle kiss on Piper's lips.

Pip dimmed the lights overhead and came around to the edge of the bed and started to tuck Piper in the way that her mom used to do when she was a little girl.

"Why don't you close your eyes for a bit? I will stay right here and listen for the babies."

"I am pretty tired," Piper yawned and rubbed her eyes. "I will just rest for a minute."

Piper could hardly get her words out before she drifted into a deep sleep. Pip bent down and kissed each of the babies. She sighed softly as she looked down at their sweet faces.

Sixteen

*   *   *

Pip reappeared in her bedroom, the moonlight streaking in through the open windows and the curtains blowing lazily from the light breeze. Toby lifted his head and whimpered at her before lowering his head back down on his paws and breathing deeply.

Joe was sound asleep on his side, softly snoring. She went over to his side of the bed and quietly stroked his hair. He looked so peaceful sleeping there, and her breath caught just by looking at him. She smiled as she thought about how after all of these years he still made her insides churn with pleasure.

"Joe, wake up. I'm back and have had the most amazing experience with Piper and Joe. Wake up. I need to talk to you." She shook his arm and felt like she was trying to awaken the dead.

Joe inhaled sharply and sat upright in a panic. "I'm up. Shit, Pip! You scared me. Are you okay?" He rubbed his hand over his face and mouth pushing himself to wake up. He glanced over at the clock and read 3:18 AM.

"Did you just get back? Where did you go this time? I was worried about you," Joe asked her concerned.

"I know that you were probably worried. I was with Piper. She had the babies—Graham and Arie. They are absolutely perfect and beautiful. I was in the delivery room the whole time. Piper did such an amazing job. Joe was really supportive too. Whew! I just can't get over it."

Pip was talking wildly with her hands and bubbling with excitement. Joe smiled as he watched his wife and marveled at how he seemed to fall more in love with her every day. Her personality was such a perfect mix. She was so stubborn that she would persist and persist until she got her way. He smiled as he watched her eyes light up with the passion he had seen so many times before. He was so intrigued how she could still smile so sweetly to him all the while she was giving him a bad time or teasing him. He loved the way she could pull off being so spontaneous and structured at the same time—everything carefully planned—but in a way that made it seem like she was comfortable flying by the seat of her pants. He loved seeing her like this, lit from the inside out, her words having trouble keeping up with her passion and fire within.

"And then Joe cut Graham's cord, and I thought he was going to pass out!" She tilted her head back and laughed a deep throaty laugh. "It was something. I wish you could've been there." She looked down at Joe, and his eyes were a deep blue as he was taking in everything that she was saying.

"Do you know how much I adore and love you?" He reached up and cupped her neck in his hand pulling her head down so he could crush his lips on hers. She breathed a soft moan into his lips and parted her lips so he could deepen the kiss. His tongue plunged into her mouth, and his hands skillfully roamed her back and slid down to her hips and to her toned rear. He gripped one of her cheeks in each hand and pulled her on top of him.

"Now what were you saying?" Joe asked her, a tiny glint in his eye.

"I have completely forgotten. Why don't you show me instead how much you missed me?" She lay down and scissored her legs around his and rolled him on top of her.

He took his fingers and traced them down the side of her face and tangled them in her hair that was fanned out on the pillow. "I will gladly show you—twice."

The sunshine streamed through the window and warmed her face. She inhaled the soft scent of lily of the valley that sat in a rose-colored vase on her window ledge. She raked a hand through her mane of tousled hair and sighed. She reached over to Joe's side and felt that she was alone. She slowly opened her eyes and glimpsed at the clock. It was ten thirty. Almost in a panic, she flew out of bed and hurried downstairs. Joe was sitting at the kitchen table working on his laptop and drinking a cup of coffee. He looked up and smiled at Pip when she came sailing into the kitchen.

"Good morning, sleepyhead. I made you eggs and sausage. It is on the stove."

"I can't believe that I slept this late! We are going to be late for our open houses. I never sleep in this long." She stifled back a yawn and moved over to the coffeepot and poured herself a cup.

"You probably slept this late because you were up half the night delivering babies and the other half trying to make babies." He chuckled at his own joke and winked at her. "I am definitely not complaining."

She flashed him a big grin and snorted out a laugh.

"You know, that's just it. We have been trying to have a baby for over a year now. I am starting to think that something isn't right. Would you go with me to the doctor just to have things checked out?"

"Sure, babe. I want kids as much as you do. Let's see what the doctor says. In the meantime, we could always practice again, in the kitchen, or I'm open to the couch."

Pip slugged him in the shoulder. "Geez, let me at least eat first," she chuckled at the pretend scowl he was giving her, "and then we can talk about it."

Pip sat in the passenger seat next to Joe and was silently fidgeting with her bracelet. This would be her first open house since the attack. Joe had tried to talk her out of doing it, but she was determined not to let

Chad ruin her life or change who she was. At least she had agreed to do the open house in the model house that was right across the street from the house he would be at. Chad was rotting in prison, but Joe still had an uneasy feeling about having Pip in a house alone. He worried that what she had gone through would creep up on her when she was at the house by herself. She was too proud and stubborn to listen to his arguments, so he gave in but promised himself that he wouldn't be too far away.

He helped place the open house signs along the road that pointed into the development. She gave him a quick peck on the lips.

"I will be fine. I will keep my cell in my hand at all times and my pepper spray in my other hand. Promise. Please try not to worry." She smiled at him and turned away, her blonde hair shining in the sunlight as she walked across the street to her open house.

He watched her walk away and felt his heartstrings pull as he vowed to do anything to keep her safe.

It was Sunday, and that meant that Pip was probably holding a house open for the afternoon. Chad thought of her as he had every day since the day they threw him in this hellhole cell. He would play it cool and talk in his group meetings about how what he did was wrong, how he had changed. He would convince them that he was a changed man and wouldn't hurt women again. It was really just one woman that he wanted and wanted to hurt. He needed to feel her warm body pressed up against him again. He needed to hear her soft whimpers and see her pleading eyes. He would not stop next time. There would be a next time—for that Pip could be sure of.

They sat in Dr. Water's office; Joe was quietly stroking Pip's arm as his knee bounced up and down nervously. He couldn't help but feel anxious while waiting for the doctor to come in and give them the test results about what they had found. He hoped that they would be able to get some answers as to why they hadn't been able to get pregnant. He glanced over at Pip and noted her calm face. She was an amazingly strong woman who kept him grounded. She patted his knee and nodded, reassuring him with her touch.

The door opened, and Dr. Water's walked into the office carrying a file folder. He took a seat behind his desk and greeted the Reynolds.

"Hello Pip, Joe. It is nice to see you again. I have the results back from your tests." Joe tensed his body and leaned forward, anxious to hear what Dr. Water's had found.

"After the first round of tests, it would appear that Pip has a normal-functioning uterus and healthy eggs. Joe, after evaluating your sperm, it looks as though you have a low sperm count. The few that you have don't seem to be very fast moving. If you continue to try and get pregnant without fertility help, I am giving you about an 8 percent chance of becoming pregnant on your own. It is not entirely impossible, but I think it will definitely be a challenge. There are certainly many different options available for you to become pregnant. We have an excellent fertility clinic here that would be happy to assist. Here are some brochures about some of the services that they offer. Why don't you take them home and look over them? I am available any time that you have questions and would be happy to go over your options in more detail at a later time. Take some time for this information to sink in and process."

Pip stood up and gathered the brochures in her hand. She shook Dr. Water's hand and thanked him for his time and for the information. She slipped her hand into Joe's and pulled him through the door.

Joe waited until they were inside the car before he turned to Pip.

"I'm the reason that you can't get pregnant." Saying those words out loud sounded even worse to him than when he thought them. He was raging with guilt and anger and didn't really know how to deal with the information they had just been given.

"Stop. Joe, look at me." Pip took his face and looked him lovingly right in the eyes. "I love you. You heard the doctor. There is still a chance that we can get pregnant naturally. We just need to try more. Practice makes perfect." She smiled at him and brought his hand up to her lips. She softly kissed his fingers and then laid them in her lap.

Joe stared at Pip and wondered what he ever did to deserve this amazing woman? She had just basically been told that she would not be able to get pregnant naturally, and she was making light of the situation to make him feel better. She was always looking out for other people's feelings and thinking about them before she dealt with her own feelings.

"I think we both need some time to think about this and process what it means. We will figure this out together. I love you." She squeezed his hand reassuringly. "Let's go home."

*   *   *

There had been a constant stream of visitors that first month. Neighbors and friends bring over meals, fussing over Piper and the babies and telling Joe what a big help he was being.

Joe's mom had come their first week home and had jumped right in, helping by fixing the meals and changing diapers. Piper's mom had been at the house constantly too. She often stayed overnight in the guest room to try and give Piper a little bit of a break when the babies were up in the night.

Piper woke with a start and had to think a second where she was. She quickly patted down the sheets around her, feeling for the babies. She could've sworn they had been in bed with her. She must have nodded off and woke in bed alone. She got up quickly and went in search of Joe.

She heard him softly singing from the nursery, and her heart nearly burst from the love she felt as she watched him from the doorway. He held Graham in one of his arms and Arie in the other. Graham was fast asleep, but Arie was wide awake, and her small baby blue eyes stared up at him with fascination. He was quietly singing "You Are My Sunshine" to her and her sleeping brother. He had changed the words to their names in part of the song and was softly rocking them in the rocking chair with just a small lamp on that put out a faint glow.

He looked up when he noticed her standing in the doorway and smiled at her; the love that he felt for his children and his wife flowed out into the song he was singing to them and to her. He loved Piper dearly when he married her, but after the babies were born, he knew he loved her even more than he thought possible.

She crept silently into the room and took the sleeping Graham from his arms and laid him in the crib.

"What are you doing, babe?" she whispered sweetly.

"You looked exhausted, so I thought I would let you sleep. We have a real party girl on our hands with this one." He looked down at his daughter that lay nestled in his arms. She looked so much like Piper. She had a full head of dark hair that was slightly wavy. She had a little rosebud mouth and a turned-up nose. Her features were petite and dainty unlike her brother. Graham was structured more like him. His head was also covered with a full head of dark hair. He had a fuller mouth and big eyes. Joe was so in love with his children and wondered how he had ever made it this far in life without them.

Piper smiled down at Arie. Her eyelids were getting heavy, and she contently sighed as she began to drift to sleep in her father's arms. Joe carefully stood up and placed her next to Graham in the crib. He wrapped his arm around Piper, and they both watched the sleeping babies.

"We should go and get some sleep while they are sleeping," Piper whispered, and both hesitantly left the babies to their sweet dreams.

Seventeen

Present Day

"Knock, knock! Anybody home?" Pip called as she opened the front door.

"Auntie Pip! I knew you would come." Arie ran and jumped into Pip's arms. Pip swung the young girl around in circles, and her throaty laugh rolled easily off her tongue.

"Of course I was planning to come. I wouldn't miss the princess and prince's fifth birthday party."

"I'm not a prince, Auntie. I'm a pirate. Arrrgg!" Graham rounded the corner dressed in a pirate's costume complete with an eye patch.

"You most definitely are a fierce pirate. Where are your mom and dad?" Pip asked looking around.

"Mom's in the kitchen getting the last few things ready, and Dad is lighting the grill," Arie explained as she joined her little hand in Pip's. They walked hand in hand into the kitchen.

"Look who just got here, Mom." Arie turned her face up to Pip and smiled sweetly at her.

Piper put down her spoon and dried her hands on her apron that she wore clinched around her waist. She walked over to Pip and gave her a quick hug.

"I am so glad that you made it back in town," Piper winked at her friend and smiled. "The kids have been pestering me all week if you were going to make it to their party. I told them that you might be out of town. I am glad that it worked out. I have their gifts upstairs in the bedroom that you asked me to get."

"I will go get them!" Graham hollered as he made a mad dash for the stairs.

"Babe, the grill is all fired up. When do you want me to put on the meat?" Joe came in through the back door, and the screen slammed closed behind him. "Hi, Pip. Good to see you. How was your trip?"

Pip laughed, and her green eyes sparkled. "It was uneventful and quick."

The front door opened, and family seemed to pour through it all at once. Claire and Henry were the first ones through the door followed by Greg, Anna, Charlie, and Eve.

Arie and Graham spotted their cousins at once and quickly grabbed them by the hands and pulled them off to the backyard and into their tree house.

Their squeals of delight and laughter flowed down from the tree house and through the screen door, making Piper's lips curl into a smile as she began cutting up the carrots for the salad.

The men had made their way outside on the back porch and were talking about the latest baseball game. Joe took a pull on his beer, and then checked his watch to see how many more minutes the burgers needed to cook.

Inside the cheerful kitchen, the women had poured themselves a glass of wine. Claire walked around the island and placed her hand on Pip's arm.

"You know, after all of these years of seeing you at important events, it still surprises me when I see you here," she said and looked at the pretty blonde woman that looked identical to her own daughter. She had been shocked when Piper had told her about the woman that looked like her and how they jumped in and out of each other's lives. She had believed her daughter, but it wasn't until she first met Pip, when the babies were just a few weeks old, that she fully understood how the two women's lives were interconnected.

"It is the same way for me when I see you here. You look so much like my own mother, but with subtle differences. I really love watching you interact with the kids. I always thought that is how my mom would be if I ever had kids." Pip smiled at Claire.

Piper studied Pip's face as she listened to her talk to her mom about having kids. She would have to remember to ask her about her having children later when they were alone.

The kids came running through the house at top speed and headed into the family room.

"Go wash your hands for dinner!" Piper called after them. She began pulling out the different salads that she had already prepared and put them on the counter. Joe walked into the kitchen carrying a tray of burgers, some with cheese and some without.

"Did the kids hear from Peter today?" Claire asked Piper.

"He called earlier in the day to wish them a happy birthday. He told me that the project that he has been working on will be done in three weeks, and then he will be home. He sounded pretty excited about it." Piper pulled the lids off of the different salads and placed serving spoons in them.

"Time to eat, kiddos," Piper called.

"Auntie Pip, will you sit by me?" Arie asked as she walked into the room and immediately went to Pip's side.

"Of course, birthday girl. I would love that."

"Will you tell me the story again about the day I was born? Don't forget about the part where Dad almost passed out."

"We can't forget the best part of the story now, can we?" Pip laughed as she caught Joe rolling his eyes.

"That isn't quite like I remember how it went," Joe protested as he was piling toppings on his burger.

"Babe, I agree with Pip on this, so I guess you are outnumbered. Besides we are always right." Piper stood on her tiptoes and planted a kiss noisily on his mouth. He grinned and swatted her behind as she walked by.

Graham was sitting quietly at the table and hadn't touched his dinner at all. His face was pale.

Piper walked over and sat down next to him. She ran a cool hand along his forehead and face. He felt warm and slightly feverish.

"Are you feeling all right, sweetie?" she asked quietly.

"I don't know, Mom. I am really tired. I don't feel like eating at all."

Joe overhead their conversation and moved over to where they were sitting.

"Bud, why don't you go lay down on the couch for a little bit and rest? Mom can save your dinner for later. Do you need help getting onto the couch?"

Graham just nodded quietly. Joe scooped him up in his arms and swiftly carried him into the family room and laid him down on the couch. He covered Graham with a blanket.

Piper leaned down and kissed him on his forehead.

"Just close your eyes, sweet boy. I will go and get my dinner and eat it in here with you. Be right back."

Joe sat on the end of the couch and looked over at his son. Graham had felt fine just an hour before. Now he was pale and had dark circles under his eyes. He thought what a bummer this was for him to get sick on his birthday.

Graham slept for the next hour while the family finished their dinner. Pip watched as Arie took her fork and just pushed her food around on her plate.

"What's up? Why aren't you eating your dinner? Are you sick too?" Pip leaned over and asked Arie.

"I feel fine. I just want Graham to feel better so he can help me blow out the candles on our cake." She bent her head down and slumped her shoulders forward making her tiara slide down on her forehead.

"I bet that Graham will still be able to blow out the candles with you. He has been resting for a while now. I bet your dad can carry him back in. Why don't I go and ask your dad if he can help?" Pip patted Arie's shoulder and set off to find Joe.

Pip found Joe sitting on the coffee table quietly stroking Graham's arm. Graham's eyes were open, but he looked pretty tired.

"Hey, bud. Your sister is hoping that you will be able to help her blow the candles out on your cake. Do you feel like doing that?" Pip crouched down and brushed a piece of his hair back off of his face.

"Yeah, I think so. Mom just left to go and get the cake ready. She asked me the same thing." Graham sat up and reached for his dad's hand to help pull him to a standing position.

They walked into the kitchen, and the family cheered. Graham gave a half smile and went to sit down by his sister.

Arie leaned over and kissed Graham's cheek and whispered in his ear, "My wish is going to be for you to feel better." She grinned at her twin, and he nodded at her.

Piper came in with the cake lit up with five candles. Anna had made the cake and decorated it with a princess dressed in pink in a castle and a pirate charging over the drawbridge. The kids had laughed when they saw it. It was a chocolate cake with a butter-cream frosting but was so cute that Piper hated to cut into it.

The family sang happy birthday to Graham and Arie. Joe videotaped the whole thing, and then told them to make a wish.

Both kids took a big breath and blew out the candles.

Arie smiled at Graham. "My wish will come true since we blew them all out."

Piper began slicing up the cake and serving it with ice cream. Graham seemed to be doing slightly better and even had a bite or two of the cake and a few spoonfuls of ice cream.

Anna picked up her plate of cake and moved over to where Piper was standing.

"Thank you again for making the cake. It is so moist and good. You know how picky Mom is about her cakes. I don't see how she could say one bad thing about this one," Piper told Anna in between bites of cake. She laughed when she overhead Claire telling Henry how moist the cake was.

Pip had made her way over to where Anna and Piper were standing. Anna turned and looked at both women.

"You know, it still kind of blows my mind when I see the two of you together. The kids really think that Pip is their aunt, don't they? What did you tell them about Pip?"

Piper set down her cake and thought back to the first time that Graham had asked about Pip. He had been learning about twins in preschool since a pair of his classmates was twins. He came home from school that day and was curious about his mom and the woman that looked like her.

"Well, we thought it was easiest to just explain to the kids that Pip was my sister, my twin sister. We told them that she travels a lot but usually makes it to important events. Luckily for us when Pip was younger she started going by the nickname Pip. Her real name is Piper, but her brother started shortening it. It is a good thing too because the kids would think that even as crazy as their grandma Claire is sometimes, even she wouldn't name her two children the same name. The kids seem to believe that Pip is my sister."

Anna turned to her sister-in-law and asked, "Have you jumped to Pip's world lately?"

"I really haven't. Strange. I haven't really thought about that until you just asked that. Pip has been jumping here whenever there is a big event happening in our lives."

"My life is just so boring that you haven't needed to come," Pip teased as she tucked a stray piece of blonde hair behind her ear. "I should probably say good-bye to the birthday kiddos though just in case I go home soon." She broke away from Anna and Piper and went to sit with Graham and Arie.

"I have to be going home pretty soon. I wanted to wish you a very happy birthday to both of you. You know that you are my favorites." She grabbed both of them and enveloped them in a big hug. "I hope you feel better, Graham."

Graham's cheeks were starting to get a little bit rosier.

"I'm feeling a little bit better. I think Arie's wish helped." Graham smiled at his sister. "When will you be back, Auntie? I have a soccer game next weekend that I would like you to come to."

"I will do my best to be there, bud." Pip tousled his hair and stood up. "I love you both. I hope to see you soon."

Pip was starting to feel her heart starting to race. She promptly stood up and hurried out onto the front porch. She had just shut the front door when the blackness took over.

* * *

Joe sat stretched out in the rocking chair on the front porch listening to the crickets chirp. It was a clear night, and he could make out every star in the sky. The air was crisp and smelled clean. The rain had stopped an hour ago, but the grass still held the last of the drops.

He knew that today was the twin's fifth birthday. He found it hard to believe that five years had passed since they had been born. Although he had never met them, he felt like he knew them from how much Pip talked about them. He wished that he could jump like Pip to get to experience what she did.

Joe took a sip of his coffee and thought about Pip. He wondered how long she would stay in the other world this time. She had been jumping a lot lately and sometimes staying away for a few days at a time. She had told him that she didn't have any control over the length of time she stayed. He wished that she had some way to get word to him that she was okay. When she was gone for a while, his mind automatically went to the day when Chad had almost gotten to her. He shuddered thinking back to that day.

He knew that Chad would be released in a few months. He felt so much more secure knowing that Chad was locked up in prison. How would he be able to protect Pip from him when he was out of prison? The guilt that he hadn't been able to protect her from him the first time gnawed at him.

He was still thinking about Chad when Pip reappeared on the porch. She had never looked better. Her hair was slightly tousled, and her eyes sparkled with happiness. She seemed to be glowing.

"Hi, babe. I made it back for the twin's birthday party. It was so fun to see them dressed up. Arie was a princess, and Graham was a pirate. They were so stinkin' cute! Graham ended up getting sick, poor thing. I hope Arie doesn't get it."

"I was hoping that you would make it home tonight. How was the party? Who all was there?"

"Greg's family was there, and Anna made the most delicious cake and decorated it for them. Henry and Claire were there too. Peter couldn't get away from a project that he was working on."

"My folks weren't there? I mean Joe's parents," Joe asked.

Pip sensed what he was feeling and what he didn't say out loud. "No, Joe's parents weren't there. Are you thinking that it sounds like your parents?"

"I just always wondered what they would be like when we have kids. I know that they love me, but they are caught up in their own lives. I know that they are busy. I always seem to be making excuses for them, don't I?" Joe sighed heavily and seemed distracted by his own thoughts.

"You know another thing, Pip, I know that you want a baby as much as I do, and it just doesn't seem to be working. What do you think about adoption?"

"I guess that I am open to it, but a part of me really wants to experience being pregnant and having our own children. Biologically. Let's give it a little more time." She walked over to him and took his face in her hands. "I love you so much. Please don't get discouraged. It will happen like it is supposed to happen." Pip bent and slowly took his lips onto hers.

The kiss started as sweet and loving and quickly turned into a hungry need that drove from deep inside of her. The wanting, the needing, and the desire threatened to take over control of her. She didn't know how much she needed Joe to stabilize her emotions until that moment. She poured all of her passion and devotion into that kiss.

"Let's go in and take this upstairs," Joe huskily whispered into her neck as he slowly sucked and kissed his way down from her ear lobe to her collarbone. He took her hand and led her inside, pulling her impatiently up the stairs. She tilted her head back and laughed as she struggled to keep up with him as he was climbing the stairs two at a time.

*　*　*

"Run, Graham!" Joe hollered at the little boy in the blue jersey running with all of his might with the soccer ball. He dribbled around the blonde boy that was a foot taller than him and headed straight for the goal post. He glanced around and studied his opponents, and then with a swift kick sent the ball soaring over the goalie's head scoring a point for his team.

Piper jumped up and cheered, clapping her hands. Graham flashed them a big smile, and Joe gave him the thumbs-up signal. He was so proud of himself as his teammates slapped him on the back. He started to run up the length of the field again.

Graham stopped suddenly. He leaned down and rested his hands on his knees. He felt so light-headed and weak. He looked over at his parents, and then collapsed onto the ground.

Piper and Joe ran over to him. He was lying in a crumpled heap on the grass. His nose was bleeding slightly, and he felt hot to the touch.

"Oh my god, Joe! What is wrong with him?"

"I don't know, but let's go and have him checked out." Joe scooped Graham up and started to carry him to the car.

Graham's coach ran up to them. "Is he all right?"

"We aren't sure. We will keep you posted. We are going to run him to the doctor," Piper explained as she was quickly gathering up their chairs and the blanket that Arie was sitting on.

"Come on, Arie. We have to go."

They hurried to the Range Rover Sport and threw the cars and blanket in the back. Arie climbed in next to Graham. She buckled her seat belt and looked over at her brother. His head was resting back against the headrest, and his eyes were glassy. He was pale, and his nose was still bleeding.

"Mom, is he going to be okay?" Arie asked with concern.

"We are going to take him to the doctor and find out. Graham, hang in there. We will be to the hospital soon. Try and tilt your head back and keep the towel on your nose."

Graham did as he was told because he really didn't have any energy to argue about it. He glanced out of the window at the buildings that were passing by in a blur. It was getting harder to keep his eyes open. He was so tired.

Joe pulled up to the Belmont Hospital, which had a children's wing attached to the main hospital. He brought the car to a stop outside of the ER.

"I didn't know where else to go since the doctor's office is closed on Saturday. Do you think this is okay?" Joe asked Piper.

"This is great. Why don't I take Graham in, and you can park the car? I will start on the paperwork."

Piper ran around and threw open Graham's door and unbuckled his seat belt. She scooped him up and walked in through the sliding doors with Arie close by her side.

"Hi. We need to have him checked out please," Piper explained to the woman behind the front desk.

"Sure thing. Please fill out this paperwork, and I will also need a copy of your insurance card." The woman gave Piper a clipboard and a pen. "Go ahead and take a seat."

Piper glanced around at the few people sitting in the waiting room. She felt fortunate that there weren't more people waiting to be seen. Piper set Graham down in a chair next her and started filling out the paperwork.

Graham moaned softly, and Piper looked over at him. She spotted Joe coming through the sliding doors. He hurried over to where they were sitting.

"Graham, what can I get you? Do you need anything, buddy?"

Graham just shook his head. Piper hated the feeling of helplessness that she felt. She got up and turned the clipboard over to the woman at the front desk.

"It shouldn't be too much longer now," the woman at the desk assured her.

Piper went and sat back down in between Graham and Arie. She patted Arie's hand and put her arm around Graham. She kissed the top of his head.

"It's going to be okay, baby. Don't worry."

"Graham Reynolds?" a young nurse called from the doorway.

Joe stood quickly and helped Graham to his feet. He steadied the small boy and then helped him walk back into the examination room. Piper and Arie followed and took a seat in the small examining room.

"Hi, I'm Suzanna. So what brought you in today, Graham?"

"I don't feel well. I was playing soccer, and then got really tired all of a sudden. My nose started to bleed too. I feel really sleepy right now."

The nurse began taking his blood pressure and getting his vitals. "I'm going to take your temperature with this little wand," she explained as she ran the wand over his forehead. "It's 102.8."

"Have you been sick before this?"

"He was sick last weekend with a fever and really tired. It just went away on its own though," Piper explained to Suzanna.

"Okay. The doctor will be in shortly." Suzanna closed the laptop and placed it on the counter.

"Now what happens, Mom?" Arie asked, her eyes big as she watched her brother lie in the big bed.

"We sit and wait. I am sure that the doctor will be in soon."

The door swung open, and a tall man with brown hair walked into the room. He walked over and shook Joe's hand.

"Hello. I am Dr. Horsch." He turned toward Graham and took a seat on the small stool in front of him and started to read through the information on the computer screen on his lap. "What seems to be the matter, Graham?"

"I have been feeling really tired lately. I was playing soccer, and all of a sudden I felt like I couldn't stand up. My nose started to bleed too."

Dr. Horsch started to examine him and felt his lymph nodes along his neck. He looked in his ears and in his mouth.

"I am going to have the nurse come back in and draw some blood. I am going to test your blood for a few different things. Once the results come in, I hope that we will have some answers as to what you have."

"Do you think it is an infection or a virus?" Joe asked the doctor.

"I'm not sure yet but will know more when I get these test results back. I should have the results back on Tuesday. I can pass along the results to your regular pediatrician if you would like. Until then I would suggest that Graham gets plenty of rest and keep pushing the fluids. Maybe take it easy on the sports for the next week and see how it goes."

"Thank you, Doctor."

"Sure. My nurse will be back in to get some blood, and then you can go home. Take care and I will make sure that Graham's regular doctor calls you in a few days."

Dr. Horsch walked out of the room, and the door slowly closed behind him with a click. Graham lay down on the examining table and closed his eyes. Piper hated seeing him like this. She went over to him and ran her hand over his forehead.

The nurse walked back into the room carrying a tray with the necessary blood-drawing equipment.

"Has he ever had his blood drawn before?" she asked Piper.

"Not lately. He is usually pretty good though with stuff like that."

The nurse pulled on her latex gloves and went over to the table where Graham was lying.

"Can you sit up for me, sweetheart? I promise to do this as quickly and as painlessly as possible."

Graham sat up and was a brave boy as the nurse drew his blood. He didn't even make a peep but kept his eyes on his mom while the nurse was taking his blood. After she was finished, she told them that they were free to go home.

Graham slipped his hand in Piper's, and they all headed out to the parking lot. Joe opened the door for them and got Graham all situated in his seat and helped him with his seat belt.

"Well, I guess now we just wait," he said to Piper. She nodded her head, and he pulled the car out of the parking lot and headed toward home.

* * *

He was fidgeting and couldn't sit still. He continued to wring his hands together and cleared his throat. He ran his hand through his sandy blonde hair, and then shoved his hands in his pockets.

"Chad Barns? The parole board will see you now."

He nodded quietly and allowed himself to be led into the brightly lit room. Sitting behind a table sat four people that ultimately would decide his fate.

He tried to clear his mind and put a smile on his lips as he walked up to the lone chair that sat in the middle of the floor facing the table.

"Good afternoon, Chad. You sit before us, and we are to determine whether or not you will be eligible for parole. I see that you have been a model citizen since you arrived in prison. You have done your group therapy as requested, and your therapist said that you have made great strides to become a better man. Do you agree with these statements?"

Chad pushed the image of Pip and the delicious scent of her out of his mind. Now was the time to focus.

"Yes, sir. I am now able to see what a horrible person I was, and what I did to those women was wrong. I feel that the time that I have spent in prison has allowed me to grow as a person. I feel confident that if I were released, I would excel in society and make a difference. I have come to terms with my feelings and emotions about women, and with my therapist's help, I have been able to see that my actions were wrong. I will not do those things again."

Chad's eye has been twitching, and he swallowed hard to keep himself under control. Only a few more minutes and he would have them fooled. He would not let his temper take control of this moment. He had been planning it for too long.

The three men and one woman whispered among themselves. The one on the far right spoke first.

"Mr. Barns, on behalf of this committee, we are granting you parole. You will be released to your own accord within the time period of two months. Thank you for your hard work and willingness to make a contribution to society." The man scribbled something down on a piece of paper. "Guard, please take Mr. Barns back to his cell. Good day."

Chad rose from his chair slowly and nodded to the committee. His mind was already whirling as he made his way back to his cell. Two months. So much planning to do so little time. His lip twitched up on one side of his mouth, and his eyes glistened with delight as he was led back to his awaiting cell.

*　*　*

Piper was scrubbing the kitchen floor and smiled to herself as she heard the children laughing in the other room. She glanced over her shoulder and watched her kids for a moment as they plotted and planned where the next Lego piece should go to make their vehicle. They had always been the best playmates. Graham seemed to be feeling better, and his fever had gone away yesterday. He still complained of being tired, but maybe that was still lingering from whatever illness he had.

The phone rang, interrupting her thoughts, and she stood, wiping her hands on the front of her jeans.

"Hello?"

"Hi, Mrs. Reynolds? This is Stoney Creek Pediatrics calling. We have the results of Graham's tests. Dr. Larson would like to go over them in person. Are you available this afternoon?"

"Oh, wow. This afternoon?" Piper glanced at her watch and quickly thought about what to do with the kids. "I think I can make that work. What time are you thinking?"

"The doctor has some time available at three. Should I go ahead and schedule you for that time?"

"Sure. I will call you back if I can't make that work. Thank you."

"That sounds fine. We will see you this afternoon."

Piper hung up the phone and immediately called her mom and asked her if she could watch the kids. After she hung up the phone with Claire, she sent a text to Joe asking him to meet her at the doctor's office. She tried not to call him in the middle of the day in case he was with clients.

The appointment was in an hour. She washed her hands and decided that she would have to finish cleaning the floor when they got home. She needed to change her clothes too before they left.

"Hey, kiddos. I am going to change my clothes quick, and then we are going to Grandma's for a little bit. Please go to the bathroom and get your shoes on. I will be back down and ready to go in a minute," she hollered at the kids as she hurried upstairs.

She heard her phone make a small beep. She dug it out of her pocket as she was climbing the steps. She glanced down and saw that it was a text from Joe saying that he would be able to meet her at the appointment.

She had changed her clothes, and she and the kids were out the door in five minutes flat. Her mind started to race as she drove toward her mom's house. Why did the doctor want to tell us the results in person? That was never a good sign.

Claire was waiting for them and stepped out on the porch when she saw the black Range Rover pull into the driveway. Piper put on a brave face for her mom and quickly climbed out of the car.

"Thanks for watching the kids, Mom. I hope that the appointment isn't too long. I will be right back to get them as soon as it is over."

"Don't worry, honey. Your phone call got me out of going to see your crazy aunt Betsy, so take all the time you need." Claire winked at her.

Piper chuckled and kissed Graham and Arie on the head. "Be good for Grandma. I will be back shortly."

"We will, Mom," Arie told her and went around to where Claire was standing. Graham waved as Piper backed out of the driveway. "Love you, guys!" Piper called out the window, and then sped down the road toward the doctor's office.

Piper and Joe were seated in the doctor's office. Piper nervously wiped her hands on her pants. Her palms were sweating, and she started to chew on her lip. Joe reached over and patted her leg, and then took her hand in his.

"It's going to be okay, babe." He sounded so reassured.

Dr. Larson came breezing into the room. The petite blonde doctor had always been such a support person to them both as the twins were growing up. She was always the first person to offer gentle advice and had a way of making those around her feel at ease.

"Hi, Piper and Joe. Thanks for coming in on such short notice today. I received Graham's tests results back from the lab. The ER doc had them sent over to my attention. I spoke with him this afternoon after seeing the results, and he wanted to be sure that I would get you the results as quickly as possible."

Piper realized that she was holding her breath. She blew out a deep breath through her mouth and sat frozen, waiting.

"Graham's tests results came back that he has pediatric acute lymphoblastic leukemia or ALL for short. That is why he has been feeling extremely fatigued and has had a fever and some bloody noses.

We want to be able to take control of this right away and will need to start chemotherapy to help kill off the leukemia in his blood cells . . ."

Dr. Larson continued to talk about the causes of the leukemia and what the treatments were for Graham, but Piper didn't hear any of it. She had stopped hearing what the doctor said after the word "leukemia" had been spoken. She sat dumbfounded and seemed to stare at the doctor's mouth and watched it moving but didn't hear any of the words that were coming out.

Her son had leukemia, her baby. How did this happen? Was he going to be okay? What would they do? Her mind snapped back into the conversation. She needed to be focused.

"I'm sorry, Dr. Larson. I kind of zoned out for a minute. I am shocked by what you said. What is your course of treatment for Graham? I'm afraid I missed it," Piper voice was shaky as she spoke to the doctor.

"We will start a round of radiation and chemotherapy. We will also start testing family members for a possible stem cell transplant match if that is something you are interested in. Once Graham goes into remission from the chemotherapy, we will do a stem cell transplant into his bone marrow from a matched donor," Dr. Larson continued on, and Piper hoped that Joe was grasping everything that she was saying because Piper was struggling to hold on. She fought back tears as they began to brim in her eyes, and her throat got tight.

"We would like you to bring Graham to the Belmont Children's Hospital this evening if possible. We want to get started on his treatment right away."

"Yes, of course. We can do that," Joe answered and squeezed Piper's hand.

"Check in on the fifth floor, and the nurse at the front desk will direct you where to go. I will be by after my office hours to visit with Graham and answer any questions he may have. I know that this is a complete shock, but we are fortunate we caught it when we did. I think that if we get started on the treatment right away, we will have positive results. I will be in touch."

"Thank you, Dr. Larson." Joe took a hold of Piper's arm and led her to the door. He held onto her through the waiting room and didn't let go of her until he opened her driver's side door for her.

"Are you going to be okay to drive?"

"I think so. I am in shock. What are we going to do?" She had held in her tears and now let them flow freely as they poured down her cheeks.

"We are going to take care of Graham and give him the best treatment that we can. We are going to be strong for him and each other. We will get through this, all of us. We are not going to lose our little boy." Piper nodded, and Joe looked down at her pleading eyes filled with worry. He heard his words said out loud and hoped that they would make him feel reassured as well as Piper. Graham had to be okay; he just had to be.

Eighteen

Piper looked at her little boy who was resting with his eyes closed. He looked so tiny in the hospital bed. He had insisted that he bring his favorite stuffed animal. His arm was draped over the whale that he lovingly called Walter. He was breathing deeply and steadily and seemed not to be in much pain.

Graham had reacted so mature when they told him that he was sick. He just looked at them with his big blue eyes and nodded his head. He had looked directly at Piper and told her not to worry, that he was strong and would fight to get better. Piper had struggled not to shed the tears that had been close to the surface ever since Dr. Larson had given them the news. If Graham was trying to be brave, she had to be too.

She fussed and tucked his blanket around him. Arie looked up from the picture she was drawing and watched her mom.

"Mama, Graham is going to be okay. I made a wish for him to get better on our birthday. We blew out all of the candles, so it has to come true. He will get better, right?"

Piper walked over to Arie and sat down next to her on the small couch that pulled out into a bed. "Yes, I hope so. Graham is strong and a fighter. We are going to do everything we can to make certain that he gets better," she said and leaned down and kissed the top of her head, inhaling in the strawberry scent of her shampoo.

The doctor had already been in to see Graham. He would start chemotherapy at 8:00 AM tomorrow. Piper was going to stay with him in the room tonight, and Joe would take Arie home. Claire was going to watch Arie in the morning so Joe could be with Graham and Piper. No one knew quite what to expect.

Joe rubbed his hand across his mouth and itched the stubble on his face. He stifled back a yawn.

"Why don't you take Arie home? You both look tired and we have an early start in the morning. I bet Graham is asleep for the night anyway. I plan on going to bed soon too." Piper walked over to Joe. He pulled her into his arms and just held onto her for minute without saying anything. She rested her cheek against his chest and breathed in his scent. It was a mixture of soap and cologne. She felt so comforted being in his arms and wished he could make this all go away.

"All right. Let's go, Arie. I need your help letting Toby out anyway, and it is close to bedtime."

Piper went over to where Arie was sitting and helped her put her crayons back into the bag.

"I love you, sweetheart. I will see you tomorrow afternoon. Please be good for Grams and Gramp." Piper kissed Arie on the cheek and gave her a tight hug.

"I love you, Mom. See you tomorrow."

Piper blew a kiss to Joe and Arie as they walked out of the door. She was left in the dimly lit room alone with her thoughts and a sleeping Graham.

"I guess that I should try and get some sleep," she mumbled to herself as she began to yawn. Tomorrow was going to be a long day.

*   *   *

It was a beautiful spring day, and Pip was glad that she had gotten up early to go for a run before her busy day of client meetings started. She had easily run six miles this morning without giving it a second thought.

Her muscles were toned and used to her pushing herself nearly six days a week.

She had felt good this morning and had come home to a big breakfast that Joe had waiting for her. She had quickly gotten showered and dressed and was just putting her jewelry on when she suddenly felt queasy. She clutched her hand to her stomach, and her eyes drifted to the clock. It read 6:57 AM.

She hoped that she wasn't getting sick. She had too many meetings today to be sick. She had felt fine earlier but now had a sick feeling of dread in her stomach, and her head was beginning to pound.

She grabbed the water bottle that sat on her bathroom counter and took a long drink. Maybe she was dehydrated? She had never had a feeling like this that came on so quickly

Pip sat on the edge of the tub and rested her head in her hands. Joe walked into the bathroom to brush his teeth.

"Are you okay, Pip? You look a little pale."

"Something's wrong, Joe. I have such a nervous feeling in the pit of my stomach."

"Are you worried about any of your clients today? I sometimes feel like that when I am meeting new people."

"No. That's just it. All of the people I am meeting with today are repeat clients. No one is new. I just can't explain it." Joe sat on the edge of the tub with her and softly stroked her back. The heat from her body was coming through the silky material of her blouse.

He continued to rub his fingertips in circular motions on her back. He had taken a handful of her hair and pushed it over her shoulder. He had no sooner done that, and she was gone. She was literally under his fingertips one minute and gone the next.

Joe was left sitting alone in their bathroom. He could still smell her vanilla perfume lingering in the room. He looked around the bathroom and sighed heavily. How long would she be gone for this time?

*   *   *

"Mom, I'm scared." Graham turned his head, and his big blue eyes looked into his mom's.

"I know, baby. Remember what the doctor told us about what would happen. They are going to give you the medicine, and it will make you feel sick, like you have the flu. The medicine will help kill off the parts in your blood that are making you sick. We will have to hopefully do it only a few times before you will start to feel better. Dad and I are going to be with you the whole time. You are such a brave boy. You can do this."

Graham took a deep breath and nodded his head, willing himself to be strong for his mom.

"Where is Dad?"

"He will be here any minute. He had to drop Arie off at Gram's house. We still have a few more minutes until they will come to get you. He will be here. Here, why don't you draw in your sketchbook while we wait?"

Piper reached into her bag and pulled out a sketchpad with a deep blue cover. Graham's uncle Peter had sent it to him for his birthday. They both shared a love of drawing, and Graham had already begun to fill the pages with sketches of all different things from animals to space vehicles.

Piper walked over to the bed and handed Graham the sketchbook. She blew a piece of hair out of her face and caught some movement out of the corner of her eye. The blonde-haired woman was walking briskly down the hall looking into each room on her way by.

Piper's face lit up when she saw her. Thank goodness Pip was here. She needed her friend's support and her positive outlook on things. She needed to hear that her son was going to be all right.

Pip caught sight of Piper and rushed into the room. It took her all of five seconds to see Graham in the hospital bed and immediately get worried.

"What happened? Graham, are you sick again?" She scooted over to Graham's bed and promptly sat on the edge reaching out to take his little hand in hers.

The door swung open just as Piper opened her mouth to fill Pip in on what was happening.

"Dad!" Graham was delighted to see Joe and flashed him a big grin.

"Hi, buddy. Your sister sends this for you." Joe planted a big wet sloppy kiss on Graham's cheek. Graham squirmed away from his dad and giggled.

"Hi, you two. When did you get here, Pip?"

"I just got here. Now will someone please tell me what is going on here with Graham?"

"Joe, do you mind sitting with Graham for a minute? He was about to start drawing in his book. I will go and talk to Pip out in the hallway."

"Sure thing." Joe went and pushed Graham over in the bed. "Scoot over. You are hogging the whole bed." He winked at Graham. Graham laughed and moved over so his dad could sit with him. He opened his sketchbook and was about to draw.

"Aunt Pip? Will you stay here until I get done?"

"Sure, honey. I will be here. Be right back." She followed Piper out of the room and into the hallway.

"What happened since I was here last? What is Graham talking about till he gets done?"

"We just found out that Graham has leukemia." Pip gasped and brought her hand to her mouth. "That is why he has been so tired lately and has been getting those nosebleeds. We are starting his first round of chemotherapy in about fifteen minutes." Piper glanced down at her watch.

"My God. No wonder why I felt sick this morning. I had such a knot in my stomach. I was filled with a nervous feeling. I must have been feeling what you were feeling. What did the doctor say would happen?"

"We are going to do the chemotherapy first, and hopefully that will kill off the leukemia. Then if we can find a match, we will do a bone marrow transplant and transplant the donor's stem cells to help regenerate new ones for Graham. Healthy ones."

"You must be going out of your mind. How are Joe and Arie holding up?"

"Joe has been my rock through all of this. He is strong and isn't showing what I know he must be feeling. You know Arie. She doesn't really understand what is happening and just wants her brother to be healthy again. She is at my folks and will probably spend a lot of time with them while we are getting the chemotherapy done with Graham. They have been wonderful—my mom is trying to fix things in her own way, and you know how quiet Dad is. He has been supportive and reminds me to keep a positive outlook on the situation. We haven't been able to get a hold of Joe's parents. They are on a cruise to Alaska for the next ten days and have been unreachable."

"I want to get tested to see if I am a match for Graham's bone marrow. What else can I do to help?"

Piper hugged her friend and held onto to her tightly for a moment.

"You being here is helping me. Who knew that when I first saw you in Mom's house all of those years ago that I would come to depend so much on you? I love you, Pip. I feel badly that my life has been pulling you away from yours so much lately."

"Oh, please. My life is so dependable. You really aren't dragging me away from anything too important. You know that I feel the same way about you. And I would do anything to help out your kids. I love your whole family." She stopped talking when she saw a doctor and nurse with a wheelchair rolling to a stop in front of the room.

"Good morning, Dr. Larson. This is my sister. Are you ready for Graham?"

"I can definitely see the resemblance. Yes, we are ready for him. I'm glad that you have some more people to support you through this. It will be hard for you to see Graham so sick, but remember it will hopefully help him in the long run."

Piper stepped aside so that the nurse could wheel the chair into the room. Joe got up from the bed and collected Graham's sketchbook and pencil.

"Hi, Graham. I'm Nancy, and I will be taking you down to get your first round of chemotherapy. Are you ready?"

"Yep," Graham inhaled deeply through his nose and held out his hand for his dad to help him into the wheelchair.

Joe took a hold of Piper's hand, and they followed the wheelchair out of the room. Pip was right behind them, and her heart tugged as she watched Graham trying to be brave for them.

"Mom, I'm going to be sick again!" Piper rushed over with the pan and held it for him as he vomited again. She sat on the edge of the bed and held his forehead and softly crooned to him that he was going to be all right. When he finished, Pip came over with a cool, wet washcloth and dabbed his cheeks and back of his neck with it.

Joe was standing in the corner with his arms folded across his chest. Piper walked over to him.

"Babe, why don't you go home and get some rest? I know how you are with vomit. I am surprised that you have vomited too," Piper smiled weakly as she tried to make a joke.

Joe half smiled. "How long do you think this is going to last?"

"I'm not sure, but I think it is normal based on what the doctor told us. Why don't I stay with him tonight, and we can switch tomorrow night? I am sure that Arie is ready to go home too."

"I hate to leave you both here alone."

"Pip is here with us. I hope that she will stay for a while. Can you please tell Arie how much I love her, and am looking forward to seeing her tomorrow?"

"I will. I love you. Try and get some rest." He leaned down to press a quick kiss across her lips.

"Graham, I will be back in the morning. Hang in there, buddy. I love you." He ruffled Graham's hair and gave a quick pat to Pip's shoulder. He mouthed thank-you to Pip as he walked out the door.

Graham was exhausted and was asleep in a moment, breathing deeply.

"Piper, you look so tired. Can you try and get some sleep? I will stay here as long as I can."

"I'm pretty worn-out. I may just close my eyes for a little bit if you don't mind," she whispered and climbed into bed with Graham. She curled up besides Graham and wrapped her arm protectively around his little frail body. She stroked his hair back from his forehead and kissed his head, letting her lips stay on his warm skin for a few moments. She closed her eyes, and it wasn't long before her breathing matched that of Graham's.

Pip sat in the dimly lit room and looked at her friend and Graham. Piper was such a good mother, and it was easy to see how much Graham adored her. It broke Pip's heart that they had to go through this. She wished that there were some way that she could fix it and make everything better.

She sighed and rested her head on the back on the chair, watching the two of them sleep. Graham had to get better. That was all there was to it.

*   *   *

Joe sat on the couch stroking Toby's soft ears with the TV blaring in the background. It had been three weeks since Pip had disappeared that morning in their bathroom. He ran a jagged hand through his hair.

"Where is she, Toby?" Toby lifted his head and cocked his face to the left. He let out a small whimper.

He hated this. He had been with her when she jumped this time so at least he knew where she was. It would've been horrible if she had jumped when they weren't together, and he would have had to worry about where she was.

Something must be really wrong for her to have stayed in Piper's world for this long. He was making himself nuts worrying about it. He felt so helpless sitting on the couch by himself.

He had explained her absence at work by saying she was visiting a sick friend. He hoped that wasn't true but really couldn't understand what else would be keeping her from coming home.

He picked up a framed wedding picture that sat on the end table. They looked so young in the picture. It amazed him that he loved her so much more now than he did on the day that he married her.

She hadn't jumped until they had been married for about five years. He wished that she wouldn't jump. He felt selfish admitting that to himself. He blew out his breath and ran a finger down Pip's face in the picture trying to will her to come back to him.

*   *   *

Pip sat at the kitchen table with Arie and was lightly coloring a picture of a princess and a frog. She searched through the crayons for a green one, and then just held it in her hand. She rested her chin in her hand and gazed out of the window.

She missed Joe. Sure, she saw Joe every day, but it wasn't her Joe. It was strange to be able to look at him and not see the man that she fell in love with and married. Although they looked identical, their personalities were just enough different that it was really more like they were brothers than the same man. This Joe had been very sweet to her and kind, but she ached to get home and to feel her husband's arms around her.

"Aunt Pip? Can you please pass me the purple crayon? Aunt Pip?"

"Hmmm? Oh, sorry, sweetheart. I was thinking about someone and something else. Here you go."

"Do you think that Mom will be home soon? I am getting hungry."

"Why don't we get dinner started for Mom? I think she should be home from the hospital soon. I think it is your dad's night to stay with Graham. What should we make for dinner?"

"Pigs in a blanket? I think that is Mom's favorite," Arie quipped looking up at her.

"Are you sure that it is Mom's favorite, or is it yours?" Pip grabbed the little girl and began to tickle her until she was howling with laughter.

"Okay. Stop! It's my favorite. Stop!" Arie confessed out of breath.

"I thought so." Pip thought how good it felt to laugh that hard. "So we can whip up pigs in a blanket for you, and maybe I will make some chicken salad for Mom and me. How does that sound? Go wash your hands if you want to help roll up the pigs in the crescent rolls."

"Okay. I will!" Arie skipped out of the room and left Pip smiling after her. She was such a sweet little girl. She wondered how her brother was doing right now.

"I want to go home, Mom." Graham complained to his mom. He was getting so tired of being in the hospital.

"I know, sweetheart, but we have to do what the doctor says so you feel better. Dad is going to stay with you tonight. I feel like I haven't seen Arie for a while and need to spend some time with her. Is that okay?"

"Yeah. Dad lets me watch PG movies when it is just the two of us. Oopps!" Graham clamped a hand over his mouth catching himself.

"He does, does he? I will have to have a talk to him." Piper smiled down at him and fluffed his pillow. "Can I get you anything before I go?"

"Who's going?" Joe strode through the door and grabbed Piper by the waist. He planted his lips on hers and kissed her until her breath caught.

"Geez, Dad. Gross!" Joe picked up Walter off of the couch and threw it at Graham. He laughed and hugged the whale to his chest.

"Now, are we ready to watch a movie or what?"

"I heard about your movies. Please nothing scary and how about some G movies this time?"

"You sold us out, man? Totally not cool." Joe winked at Graham.

"I love you both. See you in the morning." Piper waved as she pulled open the door. She blew them a kiss from the doorway, and then headed toward the elevators.

"I thought she would never leave. Great! Now what movie should we watch?" Joe asked Graham as he rubbed his hands together mischievously.

"Arie was asleep in two minutes flat," Piper explained as she handed a glass of wine to Pip. Piper sat down on the couch next to Pip and folded her legs up underneath her.

"Thanks so much for making dinner. It was such a treat to come home to dinner already made and eat something besides hospital food."

"Sure. You almost got pigs in a blanket. Arie told me that they were your favorite until I tickled it out of her."

Piper smiled and took a sip of her wine. She felt somewhat relaxed for the first time since all of this started with Graham.

"I can't tell you what it means to me to have you here. I am sure that your Joe is going out of his mind."

"I think he is too. I feel so badly that I can't let him know that I am all right, but you know how it is. We have no control when we jump or for how long we stay. I miss him though—a lot. I am glad that I can be here for you and your family."

"Your support has meant so much to me and Joe. You are amazing. It is so hard to explain how I have been feeling lately. I love my kids so deeply, and it is so hard to see Graham feeling so badly. I also feel guilty that I haven't been able to spend much time with Arie. I think it helps that you look like me, so in a way, she feels like a part of me is still with her even when it is you playing with her."

"You have amazing kids and have done an excellent job raising them. You are a wonderful mother. I have really enjoyed watching you interact with your kids over the years."

"I hope that this isn't too personal for me to ask, but I am surprised that you don't have kids."

Pip took a deep breath and blew it out slowly.

"I would love kids, and so would Joe. We have tried to have a baby for years. The doctor gave us a very slim chance of getting pregnant naturally. Joe has a low sperm count. He asked me once about adoption, but I haven't given up hope that it will still happen naturally for us some day. I do want what you have with your kids. I can see how much you love them. It is in your eyes the way that you look at them, and I can hear it in your voice when you talk to them or talk about them. It must be an amazing feeling."

"I'm so fortunate, Pip. It is pretty amazing, and I never take for granted what I have. Even with Graham being sick, I feel in my heart that he will get better. Do you think that is silly?"

"Not at all. Things have a way of working out as long as you stay positive. I have a feeling that Graham will be healthy again too. Just hang in there." Pip reached over and squeezed Piper's hand.

"I hope you're right." Piper smiled at Pip and took another sip of her wine. She just had to stay positive that everything would work out the way it is supposed to.

"Arie, could you please go and wake up Aunt Pip? Tell her that the pancakes are ready."

"Sure, Mom." Arie skipped out of the kitchen and headed up toward the guest room. Arie returned a moment later.

"She's gone. Her bed isn't made, but she isn't here."

"Oh, shoot. Okay. She must have had to get back home and get to work. Let's sit down and have breakfast. Then we are going to head to the hospital. Today is the day that we are all going to be tested to see if we are a bone marrow match for Graham."

"Will it hurt? Where is Dad?"

"I hope that it doesn't hurt too badly, but I will be glad to do it for Graham. It could really help him so he isn't sick anymore. Dad spent the night with Graham at the hospital. He is waiting there for us."

"Can I have Aunt Pip's pancakes too? I'm starving." Piper smiled at her beautiful daughter. She passed her the plate of pancakes and poured some more syrup on them.

Arie began talking about one of her little friends that had come over to play when she was at Claire's house last week. She was telling a story about a frog that they had caught. Piper was only half listening. She was thinking about Pip. She was so grateful that she had stayed all of those weeks. She was sure that Joe was really missing her, but it had been so nice to have her there. She was such a big support and always knew the right things to say to keep her positive. She was going to miss her.

They had a big day ahead of them with getting tested to see if they were a match for Graham. Hopefully in a few days they would find out if one of them could donate their marrow to help Graham. He was doing so well with the chemo, and the doctor had said that they were getting close to the time when they could do the transplant.

Piper really hoped that either she or Joe would be a match and not Arie. She really didn't want both of her children to be in pain. She knew that Arie would gladly do it for her brother, but Piper hoped that she wouldn't have to.

"I am all finished, Mom."

"Run up and brush your teeth and comb your hair. I am going to throw these dishes in the dishwasher, and then we will go. Toby, let's go out," Piper shooed the dog out of the door and took the dishes from the table to the sink. She quickly loaded the dishwasher and had just finished when Arie walked into the kitchen.

"Can you let Toby in please and get your shoes on?" She stooped and picked up her purse off of the floor.

"Ready? Let's go." They both piled into the Range Rover and headed to the hospital. Piper was hopeful that at least one of them would be a match.

*   *   *

Joe blinked his eyes and rubbed them as the sunlight poured in through the open bedroom window. He yawned and rolled over and bumped right into Pip.

"Oh my god! You're back! Wake up, Pip, wake up." Joe was shaking her with a little more force than he had intended. He was just so relieved to have her home.

"What? Hmmmm," Pip quietly murmured. She slowly opened her eyes and then realized where she was. She bolted straight up and was sitting in the middle of the bed.

"I'm home. I didn't know if I was ever going to make it home or ever see you again." She grabbed a hold of Joe and began kissing his face all over. Joe started to laugh.

"Okay, let me up for air!" He wrapped his arms around her and pulled her close. "I have missed you so much. Are you okay?"

"I missed you too. Graham has leukemia and has been having chemo treatments." Pip's face got sad, and her shoulders slumped.

"That is so horrible. I can't even imagine what they are going through. How is he holding up?"

"I think he is doing as well as can be expected. They were all getting tested today to see if any of them are a bone marrow match for Graham. I was planning on getting tested with them."

"I hope that one of them is a match for Graham's sake. No parent should ever have to see their child go through that."

"I can't believe that I was gone for that long. I am so sorry. You must have been so worried.

"I was really worried, but I knew that you had to be with Piper since I was with you when you jumped. I would have been a mess if you would have jumped and I had not known if that is what happened to you."

"I wish there was a way that I could get a message to you that I am okay. How have you been? How is work going?"

"It has been busy since you were gone. I was trying to help out all of your clients too. Do you feel up to coming into the office today and working?"

"Sure. I feel up to it. What time is your first meeting?"

"It isn't until nine. Why?" She was smiling a crooked little smile and was running her finger down his arm.

"Good, then we have plenty of time." She pulled him down on top of her and tenderly began kissing him. He felt her kiss stir all parts of him. He chuckled into her mouth.

"I like how you think. We should definitely make up for lost time." He buried his head in her neck, and she let out a soft moan.

Nineteen

P ip climbed into the shower and yelled to Joe who was getting dressed in the bedroom.

"Hey, whatever happened to the Creightons' house? Did they make an offer on that house on River Street while I was gone? Fill me in on my clients so I know what I am in for today."

Joe walked into the bathroom and was busy tying his tie. He squeezed out some gel onto his hand and ran it through his hair.

"Yes. The Creightons did make an offer on that house, and the inspection was clear. It is set to close in three weeks. We have a closing on Friday for the Winstons. Could you please check on the HUD? It is supposed to be done this afternoon. I have a listing appointment this afternoon with a new couple. I thought we could co-list it."

"That all sounds fine. Did you hear from either Jack or Hannah at all while I was gone?"

"They called about a week ago, but Jack said that they were going on vacation and would call you when they got back. I think that some of your other clients were just waiting for you to get back. You may want to check your messages on your desk when we get there. I know that Rose has been piling them up for you to review."

Pip shut the water off and climbed out of the shower. She began towel drying her hair.

"I had forgotten how beautiful you were. Man, I missed you. I am so glad you are home. Do you think that you will stay for a while now?"

"I can never be too sure. I hope so. Thank you so much for doing all of the work with my clients. I know that the Creightons are a little bit of a pain. I am sure that you had to bite your tongue and smile a lot with them."

"No doubt about it, you owe me big-time for them." She laughed and whipped her towel at him.

"I will be ready in about twenty minutes. Should we ride together?"

"Sure. I will go down and make some coffee. It is a darn shame that you have to get dressed and cover up that body of yours." Joe walked by and pinched her butt.

Pip had a stack of pink memo sheets that were piled up on her desk. She set down her briefcase and sighed when she started leafing through them. She noticed the date on some of them. A few were dated from three weeks ago. It was hard to believe that she was gone for that long. The time over there had gone so quickly.

She had a hard time concentrating on her work and found that she kept thinking about Graham. She hoped that he was continuing to do well. She wanted to get tested to see if she was a donor match for Graham. Pip wondered what the results were—if any of them would be able to help him with the stem cell transplant. She felt so sad for Graham and all of the needles and chemo that he had to endure. He already had to go through so much at such a young age. He was one of the strongest little boys that she knew.

Her time with Arie and Graham had proven one thing to her. She really wanted to have children. Maybe she was getting closer to being ready to adopt. She thought that she would surprise Joe with the topic this weekend on their date night. He would be excited but a little bit shocked that she was thinking this way. They had tried for five years to get pregnant on their own.

She found how much she loved Arie and Graham after spending the month with them. She thought about how she loved them like her own and hoped that she would feel that way about a child that they would adopt. She was beginning to get more excited about the idea.

She shook her head to clear her mind and knew that she needed to focus at the task at hand. She would put adoption on the back burner until lunchtime when she could research it a bit more.

She smiled to herself and picked up a pen. She looked down at the HUD that had just been faxed over. She needed to review it, and then call the Winstons. She flipped on the radio for a little background noise and got to work.

*   *   *

Piper was getting anxious waiting for the results to see if any of them were a match for Graham. The nurse had told her that they would rush the results, but they still hadn't heard anything.

Claire had brought Arie down to the hospital for the day, and they had just left for dinner. Graham's spirits were up, and they had all enjoyed the card games that they had played. Piper smiled as she thought back to how they had all laughed when she ended up with the Old Maid card three times in a row.

"Are you getting tired, bud?" Piper sat at the foot of his bed and rubbed his foot.

"Yeah, a little. I am not quite ready for dinner. Are you or Dad staying with me tonight?"

"I am, but I have to go back home and get a change of clothes. Your favorite nurse is on duty tonight. I can see if she minds coming in to play a game of cards while I run home quick. We can have dinner together when I get back. Does that sound good?"

"Sure. Can you please bring me my other spaceman PJs? These are too itchy."

"Of course I will. You know how much I love you, babe?"

"No. How much do you love me?" This was a game that they had played since Graham was old enough to talk. They would say how many objects they loved each other, each one trying to outdo the other one.

"I love you 153 green M&Ms."

"Wow, Mom. That's a lot. I love you 284 gray elephants." Piper leaned down and kissed his forehead.

"I will be right back. Then we will get dinner, okay?"

"Okay. Bye, Mom." Piper waved and pulled open the door. She stopped at the nurse's station on her way out and asked if Holly could go in and sit with Graham until she got back.

She decided last minute to run by the lab and see if by chance the results were in.

"Hi. I am sorry to bother you, but I was wondering if you could check on some donor match results that we had done a few days ago?"

"Sure. What is your name?" the front desk nurse asked.

"It's Piper Reynolds, and my husband and daughter were tested as well. Joe and Arie Reynolds."

"Do you mind giving me a few minutes? Some of the results were just sent over, and I haven't had time to get them all processed yet. Let me see if I can find yours." She disappeared around back for a few minutes.

Piper was fidgeting with her phone and checked her watch. She had told Graham that she wouldn't be long. She was getting nervous about the results too. What if none of them were a match?

The nurse came back and interrupted her thoughts.

"Mrs. Reynolds? I have the results right here. Do you want to take a look?"

She set the piece of paper down on the counter. Arie was listed first, and Piper's eyes followed the numbers and graph over to the column on the right. Not a match. Next was Joe. She did the same, and the outcome was the same—not a match. She was getting a sick feeling in her stomach. She looked at her own name and followed it over to the far right column—a match.

Had she read that right? She was a match?

"Excuse me. Because I am a little bit crazy, could you double-check this for me? Does it say that I am a match?"

The nurse took the sheet of paper and followed the results under her name.

"Yes, dear. Looks like it."

"Holy shit! Yes! I'm sorry. This is just wonderful news. Can I take these results with me?"

"We will be mailing you out a copy. That one needs to stay here because I haven't inputted it into the system yet."

"Thanks so much for your help. Have a good night."

"You're welcome. Take care."

Piper practically floated down the hall and flung open the door that led to the parking lot. She needed to call Joe right away and tell him. She couldn't even wait until she got home.

She punched the home number into her cell and listened as it rang and rang. Her voice came on, and the voice mail picked up.

"Thanks for calling the Reynolds' residence. We can't come to the phone right now, but if you leave a message we will get back to you. Have a good day!" Beep.

"Babe, are you there? Pick up. I have the best news! The best! I can't wait to tell you. Everything is going to be all right. I love you so much. I will be home soon. I am just leaving the hospital now. See you soon. Bye."

Piper clicked the phone off and shoved it in her pocket. She couldn't wait to get home and tell Joe about the results.

It was a beautiful day, and so Piper had decided to drive her Mazda Miata to the hospital. She rarely drove it anymore since it was only a two-seater, and she always had the kids with her. She had that car for twenty years. Joe always gave her a bad time about it, but she loved it. She told him that she wasn't getting rid of it—ever. He couldn't drive a manual transmission, so she always teased him that is why he didn't like the car because he couldn't drive it.

It was one of the last cars in the parking lot and was just starting to turn to dusk. The sky had been painted a brilliant orangish red as the sun was starting to dip down below the horizon. She tilted her head back and admired the beautiful colors and felt like finally things were going to be all right.

She climbed into her car and threw her purse onto the passenger seat next to her. The engine roared to life, and she turned on the lights making the little headlights pop up. She loved this car and finally felt like celebrating, so she turned the radio on and turned it up.

She couldn't wait to tell Joe the news. She wished that she could somehow get word to Pip and let her know that hopefully with this stem cell transplant, Graham would be healthy again.

She stepped on the gas, and the little car zipped onto the interstate. A song came on the radio that she liked and she couldn't help but to tap her hand on the steering wheel and sing along.

It was late enough in the evening that she had just missed rush hour. The traffic wasn't bad, and she was getting close to her exit. Just a few more minutes, and she would be home.

"No brakes!" Those words screamed in her head as her neck rolled around and slammed into the headrest. The radio that she had been singing to just a few seconds before suddenly was quiet. The silence was deafening as she watched a road sign slowly pass in front of her eyes. She had lost her traction on some loose rocks on the side of the road just as she was pulling off on her exit from the interstate. Everything seemed to be in slow motion as she watched the road sign come inches from the hood of her car for the second time. The third time that she passed the sign she wasn't as lucky.

Pip had been wrenched away from the dinner table and woke up on the side of the road. She was confused as to what she was doing there until she looked across the street and saw the white Mazda Miata. Oh, God, no! It seemed to be happening in slow motion as she watched the car spinning and narrowly missing the sign a few times before plowing into it. She sat frozen in fear as she watched the car's hood rip in two.

She began running to help Piper, but as quickly as she was brought into the scene, she was taken back out of it again.

The force that propelled Piper into the steering wheel knocked the wind out of her and left her gasping for breath. The crunching of metal echoed in her ears as the road sign split the hood of the car in two. The dashboard seemed to crumble like tinfoil as it collapsed onto her stomach and legs, penetrating her abdomen in one swift movement. The car had stopped moving, but her head was still spinning as she reached down and felt her stomach. She pulled her hand away and looked down at the warm red liquid that covered her fingers.

She had never felt this intense pain before in her life. Her stomach had a gaping hole that blood was swiftly running out of. She tried to move her legs to get out of the car and cried out in pain.

Piper struggled with the seat belt to get it to release but was getting so tired that she could hardly keep her eyes open. She felt herself drifting into blackness with the sounds of wailing sirens fading into the background.

"Unit 5, we have a car accident that just occurred on the 17 Northbound. The man that called into 911 said that it was only one vehicle involved. A Mazda Miata collided with a road sign. The firefighters have been called to the scene and will be available with the Jaws of Life if needed. Radio into me after you access the accident. Over."

"10-4. Will do. Over."

The ambulance rolled to a stop, and Tommy jumped out. He was the first person to get around to the driver's side door. The door was jammed shut, and he tapped on the glass.

"Madam. Can you hear me? Help is here. We are going to get you out."

"Did you get any response?" Rick yelled as he was running up to the driver's side.

"None. Give me your knife. I am going to cut open the convertible top and check for a pulse. I can see that she is losing a lot of blood."

Rick handed Tommy his knife. Tommy flipped it open and skillfully tore into the top with no resistance. He reached his hand down inside the car and felt Piper's neck.

"She's alive, but her pulse is very faint. We have to get her out of here fast."

The fire truck pulled to a stop behind the ambulance, and two men slid out and went to the back to retrieve the Jaws of Life. They brought it over and quickly began cutting the car away from Piper. Once they had gotten enough of the car removed, Tommy held pressure to her abdominal wound. His towel was quickly becoming saturated.

"Just a few more cuts, and we should have her out."

The saw made a buzzing noise, and after a big crunch, one of the firefighters pulled the door away from the car. The dashboard was cut into next, and the Jaws of Life ripped away at the tangled mess of metal.

"We have to be careful when we move her. We need to get her secured to the backboard and her neck immobilized. On my count—ready, one, two, three, lift!"

They eased her onto the stretcher and swiftly wheeled her to the waiting ambulance.

"I need vitals now!"

"Her heart rate is 130. Her BP is 70 over 30. Female in her midthirties. Unconscious. Losing a lot of blood. I assume that she has massive internal injuries and a broken pelvis."

"Hold on, madam. We are going to get you help."

Rick saw Piper's cell phone sticking out of her pocket. He eased it out carefully and slid it on. He went to the call log and saw that home was the most recent call. He punched that number to call again.

Joe was getting out of the shower and ran a brush through his wet hair. He peeked his head out of the bathroom door to check on Arie. She looked up at him with her bright blue eyes and was still playing with her babies on their bedroom floor. He smiled down at her.

"Mom should be home soon. After she leaves to go back to the hospital, I will get us dinner."

"She called a little while ago when you were in the shower. I saw her number on the caller ID. She must've left a message because I heard her voice, but I couldn't tell what she was saying from up here."

"Maybe she is not coming home? I will check it in a sec after I get dressed." Joe pulled on some shorts and yanked a T-shirt over his head.

The phone began to ring, and Arie yelled, "Dad, it's Mom again!"

Joe rushed over to the phone and picked it up, "Hello, gorgeous."

"Sir, this is Rick, and I am an EMT. The woman whose phone this is has been in a serious accident. We are in route to Belmont Hospital. Can you meet us there?"

Joe quickly hung up the phone after giving the EMT as much information about Piper as he could. He was stunned and stood for a moment with the phone in his hand.

Piper had been in an accident? Something about the hood of her car being split in two?

Joe snapped back to attention. "Arie! Arie, we have to go. Mom's been in an accident. Get your shoes on."

Arie ran over and slipped into her shoes. They headed out the door, and Joe opened the back car door so she could slide in. Next to his car sat the Range Rover. Damn it! Now it made more sense. She had been driving the Miata. He always hated that car. When she got better he was going to have a serious talk with her about selling it. He thought that maybe he wouldn't have to. It may be totaled.

Joe punched in the phone number for Claire and Henry. The phone rang through the car speakers. Claire answered the phone with a cheery, "Hi, Joe."

"Claire, Piper has been in an accident. She was in the Miata, and the accident had something to do with a road sign. I am not sure on the details. The EMT called me from the ambulance. They are taking her to Belmont Hospital. He told me that she was unconscious."

"Oh my god, Joe! Is it bad?"

Joe looked up into the rearview mirror and saw Arie looking at him waiting for an answer.

"I'm not sure yet. They will know more once they get her to the hospital. Can you meet us there?"

"Of course. Henry just got home from work. We will leave right now."

"Oh, and, Claire, Graham doesn't know and is expecting his mom back for dinner. She called when I was in the shower. I am assuming that she was calling to say she was coming home for a change of clothes and then was heading back. Could you please go and check on him and make sure he is okay? I will be waiting with Arie in the waiting room at the ER."

"Yes. We will check on Graham. Don't worry about him. Just find out any information you can on Piper."

"Okay. See you soon. Bye." Joe switched the phone off in the car and was thankful that he would be to the hospital in the next few minutes.

"Arie? How are you doing, sweetheart?"

"Is Mom going to be okay?" Her lip was quivering, and a few tears were starting to fall down her cheeks.

"The doctors will do everything they can to help her. They will get her fixed up as best as they can. Hang on, sweetie. We are almost to the hospital and will find out more once we get there."

"This is Unit 5 calling Belmont. We are in route to the ER. The accident victim is a thirty-five-year-old female with severe abdominal injuries. She has lost an extreme amount of blood. Alert the trauma team. Over."

"10-4. Over." The radio crackled and then was silent.

Tommy looked over at Rick who was monitoring her vitals.

"This doesn't look good."

"No. No, it doesn't."

The ambulance rolled to a stop at the ER entrance, and Rick and Tommy jumped out of the back. They swiftly pulled the stretcher from the ambulance and began wheeling her into the hospital.

A blonde-headed nurse with her hair in a ponytail greeted them and asked what her vitals were. She directed them to Trauma Bay One where a surgical team was standing by.

They pushed her through the doors that swung open. They moved the stretcher alongside the operating table. A surgeon with dark black hair and kind brown eyes immediately stepped in.

"Okay, we need to get her moved onto the table. And move together, now," Dr. Venka directed.

The nurse began to swiftly cut off her pants and begun wiping her belly with antiseptic.

"We have it from here. Thank you, gentlemen," Dr. Venka told the EMTs and then directly turned back to work on Piper.

Rick and Tommy wheeled the now empty stretcher out of the door and back toward the entrance to the ER.

Joe had been waiting near the entrance hoping to catch a glimpse of Piper when she came in. He noticed the two EMTs and immediately went to them.

"Did you just bring my wife in? Piper Reynolds, dark-haired woman that was driving a Miata."

"Yes, sir. We just took her to the operating room. She needed emergency surgery."

"What happened? The gentleman that I talked to said something about her car hitting a sign?"

"Yes, her car was the only one involved in the accident. She must have slipped on some loose rocks coming off of the exit and ran into a road sign. It literally split her hood in half and collapsed her dashboard onto her legs and abdomen. She was trapped in the car and was unconscious when we arrived at the scene. We cut her out as quickly as we could and got her to the hospital immediately."

"What now? What are they doing to her?"

"Her doctor is a trauma surgeon and is the best in the area. He will do his best to fix her up. It may be a few hours before he is done. Her injuries are quite extensive."

"Thanks for the information and for helping her." Joe shook Tommy's hand and stepped back so they could wheel the stretcher by.

Joe looked over at Arie who was sitting quietly coloring in her book. Their world had been turned upside down. Her mom was fighting for her life in the operating room, and her brother was upstairs fighting leukemia. Sometimes life wasn't fair.

He started to walk over to Arie when Claire and Henry came rushing in.

"We just checked on Graham. He is doing fine. How is she? What have you heard?" Henry asked Joe.

"They took her in for emergency surgery. The EMTs told me that her doctor was the best in the area. I guess that she was unconscious when they found her and had extensive injuries to her abdomen."

"Oh, Lord!" Claire began to sob. Henry wrapped his arm around her shoulder and squeezed her close to him.

"In the meantime, I guess we wait. The EMT told me that it could be a few hours." They all moved slowly over to where Arie was sitting and sat in a small grouping of chairs that faced each other.

"How is Mommy?"

"They are working on her now, sweetie. She is a fighter. We just have to wait and see." Joe stroked her hair and leaned down to kiss the top of her head. Damn it, Piper. She better fight.

*   *   *

Pip woke up on the kitchen floor and was trembling from head to toe. Joe was standing over her and immediately bent down to her.

"What is wrong? What happened? Pip, look at me. You just jumped but were gone literally for only about one minute."

"Shit, Joe." Pip tried to collect herself and wiped a droplet of sweat off her brow. "I saw the whole thing happen. She was spinning out of control. Oh my god! I don't know if she is all right. Her car plowed into the sign and crumbled like it was a toy." Pip brought her knees up to her chest and began to sob into her hands. Her whole body was shaking.

"Piper was in a car accident? You were there and saw it? Is she okay?"

"I don't know. I was running over to the car when I jumped back home again. Why? Why couldn't I have stayed longer? How will I get back to see if she is okay? What if she died, and I don't even know it?"

"Calm down. You need to relax. We need to talk about this. Help me understand a little bit more about your jumps. When you jump, where do you go? So you left our kitchen, and did you go first to Piper's kitchen?"

"No, I jump to wherever Piper is. Like last time when I jumped, I started in our bathroom, and I ended up in the hallway at the hospital. Tonight I jumped from our kitchen to the side of a road, right before the accident happened. It is like Piper and I are drawn to each other. She pulls me to her when she is in trouble or scared. I guess that isn't the only time I have jumped. I went for the kids' birthday and have been on other happy occasions. I can't explain it, but Piper and I have a bond, and we are drawn to each other. I seem to go to her world more than she comes to mine. I don't know why that is, just like I don't know why this is happening in the first place."

"Thanks. That helps to clarify it for me. And you jump with the clothes you are wearing?"

"Yes. Whatever is on our body goes with us. I guess that is lucky for us that we don't show up naked." Pip smiled weakly up at Joe.

"Can Arie or Graham jump?"

"I don't know, but I don't think so. I mean technically they have part of their mom in them, so maybe they will one day, but they don't have someone on our side to be pulled to since we don't have children. They don't exist over here in our world."

"You're right. I didn't think of it like that."

"I would know it if she died, right? I can't lose her, Joe. She has become like a sister to me."

"You aren't going to lose her. You will find a way to get back to her."

"I hope you know that when I'm gone, I think about you all of the time and miss you. I am sure it is hard for you when I disappear."

"It is hard. I never really know if you are safe. The last jump when you were gone for a little over a month was torturous. Honestly I could do without you ever jumping."

"I know, babe. I know."

Twenty

*   *   *

J oe sat wringing his hands back and forth. He glanced up at Henry who was pacing back and forth on the floor in front of them. Claire was holding a sleeping Arie in her arms.

The doors that led to the operating rooms swung open, and a dark-headed doctor in green surgical scrubs came walking through and headed toward them.

He pulled off his green surgery cap and walked over to Joe.

"Are you Piper's husband?"

"Yes. I am. My name is Joe, and these are Piper's folks, Claire and Henry. How is she doing, Doctor?"

"Hello. I am Dr. Kris Venka. Piper came into my operating room a little over seventy-five minutes ago. As you know, she sustained some extensive abdominal injuries and lost a lot of blood. Immediately we activated a massive blood transfusion protocol. Upon exploration, she was found to have a large pelvic hematoma, a broken pelvis, and a lacerated spleen and had severe damage to her small intestine. Her abdomen was filled with blood and enteric contents which are bowel movements."

Claire raised a hand to her mouth, and Henry gripped onto Joe's shoulder for support.

"We ended up having to remove her spleen and four feet of her small intestine. We packed her pelvis with surgical sponges. She is now on a ventilator helping her to breathe. She has been moved up to the ICU and is in critical condition. She is still unconscious."

"Thank you for taking care of her. Can we see her, Doctor?"

"You can, but if I may make a suggestion? She looks pretty beat up right now. It may be too much for your little girl to take seeing her mother like that."

"I can keep Arie out with me, and then we can take turns visiting with Piper," Claire suggested.

"I would expect her to wake up in the next day or so. We may have to keep her on the ventilator to ease the stress of breathing off of her body. I will check back in with her in a few hours. She is in the ICU, room 714."

Joe shook Dr. Venka's hand. He turned and walked back through the swinging doors.

"Joe, why don't you go and see Piper first? We will wait with Arie, and then Claire and I can go when you are done?"

"Are you sure you don't mind?"

"No. Now go. I will go up and check on Graham while you are with Piper. We can meet back here."

"Thank you. Thank you both so much." Joe headed to the left where the elevator bay was and punched the up button.

He couldn't believe that this was happening. First his son and now his wife. It was too much. He felt his throat getting tight as he tried to fight off the urge to cry. He needed to stay strong right now not only for Piper, but also for Graham and Arie. How were they going to get through this?

The elevator dinged, and he stepped inside and hit the button for the seventh floor. He watched the numbers climb and then stop when it got to seven. The doors slid open, and Joe exited the elevator and followed the sign toward the ICU with rooms numbering 701-721. He checked in at the front desk and was given a badge that allowed him to unlock the heavy doors leading to the hallway where Piper's room was. He moved quietly until he stood outside of her door and slowly pushed it open and stepped inside.

The room was dimly lit, and Piper lay in the bed with a tube sticking out of her mouth. The monitors were quietly beeping, and Joe could see the graph keeping track of her heartbeat.

The blanket was pulled up to her chest, and her arms lay on the outside of the blanket. They were already bruised and had cuts up and down her forearm. Her right arm had an IV in it with clear fluid slowly dipping from the bag that hung above her bed.

She still looked beautiful. Her chestnut hair was pushed off to one side, and she looked like she was sleeping. She had a small cut under her right eye and some bruising.

Joe went to her side and pulled up a stool. He sat down and pulled her left hand into his. He intertwined his fingers with hers and then pulled them to his lips. He kissed her fingers and then just held her warm hand to his mouth. The tears began to fall, and he couldn't stop them.

"Hey, sweetheart. It's me. You are in the hospital and have had an accident. Your mom and dad are here too. We all love you and know that you are strong. Keep fighting. Arie and Graham want you to get better too."

"I'm going to send up your mom and dad to see you. Then I am going to see if they can take Arie home. I am going to stay with you tonight. I will go down and check on Graham and then be right back. I love you so much. I know you can hear me. I will be right back."

Joe met Piper's parents where he had left them, and Arie was now awake.

"Hi, sweetie. What do you think of this plan? Why don't you both go and see Piper now? I will take Arie with me and go see Graham. When you are done, could you come and get Arie and one of you take her home while the other one stays with Graham? I want to stay with Piper tonight."

"Sure, Joe. Whatever you need us to do. We will come to Graham's room when we finish seeing Piper." They all headed back toward the elevator and rode up to the fifth floor where Arie and Joe got off.

"We will be there shortly."

"Take your time." The elevators closed and proceeded to climb up two more floors.

"Dad! Arie! How is Mom?" Graham asked as soon as he saw Joe and Arie walk into his room.

"She is hanging in there, kiddo. I am sorry that you have had to be alone tonight for so long. Mom was in surgery for quite a while. How are you holding up?"

"I am fine. I want to see Mom."

"I do too, Dad."

"I know that you both want to, but she is sleeping right now from the surgery. They hope she would be awake in the next day or so. I will take you both up to see her as soon as she is awake. I promise."

Arie climbed into bed with Graham and let out a huge yawn.

"Why don't you just go to sleep, baby, and we will all stay at the hospital tonight? We will just rotate between Graham's room and Mom's." Joe switched off the overhead light and sat down on the couch.

He looked over at his two children and could tell that they were comforted by each other. They nestled into each other, and within minutes, both of them were sound asleep.

The door pushed open, and Joe put a finger to his lips. He crept out to the hallway where he could talk to Henry and Claire.

"Arie was so tired, so I decided that we all could stay the hospital tonight. We can just rotate between the rooms. I know that you will want to be close in case Piper wakes up."

"I would like to be here when that happens. Why don't Henry and I stay with the children, and you go be with Piper for a while? We can switch in a few hours."

"I think that sounds like a good plan. Thank you, both. I don't know how I would do this without you." Joe gave Claire a quick hug and retreated back to the elevators.

It was getting close to dawn when Pip found herself back at the hospital. She was on a different floor than she was used to with Graham. She lightly tapped on the closest door, and then quietly stepped inside. Joe was a sleep sitting straight up holding onto Piper's hand.

"Oh, thank God!" Pip rushed over and gently shook Joe awake. "What happened? I was there. I saw the accident. Is she going to be okay?"

Joe woke up and was slightly confused to be looking at his wife's face above him.

"Joe, it's Pip. Wake up. What is going on?"

"You scared me. Sorry." Joe filled her in on Piper's emergency surgery and what happened in the last twelve hours. Telling Pip about it again had his head reeling. It didn't seem real to him that he was facing losing his wife.

"I want to stay here with her. Is that okay?"

"Of course, Pip. You don't even have to ask. I could use your support too."

"Look, Joe! Her eyelids are fluttering. She must be waking up."

Piper blinked a few times, and then her eyes flew wide open. She began to struggle and pulled at the ventilator. Joe jumped up and tried to grasp her hands and pull them away from the tube coming out of her mouth.

"Pip, get the nurse quick. Piper, listen to me. You have been in an accident and are at the hospital. You need to calm down. The ventilator is helping you breathe. Take it easy. That's right. Keep looking at me."

Piper's bright green eyes were opened wide and stared at Joe. She squeezed them shut and shook her head. A single tear fell from her lashes and rolled down her cheek.

Pip rushed back in with the nurse. The nurse pushed some Ativan into Piper's IV.

"That should help calm her down," the nurse explained and began checking Piper's vitals. "Piper, I paged your doctor that you were awake. He will be in shortly to discuss with you what he did while he was in surgery. I know that you are uncomfortable with the ventilator in, but try not to fight it."

"Thank you," Joe told the nurse as she turned and headed for the door.

Joe moved to the right hand side of her bed, and Pip was already seated on her left. Joe picked up her hand and tenderly stroked her arm. Piper looked at him with a cloudy expression in her eyes. The room was quiet except for the ventilator making the swoosh sound and the monitor that was beeping keeping track of her heartbeat.

"Piper, I know that you must be confused and in pain. You were in an accident and lost control of the car. You ran into a road sign. The dashboard folded down onto your stomach and did some damage. The doctor can tell you more."

Piper looked over at Pip, and her eyes filled with tears. Pip reached over and took a hold of her other hand.

"Graham is fine, sweetie. Your parents are with him now. I am sure that they will want to see you now that you are awake. I will go up and stay with the kiddos so they can come down and see you." Piper squeezed her hand. "You're welcome."

There was a knock at the door, and it slowly pushed open. Dr. Venka strode in and came to the foot of Piper's bed.

"I heard that our patient was awake. Hi, Piper. I'm Dr. Venka. I am sorry that you have to have that ventilator in, but it is less stress on your body to have it working for you. Your pelvis is broken, and we had to pack it for it to heal. I removed your spleen and about four feet of small intestine. You had quite a bit of internal bleeding. We got the bleeding under control. I am afraid that you had extensive internal damage. We really aren't out of the woods yet. The next few days will tell a lot on how you are recovering."

"I brought a pad in for you to write with so you can communicate until the ventilator can be removed." He handed Piper a notebook and a pen.

"How is your pain? We are monitoring your pain meds but can give you a stronger dose if you need them."

Piper wrote down a few words in her notebook and turned it so the doctor could read it.

"Pain is okay. Thank you." She tried to smile at him but couldn't with the ventilator in her mouth.

"You're welcome. Now get some rest. I will be back in a few hours to check on you."

"I think that I will go down and relieve Claire and Henry and send them up to see Piper. Then I think she needs to rest."

Piper quickly scratched out some words for Pip.

"Can you come back soon? I need to talk to you."

"Sure, I will be back in a few hours. Get some rest, Piper. I'm so glad to see your green eyes looking at me." Pip winked at Piper and left Joe and Piper alone.

"I'm sorry that I got in an accident. Are you mad?"

"Are you serious? No, babe. I was just so worried about you. I think that you totaled the car. I can honestly say that does make me a little bit happy. Is that wrong?" Joe chuckled. "I guess I should be glad that you can't talk or you would've just given me a piece of your mind."

Claire and Henry rushed into the room.

"I hear our girl is a wake. Oh, Piper. I was so worried." Claire moved up to the head of the bed and kissed Piper's forehead.

"The doctor said that Piper would need the ventilator for a while yet, but she can write in her notebook. The doctor also removed the surgical sponges earlier today and said that there was no bleeding or evidence of any other abdominal injuries. Why don't I go get a cup of coffee so you can have a few minutes alone? I think she is going to need her rest in a little while." Joe bent and kissed her cheek, and then headed out the door to give them their privacy with their daughter.

Joe was outside of Graham's room and about to go in when he heard Pip's laugh that sounded just like Piper's.

"No way! You cheat! That makes four in a row, Graham. I think we need to find a different game to play, Arie."

Joe closed his eyes and leaned his head against the wall. Standing in the hallway and listening to them, he could almost trick himself into believing that he was listening to his Piper laughing and playing with their kids. He had a gnawing feeling in his stomach. He wondered if he would ever hear Piper laugh again or sing at the top of her lungs to a song that came on the radio or give him a bad time about how she was always right.

Joe felt like he was losing control. He knew that he had to appear strong for their kids and for Piper, but on the inside he was drowning. It was Piper who was positive and always found the good in everything. She said that everything happens for a reason and would somehow make him believe it too. She could change the crummiest days into something he could laugh at. He needed her to help him get through this. He needed his wife.

Joe took a deep breath and pushed his shoulders back. He walked into Graham's room and fixed a smile on his face.

"Let me guess, Graham is beating everyone?"

"He is. Arie and I don't even stand a chance." Pip reached over and ruffled Graham's hair. He smiled a crooked little smile at her, and she laughed.

"Piper is asking for you, Pip. I will stay with the kids. Claire and Henry went home for a while to rest. Piper is awake now and wants to see you."

"I will head up there. See you guys later—card shark." She winked at Graham and headed out of the room.

"Hey, you. How are you doing?" Pip went into Piper's room and sat down on the stool that was next to Piper's bed. Piper's complexion was starting to look waxy and pale. Her eyes were beginning to look sunken, and she had black circles under them.

Piper began to write furiously in her notebook, and then had to rest for a moment before she started up again. She turned it so Pip could read what she wrote.

"I'm a match for Graham. I found out the day of the accident. No one else is a match, just me. Joe doesn't know. Pip, I need you."

"Okay, what do you need me to do? Do you want me to tell Joe?"

Piper continued to write.

"Don't tell Joe yet. I want you to get tested to see if you are a donor match too. I bet you are. I need you to be in case something happens to me I will know that Graham will be all right."

"Piper, don't talk like that." Pip leaned over and grasped her hand. "You are going to get better."

Piper pulled her hand away and wrote for a long time. She needed a few breaks when she would rest. Pip just watched her and waited patiently for her to finish.

"I believe that everything happens for a reason. Pip, you and I are interconnected so that if something happens to me, my family will still be okay. You will have to find a way to get back here to them if I die. I am counting on you to tell my children about me. Tell them about how much I adored and loved them. You have to let them know that my life didn't really begin until I looked down into their eyes five years ago on the day they were born. Each moment that I have had with them in my life has truly been a blessing, one that I have cherished. You have to be a part of their lives so you can help Arie pick out a prom dress and show Graham how to drive a car with a manual transmission. You need to be here so that they can experience a little of their mother through you. And Joe—oh, Joe. He is the light of my life, my fierce protector, my lover, and ultimately my best friend. You have to help him realize that if I am gone, he will need to be the rock for our children. I love them more than all of the stars in the universe, and I will need you to tell them and help them understand. I know I am asking a lot of you. I love you too, Pip, and have come to think of you as my sister."

Pip took a moment after reading this and quickly wiped away a tear that had fallen down onto the page. Piper was studying her eyes and waiting for her to respond.

"Piper, first of all you aren't going to die, so I don't know why you are talking this way. But I will humor you for a minute. *If* something were to happen, I will definitely help your memory live on. You will be forever engraved in my heart just as I know that you are in your children and in Joe. The children can feel how much you love them and are witness to your love every day in everything that you do for them. And Joe? He knows it too just by the way that you look at him or lay your hand on his arm to steady him. They all know the love that you have for them—they know, but yes, I will do what I can to make sure that they never forget."

Piper closed her eyes briefly, and tears streamed down her cheeks. She wiped them away with the back of her hand, and then picked up her pen again.

"Thank you, Pip. I love you."

"You are welcome, and I hope you know how much I love you. Now get some rest. I will stay with you until you fall asleep." Pip stroked back Piper's hair off her face and watched as Piper drifted into a deep sleep.

She picked up the notebook and carefully tore out the pages that Piper had just written. She didn't want Joe to read those words. It would just upset him, and she hoped there wouldn't be a need for them anyway. She gingerly creased them and slid them into her pocket.

She slumped down in the armchair that sat on the other end of the room. The room was quiet except for the noises of the machine. Pip began thinking of everything her friend had just told her, and her tears began to flow. She quietly sobbed and just let herself cry. She cried for herself. She cried for Graham, Arie, and Joe. But mostly she cried for Piper. She prayed that Piper was wrong just this once.

Twenty-one

*   *   *

Pip was home. She felt a little more like she was in prison locked in her world and not knowing what was happening to Piper in the other world. She had been a wreck since she got back yesterday afternoon. She had immediately pulled the pages that Piper had written on. She smoothed them out and laid them on her makeup table.

She had read them to Joe and since then had read them over again about a hundred times. She had relived everything over again as she told Joe what had happened. She explained how she had gotten tested yesterday morning to see if she was a match for Graham. She didn't know how she would find out the results since she was over here—a world away.

She had spent the night tossing and turning. Joe had reached over at one point and gathered her in his arms. He didn't say a word but just held onto her. She broke down and sobbed until there were no tears left. She had fallen asleep in his arms, completely exhausted and feeling helpless. She drifted into a dreamless deep sleep and didn't wake until the morning.

When she woke, she wondered if for a moment it had all been a bad dream. She sat up and had almost talked herself into it being a dream, until she saw the pages of the notebook lightly fluttering in the breeze of her ceiling fan. Their light rustling noise made her heart ache.

Across town Chad had awaken that morning with a new lease on life. He was to be released this morning at ten. All of the years of planning, scheming, and dreaming were all coming down to the next few hours. He just needed to play it cool and show the guards what a changed man he had become.

His right leg began to twitch and bounce. He dug his nails into his thigh to get the movements to stop. He was in control. If he had managed to be in control for the last five years, he could do so for a few more hours.

As the sunlight hit his face, he looked up toward the sky and breathed in a sigh of relief. He stepped into the cab that the prison had called for him and slammed the door behind him.

"Where to, buddy?" the cabbie asked him smacking his gum and popping it.

Chad hated gum chewers. He felt his hands balling into fists, and as he looked at the back of the bald man's head, he imagined tightening his hands around his neck and snapping his spine. He shook his head to focus his mind and cleared his throat.

"Could you please take me to the nearest Motel 6?"

"Sure thing." The cabbie pulled away from the curb and headed southwest of the prison. Chad watched as his home for the last five years got smaller out the rear window.

He tipped his hat toward the prison and whispered, "This time I won't get caught."

*   *   *

Piper was getting weaker by the day. She had developed a fever yesterday. They did blood tests and CAT scans to see if they could find the reason for her decline. She was in and out of sleep, and Joe was noticing that she was having trouble holding the pen to write much of anything.

Joe had been splitting his time between Graham and Piper's rooms. The lack of sleep was starting to take a toll on him. Claire and Henry had been amazing helping with Arie. Anna had kept her a few days too. She had loved the time with her cousins.

Joe rubbed his face and felt the last few days of stubble brush against his thumb. He had come home to get a change of clothes and thought maybe a hot shower would help him feel better. He got the mail and walked through the garage door and into the kitchen.

He threw the mail down next to the answering machine and noticed that he had nine messages. He hit play and listened as it read off the day and time of the first message.

"Babe, are you there? Pick up. I have the best news! The best! I can't wait to tell you. Everything is going to be all right. I love you so much. I will be home soon. I am just leaving the hospital now. See you soon. Bye."

Joe's knees felt weak, and he gripped the counter to steady himself. Just the sound of her voice made his insides hurt.

The answering machine called out, "Next message . . ."

Joe hit replay and listened to Piper's message again. He replayed it over and over again until he was standing in the kitchen crying. He slid down the cabinets and slumped down onto the floor. He buried his face in his hands and just cried.

Toby came over and licked his hand, and then lay down and whimpered.

"I know. You miss Mama, don't you? So do I. What are we going to do, Toby?" The dog looked up at him with big sad eyes, and then scooted closer to Joe.

Joe wrapped his hands in Toby's fur and held the warm body against his. He inhaled deeply and slowly stood up.

He idly flipped through the mail until he came to a letter that was from the Belmont Hospital Laboratory. He quickly ripped open the letter and began scanning the paper.

Piper was a match. He and Arie weren't a match, but Piper was. That must have been what she had called to tell him that day. He wondered why she hadn't told him about the results? She could've written that down in her notebook and let him know. Why hadn't she told him?

He was angry, and it felt good to feel a different emotion than what he had felt for the last five days. He stormed upstairs and got a quick hot shower and changed his clothes. He was going to head back to the hospital and demand to know why she had kept that from him.

He walked out of the elevator doors and used his key card to unlock the double doors that led to her hallway. As he was getting close to her room, he noticed nurses running in and out of her room.

He began to panic and raced down the hallway. He grabbed the nearest person he could find.

"Doctor, this is my wife's room. What is going on?"

"Your wife developed a high fever this afternoon. Her blood pressure is extremely low, and her heart rate is elevated. Her chest x-ray shows multilobar infiltrates consistent with ventilator associated pneumonia."

"What does that mean?"

"We are keeping a close eye on her, but her body is in shock. We will do everything we can for her, but you may want to go in and say your good-byes."

"Oh my god. How much time does she have?"

"It is hard to say. Her organs are starting to shut down. Her body can't withstand a second assault."

Joe took out his cell phone. He punched in Claire's number.

"Claire, get Henry and get to Piper's room quickly. We are losing her."

Joe sat on the little stool next to Piper's bed, and he grasped his fingers together. He watched the nurse as she hung another bag of fluid up to drip slowly into Piper's IV.

"We are keeping her going on fluids, antibiotics, and vasopressors. This helps to keep her blood pressure up because of the shock on her body," the nurse explained to Joe, and then adjusted the volume on the monitors before leaving the room.

Piper's eyes fluttered open, and Joe quickly jumped up and went to her.

"Babe, I know that you are scared, but hang on. Don't give up. The kids and I need you. I wish that I had told you more how much I appreciate all that you do for the kids and me. I think it all of the time but should have told you more. Do you know how much I love you?" A tear spilled down Joe's cheek, and he leaned down to kiss her on the forehead.

Piper's eyelids were so heavy that it was hard for her to keep them open. She held up her pinkie and index finger and stuck out her thumb, the sign for I love you. Her pale green eyes glistened with tears, and she struggled to keep them open.

"It's okay to go to sleep for a little while, Piper. I am going to be here the whole time. I am not leaving. Your parents are on their way too. Get some rest. I love you so much." Piper squeezed his hand and closed her eyes. Joe reached up and softly wiped away a tear that had escaped through her eyelashes.

Joe sat and watched her breathe and listened to the monitor as it was keeping track of her heart rate. He could see the graph on the screen moving as her heart pumped and beat. Piper's hand went slack, and he glanced up at the monitor in time to see her heart rate starting to drop.

Joe placed both of his hands on her shoulders and shook her.

"Wake up, Piper. Piper, I am begging you. Wake up. Don't leave me. Don't leave me." Joe ran out of the door and yelled for a nurse.

"Help! Someone please help. My wife needs help."

A nurse came running into the room. Joe watched as the heart-rate number slowly counted down to zero, and he heard the constant beep on the monitor as it flatlined.

Another nurse breezed into the room.

"She is having a systolic cardiac arrest. Call for a Code Blue!"

Joe stepped back away from the bed to allow the resuscitation team to get in and try and help Piper. He watched them work and felt like this wasn't real—he couldn't be losing his wife. They had to save her.

The resuscitation team was working hard to revive her. The door pushed open, and Henry and Claire burst into the room.

"Oh my god! What is happening?" Claire croaked out to Joe as they all watched in horror at the team that was desperately trying to bring Piper back to life.

"She had a heart attack. I can't lose her. I just can't . . ." Joe began to sob and held his head in his hands.

"Okay, team, stop. Our efforts have failed. Time of death is 8:17 PM."

"What? No, you can't stop! You have to keep working on her. Don't stop. You can't stop! Henry, make them save her. We can't lose our little girl." Claire balled up her fists and beat them on Henry's chest. He wrapped his arms around her and just held onto her while they both cried in each other's arms.

Joe couldn't stop the tears from falling. He watched the nurse switch off the monitor with blurry eyes. He went over to Piper and reached out to stroke her arm. She was still warm, and it didn't seem real that she was gone. Her tucked her hair behind her ear and kissed her forehead. He held onto her hand and lowered his head to kiss her fingers. He kept her fingers to his lips and let the tears fall, his body trembling with the sobs.

It was a gloomy day, overcast and the smell of rain in the air. Joe got out of the car and went over to help Graham get out of his seat. Arie ran over and held onto Graham's other side. He was weak but finally in remission from the leukemia. The doctors had allowed him out of the hospital just for a few hours for his mom's funeral. He was on the donor list waiting to find a match for his bone marrow transplant.

The three of them walked slowly up the soggy ground and stopped at the top of the hill. Arie carried three purple tulips in her hand, her mom's favorite flower. They stood in front of the casket that sat under a green tent. Arie went and immediately sat next to Claire and Henry. Joe's parents were there and were seated in the chairs next to Henry.

Joe helped Graham get seated and then took his place next to him. He looked around at all of the people that had shown up to say good-bye to Piper. There weren't enough chairs for everyone, and people just stood behind the family.

The church had been packed as well with people standing in the back. Many people shared stories about how Piper had touched their lives in one way or another. Joe noticed that Pip wasn't there at the church. He was surprised that she hadn't come.

Pip stood leaning on the tree for support as she watched the whole scene from a distance. She had felt sick for the last few days and had wondered why until she showed up a few minutes ago.

She was having a hard time believing that her friend was gone. She looked lovingly at little Graham who still looked pale and fragile. Arie clutched the tulips as though her life depended on them, and Joe, oh, Joe. He looked broken, his arm around each of his children as though he was trying to protect them.

She couldn't hear what the pastor was saying, but she watched as Arie and Graham walked up hand in hand and placed the tulips on the casket. Joe held onto his flower and kept his head bowed.

It started to rain, and the umbrellas began to pop open. People began moving quickly to their cars as a loud boom of thunder sounded.

"I will take Graham and Arie with me. I will get Graham back to the hospital and will stay with him until you get there." Claire laid her hand on Joe's arm and gave it a little squeeze. Joe just nodded, unable to speak.

Joe was alone and stepped out into the rain, which quickly soaked him. He stood at the foot of the casket holding onto the purple tulip.

Pip walked up to him and without saying a word intertwined her fingers with his. She looked at him with tears brimmed in her eyes and her lip quivering.

"She is really gone, Pip. She's gone." Pip just nodded, and they continued to stand hand in hand while the rain mixed with their tears that streamed down their faces.

A few days had passed after the funeral, and Pip was still there. Joe was like a zombie, just making the movements. He rarely spoke, and when he did it was always to the children and never about Piper.

It was after lunch when Joe came up to Pip holding onto an envelope. He shoved it into her hands.

"What's this?" She flipped the envelope over and saw that it was addressed to her at Piper and Joe's address. She slipped her thumb under the seal and pried it open.

She quickly scanned the letter and let out a small gasp.

"Joe, I'm a match. I am a match for Graham," Pip whispered it and barely believed it herself when she heard the words escape her lips. Joe turned and stared at her.

"Did you say that you are a match? You're a match?" A small flicker of hope lit up Joe's eyes, one that she hadn't seen for a few days. Joe went to Pip and picked her up and swung her around happily in a circle. She was going to save Graham, just like Piper was going to do. He wasn't going to lose his son too. She was a match!

*   *   *

Pip woke up in her own bed. Joe was lying beside her snoring softly.

"Shit! I'm back. Now what the hell am I going to do?"

"Hey, babe," Joe mumbled and yawned big. "What happened? How is Piper?"

"She died, Joe. She is gone." Pip sat on the edge of the bed and was just staring straight ahead without blinking.

Joe sat straight up, suddenly wide awake.

"She's gone? What happened?"

"She got pneumonia from the ventilator, and her body couldn't fight off the infection. She had a heart attack. When I jumped, I ended up at her burial at the gravesite. Her poor children and Joe. They are all devastated."

"I honestly can't imagine. Just the thought of losing you is too much to bear."

"Then to make matters worse, I found out that I am a donor match for Graham."

"I don't understand. Isn't that a good thing?"

"It is, if I was over there. How can I help if I am over here?"

"Don't worry, we will figure out something." Joe reached over and rubbed her back.

Three weeks had passed, and Pip still hadn't jumped. She had done everything that she could think of to scare herself into going over to Piper's world. She had watched scary movies, and Joe had tried to jump out from around the corner and scare her, but nothing had worked.

She was dealing with so many emotions. She had cried day and night for about four days about losing Piper. She felt like a piece of her was missing. Then her emotions switched to anger—anger over losing her friend. Anger for Arie and Graham not having a mother and anger for Joe to have lost the love of his life.

She had stayed cooped up in the house and sat around in her bathrobe all day. She had told Joe that she couldn't work. She had lost all desire to do anything. She was filled with sadness and knew that she could help Graham if she could jump, but she was beginning to think that wasn't possible anymore.

"I am starting to think that I can't jump because Piper isn't there. There isn't anything or anyone to draw me over there anymore. I can't stop thinking about Joe. He lost his wife and knows that I am a match and can save his son, but I am not there. They have Graham on a donor list but hadn't found any matches yet. He must be going through hell over there."

"I think you may be right about not being able to get back over there. You had been jumping with so much more frequency lately. This is the longest that you have been home."

"I know, and I am starting to go crazy just waiting around for something to happen. I have to move on with my life. Piper wouldn't want me to just sit around waiting. You know, I think I will do an open house this Sunday. I will do an open at the house on Water Ridge Court. They moved out a few weeks ago and are so anxious to get that house sold. I am going to call them now and make sure that is okay with them."

Chad flipped open the paper to the real estate section and began searching for her name on an open house. This was becoming his Sunday morning ritual for the past seven weeks, patiently waiting.

That's when he saw it. Pip Reynolds was holding an open house at Water Ridge Court from one to four today. He blinked and rubbed his eyes to be sure that he had looked at that correctly. Yes, today was the day.

He rubbed his hands together, and a smile crept onto his lips. He had a lot to do and only a few hours to do it. He needed to make plans so she wouldn't be able to get away from him again. He began pulling out the box in his closet that he had been saving for the past seven weeks. He gingerly pulled out the 9 mm handgun and laid it carefully on the bed. He laid out the duct tape and rope and began to hum as he went in search of a little saw. Today was going to be a good day after all.

"Are you sure you want to do this today? You could always stay home, and I could get a new agent to hold open the house for you. I don't know if you are up for it."

"Joe, I am fine. I have to get on with my life—our lives. Piper would tell me to get busy living. It is a good first step to making me feel normal again," she said and placed her hand on his cheek. "I couldn't have made it through this without you. I know that I have a ways to go yet, but I can make it with your support. You mean everything to me. I hope you know that." Pip reached up on tiptoes and tenderly placed her warm lips on his.

"You know that I am still crazy about you. I love you, babe. Close up early if you aren't feeling up to it. Let's go out to dinner tonight after our open houses. I could use a date night with my wife."

"You got it. I love you." She winked at him and climbed into her SUV. She waved at him through the windshield and headed to her open house. She flipped on the radio, and the sunlight that was pouring through the window hit her silver charm bracelet. It gleamed in the light, and Pip looked down at it and fingered the small heart. She remembered one of the first encounters she had with Piper. She was so thankful that Piper had found the small charm that her gram had given her. She sighed and felt a single tear drop down her cheek.

"I miss you, my friend. There has to be a way for me to honor my promise to you to help Graham. I will find it. I have to for everyone's sake."

The open house was a success. She had a lot of traffic through the house and had even picked up a few new clients. The house was pretty much selling itself. It was a four-bedroom two-storey house, and the owners had tastefully decorated it so when people walked in, they could easily imagine themselves living there. She smiled to herself as she thought about the couple that had just left. The wife was already placing her furniture. Pip wondered how long it would be before she heard from them.

She went through the house and started flipping off the light switches. She pulled out her phone as she was going through the rooms turning everything off. She began to text a message to Joe to let him know that she was on the way home.

"I'm about done here. Good turnout. See u soon. Luv u!" She hit send and threw the phone into her purse. She began to climb the stairs to get the lights turned off on the second floor.

She made it halfway up the steps when she heard his voice, "Hello, Pip."

She whirled around stunned and already felt the fear as it began to bubble up inside of her.

"Stay away from me!" She screamed in his face and began to bolt up the stairs because he was blocking the bottom of the stairs.

She had made it to the top step when he grabbed a hold of her ankle and pulled with such force that she fell flat onto her side. She landed with a "Hhummmph!" and it knocked the wind out of her.

Chad took that opportunity to stand above her and was holding a gun, which he had pointed right at her.

"Get up." His words were sharp and cold. "I have been waiting a really long time for this, Pip. Five years, three months, and nine days to be exact. I spent a lot of time reliving the last time that we were together. I am still not sure how you got away from me, so this time I didn't want to take that chance." As he was talking, he was wildly waving a gun around.

Pip tried to remain calm and tried not to concentrate on the gun that he was holding above her head.

"I said to get up—now."

Pip scrambled to her feet, and he shoved her against the wall. She could smell the sweat on his skin and dirty hair. She was beginning to get nauseated and tried to think about how she was going to get out of this.

He pinned her so her back was flat against the wall and kicked her feet apart so he could stand with one of his legs in between hers. He rubbed himself against her, and she felt him budging against her thigh.

Her mouth was dry, and she couldn't swallow. She was starting to have difficulty breathing. He ran the barrel of the gun down her cheek, and then rammed it into her throat, half choking her.

"What do you want from me?" she half-whispered and half-croaked out.

Chad threw his head back and laughed a high-pitched laugh that chilled her blood.

"Oh, I think you know what I want, Pip. I want you. We are going to be together forever. I have made sure of that." He roughly smashed his lips on hers and plunged his tongue into her mouth. She could taste the whiskey of his tongue and began to gag. She wasn't going to give up without a fight. She fought back and scratched at his neck and swung with both hands into his chest and face.

Chad took his other hand and backhanded her across the face. Her eye felt like it was going to explode. He took the butt of the pistol and rammed it into her skull. She began to see the darkness settling in and lost her footing. She took one more step backward and began falling and rolling with limbs failing in all directions down the stairs.

He watched her falling down each step as her head and limbs banged into the wall and stairs. Blood from her head splattered out in a fan pattern on the wall as she tumbled down the stairs. He sat stunned for a second when she abruptly came to a stop at the bottom of the stairs in a crumpled heap. She moaned quietly, and then began to start to quiver and gave off a glimmering light.

"no! You aren't going to get away from me again. Not this time!" He took aim with his gun and fired off a shot—aiming it directly at her heart. Pip heard the sound as the bullet left the barrel and heard the whizzing noise as it was coming for her.

She waited for the impact of the bullet to meet her body but instead welcomed the still of the blackness that swallowed her whole.

*   *   *

"Dad, I want to go home. I am tired of being here. I don't understand why I have to stay in this stupid hospital."

"I know, Graham. But we have to stay until a donor can be found for you to make you completely better."

"I want to go home," his lip started to quiver. "I miss Mommy. Why did she have to leave us?" Graham was crying big tears now that were falling down and beginning to soak his pillow.

Joe had to choke back his own tears and be strong for Graham. How he wished that he could climb into the bed with his son and hold him and cry with him and tell him that he didn't know why his mom was taken from him, from all of them. It wasn't fair. He resisted that urge and tried to do for his son what Piper would've wanted him to do.

"I know, buddy. I can't tell you why Mom had to go, but she will never really be gone. She will live forever in here." He tapped his finger on Graham's heart. "Mom told me once that when a heart feels love, so much love that it is bursting from it, that your heart will never forget who made it feel like that. She lives on in you and in your sister, Arie. She will always be looking out for you and your sister. You were the lights of her life. Promise me that you won't forget her."

"I'm trying not to, Dad, but I am having trouble remembering what her voice sounded like. I can still hear her laugh and what she sounded like when she would sing to me, but I can't remember what her voice sounded like."

Joe pulled out his phone and punched a few of the buttons. Piper's voice came to life.

"Go, Graham, run! You can do it. Head for the goal!" Joe and Graham watched as Piper was cheering on Graham at one of his soccer games as he skillfully kicked the ball into the goal and scored. She then turned toward the camera that Joe was holding and with the sunshine streaming into her hair, gave Joe a wide grin.

"That's our boy, babe. That's our boy. All right, Graham!" she cheered and clapped her hands, and then gave Graham the thumbs-up signal. Joe watched the video and didn't even realize that silent tears were streaming down his cheeks. He looked at Piper frozen in time at the end of the video—the sun on her face and the biggest grin on her lips that lit up her eyes and wondered how she was really gone.

"Daddy, will you play it again?" Joe snapped back and looked down at his son.

"Sure, bud." He tapped it again, and they started to watch the precious video again. Suddenly there was some commotion going on outside of Graham's room.

Joe could see from the window in the door that nurses were running about and seemed to be gathering right outside of Graham's door.

Joe pushed the phone into Graham's hands. "Here, bud. Let me go and see what is going on. I will be right back."

Joe pulled open the door and looked out. He gasped and immediately rushed to the side of the woman that was lying helpless on the floor.

"Sir, do you know this woman? I was standing at the front desk working on files and turned my back, and she was lying here." The nurse explained while the other nurse was checking for a pulse.

"Yes. That is my sister-in-law, Pip. Is she alive?" Joe was frantic and kneeling beside her. He couldn't lose both of them.

"Yes. She has a pulse. Get me another pad of gauze for her head. This one is saturated. She has a good size knot on the back of her skull. I think she is going to need stitches for her head wound too." The nurse pressed the gauze to her head, and Pip let out a moan and whimpered.

"You're hurting her," Joe said to the nurse and reached for her hand. That was when he noticed that Pip's arm was hanging at a strange angle. "Whoa. What is going on with her arm?"

The nurse glanced over and after taking a look at it explained that Pip had probably dislocated her shoulder.

Another nurse came over with a hospital bed and said that a doctor had been paged. The three nurses were working hard to get Pip's head and neck stabilized before moving her onto the bed.

"Where are you taking her?" Joe asked suddenly panicked.

"We are taking her to get a head scan to rule out any bleeding in the brain. One of us will come back here and report to you our findings." Joe watched helplessly as they rolled Pip away.

Twenty-two

Joe was quietly pacing the floor in Graham's room and kept his head down. Graham was watching him with interest.

"Dad, what are you doing?"

"Hmmm? Sorry, Graham. Aunt Pip must've had an accident. She was outside of your room. The doctor is helping her now, but I am worried about her."

"Aunt Pip is here? Why don't you go check on her?"

"You know, I think I will. I will be right back. Don't go anywhere." Joe winked at Graham and headed out the door to see what he could find out about Pip.

He tracked down one of the nurses that had helped Pip outside of Graham's room.

"Excuse me, ma'am? You were helping my sister-in-law. Do you have any idea where I can find her, or what was wrong with her?"

"Sure. She has been moved down two floors to room number 312. Just check in with the nurse on that floor and tell her that I sent you down."

"Thanks, Doreen." Joe glanced at her name tag, and then headed for the elevator bay area.

After he was directed to Pip's room, Joe pushed open the door, and that is when he saw her—lying in the hospital bed. He held his breath and had to remind himself that it was Pip, and not Piper in that bed. He was flooded with emotions as he looked at her in the hospital gown and tucked into the bed. He didn't know if he could do this again.

He walked over to her side and lightly stroked his hand down her arm. Her eyes were closed, and she was breathing deeply. He quietly said, "Pip? Are you awake?"

Her eyes opened slowly, and she managed a weak smile. "What happened, Joe? Did I have an accident on my way home from my open house?"

Joe looked at her and was perplexed. He was confused by her questions, and then it struck him. Pip thought that she was still in her world and that *he* was her husband.

"Pip, it's me. Piper's husband, Joe. You jumped and were lying outside of Graham's room. Something happened, and you were hurt. I haven't heard yet from the doctor to see what your scans showed."

"Joe? You're not my husband. My head is really foggy right now. I don't remember what happened or how I got here," Pip let out a big sigh and looked frustrated.

Joe felt sorry for her. He wondered what had happened, and then suddenly feared that Chad had done something to her. She looked somewhat defeated lying in the bed. Her hair was matted down with dried blood, and Joe could see some stitches stretching across the swollen knot on the back of her head. Her arm was immobilized in a sling, and her face was bruised and swollen. The corner of her mouth had a smear of dried blood.

The door swung open, and both Joe and Pip turned to see who was coming in.

"Hi, Mrs. Reynolds. I'm Dr. Lemer. I have the results of your MRI. You have no bleeding in the brain or skull fractures. You are extremely fortunate. However you do have a concussion. You will probably have trouble remembering the last few days leading up to the accident, and you may never recover those memories. You will also have some trouble with your short-term memory for a bit. That's a nasty knot that you have on your head, and I ended up having to put in nine stitches to close the wound. I also had to relocate your shoulder. It will have some soreness for a while. Maybe you don't remember me fixing your shoulder?"

Pip shook her head, her eyes clouded with confusion.

"That is probably a good thing. You have a good set of lungs on you, and you let me have it." Dr. Lemer smiled and looked at Joe. "Your wife will probably be confused on what happened and may ask you repeatedly what occurred. Don't get frustrated. This is completely normal."

"Oh, she isn't my wife. She is my sister-in-law."

"I'm sorry that I misunderstood. She has a dose of morphine on board, and we are going to keep her overnight for observation. After she is released, she can just go to Tylenol to help with the pain. I will check back in with her in the morning."

"Thank you, Doctor." Joe felt a fleeting moment of déjà vu. He had just been here with his Piper. This was too soon and felt as though his heart was being ripped to shreds. He was raw with emotion as he looked at the woman who shared his wife's face and mannerisms, and his throat got tight. How was he going to go on without Piper?

"Joe, what happened? Why am I here?"

Pip's question snapped him out of his thoughts.

"Pip, you were in an accident. You are safe now and will feel better in a few days." She was clearly having trouble remembering what had happened.

"I will be right back. I have to make a quick call."

Pip nodded her head slightly, and then leaned her head back on the pillow and closed her eyes.

Joe stepped out into the hallway and placed a call to Claire.

"Hi, Claire, it's Joe. I need your help. Pip has been in an accident, and she is here in the hospital. Could you come and stay tonight with Graham and Aries?"

"That is horrible. What happened?"

"I am not sure. She has a concussion, and I don't think that she remembers what happened either. Hopefully she will get her memory back in a few days—if she is here that long."

"We are just finishing up dinner, and then I will head over to the hospital. See you shortly."

"Thank you. Sounds good. Bye." Joe turned off the phone and walked back into the room. Pip opened her eyes and looked at Joe.

"Joe, what happened to me? Why am I here?"

Joe smiled at her and started to explain again to her. It may prove to be a long night.

*　　*　　*

Joe looked at his watch for the hundredth time. Where was she? He had gotten her text about an hour ago, and that was plenty of time for her to finish up at the open house and get back home.

He was done waiting around. He grabbed his keys off of the counter and jumped into his car. He backed the car quickly out of the garage and slammed his foot down on the accelerator. He decided to head to where she was holding her open house first and see if maybe a client had held her up.

Joe arrived to the house on Water Ridge Court in record time and pulled up to the house. He was relieved to see that Pip's car was still in the driveway. She must have been detained with some last-minute clients. Joe smiled to himself as he thought about his hard-working wife.

He opened his door and grabbed his sport coat out of the front seat. He slipped his arms into it as he was walking up to the front door. He would go in and see if she needed any help.

He had only taken one step onto the front porch when he could feel that something wasn't right. The front door stood wide open, and the house was eerily quiet.

"Pip! Are you here? Pip!" Joe called to her as he quickly rushed into the house. He breezed through the foyer and stopped dead in his tracks when he came to the staircase. There was a puddle of blood at the bottom of the stairs, and his eyes followed the blood splatters that fanned over the wall next to the staircase.

Joe couldn't think. He pulled out his cell phone and punched in 9-1-1.

"911. What's your emergency?"

"I'm at 857 Water Ridge Court. Send the police right away. Something has happened to my wife."

"Okay, sir. I have dispatched the police to your location. What is wrong with your wife?"

"I don't know. I can't find her, but there is blood all over," Joe's voice cracked, and he began to panic.

"Sir, I need you to remain calm. Help is on the way."

Joe hung up the phone and began frantically searching the main floor. He was constantly calling out Pip's name and opened every closet and bedroom door looking for her.

Joe had made his way through the first floor of the house and was about to go upstairs when he saw the police's flashing lights arrive at the front of the house. Two men promptly got out of their vehicle and clamored up to the front porch.

"Officers, my wife was holding an open house here this afternoon. She had texted me that she was almost done and was heading home soon. She never made it home, so I came to check on her. There is a lot of blood by the staircase, and I can't find her anywhere. I was just about to go and check upstairs."

"Sir, please leave that to us. Stay here while we go and check out the second level."

The officer with jet black hair removed his gun from his belt and, holding it skillfully in front of him, made his way up the stairs. Moments later he called down to his partner that the second floor was clear.

Scott was a tall lanky officer who had stayed on the main level. He squatted down and was taking a closer look at the blood puddle. His trained gaze slowly moved up the wall, and then stopped. There was something in the wall that caught his eye. He carefully maneuvered around the puddle and stooped down to get a closer look. Just as he thought, there was a bullet lodged in the wall.

"Ethan, we have a single shot that was fired and is in the wall. Sir, please don't touch anything. This has turned into a crime scene and will need to be dusted for prints."

Scott made his way back down the stairs and began calling in the proper teams to take over.

"Oh my god! Chad. It could be Chad. He may have her," Joe said aloud, and then began to fill in the officers on how Chad was obsessed with Pip and had recently been released from prison.

"I will call and see if I can get a hold of his parole officer. Just sit tight until I can get some more information and the crime scene investigators get here." Ethan stepped into the kitchen and began to make calls to see what more he could find out.

"I knew she wasn't ready for an open house yet. Why did I let her go?" Joe was speaking out loud but was mostly talking to himself. Scott was busy on the phone as well.

Ethan came back into the room from the kitchen first and looked at Joe.

"I'm afraid that I have bad news. Chad Barns has not been heard from nor can his parole officer get a hold of him."

Joe looked from Ethan to Scott. "Now what do we do?"

Scott turned and looked at Joe and Ethan. "If Chad does have Piper, the first forty-eight hours are crucial. We have to get on this right now."

"Joe, try to stay calm. Think back to everything you know about Chad. Anything you can think of might help us find out where Pip is and bring her home safely."

Joe hoped so but couldn't shake the bad feeling that he had in his stomach.

*   *   *

Over the next few days, Pip got increasingly stronger and was beginning to feel more like herself. She had been released from the hospital and was staying at Piper and Joe's house.

Joe had been staying at the hospital, and Claire had been staying at the house with Pip and Arie. No one said it, but everyone was concerned that if for some reason that Pip were to go home suddenly, they were worried that Arie would be by herself.

Pip rolled over in bed and was slightly startled when she saw Arie's small sleeping body all curled up next to her. She looked down at the innocent little face and smiled. Her long dark eyelashes curled up slightly, and her dark mane of curls was fanned out over the pillow. She didn't remember Arie getting into bed with her.

Arie began to stir and let out a huge yawn. She slowly opened her eyes and saw Pip looking down at her.

"I am sorry that I got into bed with you, Auntie. I just miss my mom so much. Why did she have to leave me?"

"Oh, baby girl. Your mom would've never left you if she had the choice. She loved you so much. She told me how you, Graham, and your dad were the lights of her life. Sometimes accidents happen, and we can't change what happens because of them. Your mom would've wanted you to grow up and be happy. She will always live on in your heart. You are a piece of her, and so is Graham. You will have to help each other to never forget her."

"Aunt Pip, are you going to leave me too?"

Pip felt a stab in her heart. She really didn't have a choice, but for a brief moment the thought did cross her mind about if she could choose to stay here with Graham and Arie if she would indeed stay. She dismissed that thought as quickly as it came. She wouldn't be able to stay here with them, but she felt sad that Arie had just lost her mother, and more than likely she would lose her as well. Without Piper here to draw Pip to her, Pip was worried that she wouldn't be able to jump anymore.

"Arie, I will promise you this. I will do my best to stay here with you and come as often as I can, but you have to know that if you don't see me for a while, it doesn't mean that I am not thinking about you. I love you so much, and there are only a few people in my life that mean so much to me. My heart is full of you, Graham, my husband, and your dad."

"Okay, Auntie," she said and snuggled her head under Pip's arm.

Pip kissed the top of her head and felt comforted by the warmth of her little body. She missed Piper dearly and did see parts of her friend in Arie. She wished that she could protect Arie from all of the scariness of the world.

As she thought about the dangerous people that Pip wanted to keep Arie safe from, she suddenly pictured Chad's face. Pip sat straight up in bed. That is what happened at the open house. Chad did this to her. She was beginning to remember what happened that afternoon when she had the accident. Some of the images were a little bit foggy, but they were starting to come back to her in bits and pieces.

"Arie, let's get dressed and go take breakfast to your dad and brother. I have a feeling that Graham could use a break from that hospital food." She wanted to get to the hospital to talk to Joe about what she had remembered. She also wanted to talk to the doctor about when they could do the bone marrow transplant. She thought that they better do it soon before she went back home.

The pair shuffled down the stairs together and found Claire in the kitchen having a mug of coffee.

"Hi, sleepyheads. I was wondering when you were going to get up this morning. Do you want some coffee, Pip?"

"Good morning, Claire. Yes, please. Do you mind taking us to the hospital? I want to ask about getting the transplant done soon."

"Sure thing. What about breakfast?"

"I was thinking that maybe we could swing by and pick up some muffins on our way to the hospital."

"That sounds good. I will call Anna at the restaurant and see if she can throw together a bag of different muffins and pastries for us to pick up on the way to the hospital."

"Now you're talking. Nothing beats Anna's chocolate chip muffins in the morning. Arie, go get your shoes on please. We are going to go see your dad and Graham."

Pip strode into Graham's room, and Joe looked up from the newspaper he was reading. Graham got a big smile on his face when he saw the white paper sack that Pip was carrying with his favorite chocolate chip muffins.

"Hi, you two. We brought you breakfast. We thought that maybe you were getting tired of hospital food." Pip handed a muffin to Graham who immediately began to devour it.

"Slow down, man. You are going to choke." Graham looked up at Pip and smiled, crumbs falling out of his mouth and onto his lap.

Pip laughed and handed the bag of muffins over to Joe.

"Can I talk to you for a second in the hallway?"

"Sure. Do you mind watching them for a second, Claire?"

"I don't mind. Go right ahead. Arie and I are going to have a muffin with Graham anyway."

When they were in the hallway, Pip began to hurriedly explain to Joe what she remembered from the open house. Joe could feel his blood pressure starting to rise as he got upset thinking about what Chad had done to Pip.

"I can't remember all of the details clearly, but I think that he shot his gun at me right before I jumped. I remember hearing the sound of the gun being fired, and I think that I just narrowly missed being hit."

"So he shot at you after he threw you down the stairs? Pip, you could've been killed."

"I know. I don't know why I can jump into your world, but I am so thankful that I can, or I would probably be dead now," Pip caught her breath as she realized what she had just said out loud to Joe.

"I'm so sorry. I didn't mean to say that." She cast her eyes downward, and her shoulders slumped over.

"I know that you didn't mean anything by it. I know that you must be struggling with losing Piper too. I have just been worrying about everything going on with Graham that I haven't really been able to grieve like I should. I just feel like she is going to come around every corner any minute. I don't feel like she is really gone. She can't be. I have loved her almost half of my life. I don't want to remember what life was like before her. I see so much of her in each of the kids. The way that Arie laughs and her whole face lights up or the way that Graham can crack a joke when everyone else is stressed and calm people down, that is Piper coming through in them. She will be forever a part of them and of me. I just wish that I was able to tell her one more time how much she touched my life and left her handprint forever on my heart."

"She knew, Joe. She knew how you felt just by the way that you looked at her and smiled without even being aware of it when you watched her with the children. I know that she felt the same way about you because I feel the same way about my Joe. We are so similar and shared a lot of the same feelings. She knew—take comfort in knowing that she loved you just as passionately and deeply as you loved her." Pip wrapped her arms around Joe, and he allowed himself to be comforted in the arms of the woman that looked and felt just like his wife.

Pip pulled away and tilted her head and stared into Joe's blue eyes. She wiped away a lone tear on his cheek.

"Now, let's go find the doctor and see about how I can give Graham my bone marrow so he can get healthy and go home."

"That's a deal. Follow me." Joe led her down the hallway and to the nurse's station in search of Graham's doctor.

Twenty-three

The procedure was scheduled to take place at 8:00 AM the next morning. The doctor would remove Pip's bone marrow through her hip. The doctor explained that then the cells would be transferred into Graham's blood intravenously.

Pip sat on the edge of her bed and sighed heavily. This procedure had to work. She had to stay long enough to make it through the procedure without going home. We wanted to be able to do this for Graham. She wanted to fulfill the promise she made to Piper.

The birds outside of Pip's window were chirping loudly to each other. Pip yawned and stretched and grabbed her robe on the way to the bathroom. She showered quickly and dressed in comfy clothes for the procedure. She was so anxious if she would still be here long enough to donate the bone marrow that she was sick to her stomach. She wasn't worried about the procedure itself too much, but she was worried about jumping home in the middle of it.

Pip had just finished getting her shoes on when she heard a knock at the front door.

"Good morning, Anna. Thanks so much for taking me to the hospital this morning and for watching Arie for a little bit while we are at the hospital doing the procedure."

"It is my pleasure," she said and smiled warmly at Pip and shouted up the stairs to Arie. "Hustle up, girl! Your cousins are excited to see you."

"I'm ready, Aunt Anna. Can I bring my doll with us?"

"Sure thing, hon. Now let's get a move on before we are late." They headed out the door and piled into Anna's car.

*   *   *

Joe sat at his desk, and his mind began to wander for the twentieth time today. He couldn't stop thinking about Pip. He was wrestling with so many emotions. He would surely know if she had died, wouldn't he?

He reached over and picked up their wedding picture off of his desk. God, she was beautiful. He thought that he loved her so much on their wedding day. He was amazed at how he seemed to love her more with each passing day.

An older agent stopped by his office and popped his head in. He was a kind man, and Pip had taken to him instantly.

"Listen, Joe, she is going to be all right. She is a fighter and strong. Keep the faith. She will come home."

"Thanks, Matt. She always tells me that I should listen to you more. You have always been her favorite. I will keep you posted." Matt smiled easily at the man who he could see clearly missed and loved his wife.

It helped to be at the office to keep his mind off of Pip and her disappearance. When he was at home in the quiet, his mind would go to dark places, and sometimes he would just lose it.

The police said that they didn't have many solid leads on Chad. He still hadn't been located. They were following up on a tip that he might be staying with a cousin, but so far they had been unable to find out where the cousin and Chad may be hiding out.

This was the longest that Pip had ever been away. He dreamt of her and would wake frantically in the middle of the night hoping that she had come home and would be lying next to him. He would reach out for her and find that her side was still bare and empty.

Not knowing what happened to her was eating him up inside. He would not rest until he found her, and she was home safely with him.

*　　*　　*

The procedure had gone well, and Graham had already received the stem cells into his blood. Pip was still slightly sore although the procedure had been a few days ago. Pip leaned her head back and slowly rocked herself with her toe and let out a sigh. Arie was sitting on the front porch with her and was curled up in the chair coloring in her book. Now they just have to wait and see if the procedure worked.

Arie and Pip both looked up when they heard the black Tahoe turn into the driveway.

"It's Aunt Anna." Arie set down her crayons and wandered down the steps until the Tahoe rolled to a stop.

Anna jumped down from the truck and slammed closed the door.

"Hey, girls. I have come to see if I can take Arie back to my house for a sleepover tonight? The kids are having a few friends over for pizza, and they wanted to see if Arie could come too." Anna looked over to Pip.

"Can I please go, Auntie? Please," Arie practically whined.

"Okay. Go pack your jammies and toothbrush. I will be inside in a second to see if you got everything."

"Thank you!" Arie yanked open the front door and went charging up the steps to her room.

"Well, you just made her whole night and maybe even her whole week. She has been kind of distant lately. She is worried that I am going to leave her too. I don't know what to do, Anna. I can't control when I leave. What if I go home and I can't ever come back since Piper isn't here anymore to draw me to her?"

"Or what if you are stuck here and never go home? Have you thought about that?"

"Yes. I actually have. I love the children almost like they are my own. The only problem is my Joe is back home, and although this Joe looks like him, he isn't the man that I fell in love with and married. I miss Joe so much and am anxious to get home to him."

"I know that you must be anxious to get home to your husband. I do think that your being here has really helped the kids. You and Piper are so much alike. You have such a caring and nurturing way about you just like Piper did. The children need that right now."

The screen door slammed shut behind Arie. She stepped out onto the front porch with her bag swung over her shoulder.

"I'm ready, Aunt Anna."

"All right, then let's go. Can you please tell Joe that I will bring her home tomorrow morning?"

"Sure, thanks for including her. See you tomorrow."

Pip watched the Tahoe back out of the driveway and gave them a small wave and a smile. She went back inside and started straightening up the house. She thought Joe would be home soon to get his change of clothes and grab a quick dinner before heading back to the hospital. It was just beginning to turn to dusk now, and she wondered how much longer until Joe came home.

She popped her earbuds in and turned up the music as she danced around the house dusting the furniture. She was in the guest room and was just finishing up the dusting in there when Joe found her. He reached out and grabbed her waist and spun her around.

"Pip! Pip! Turn those damn things down. I have the best news!"

"You scared the crap out of me, Joe. I didn't hear you come in. What's the news?"

"You saved him, Pip. You did it. The doctor came in and said that the procedure worked. Graham will be released from the hospital in a few days. He is going to be all right. You did it!" Joe picked her up and swung her in a big circle. Pip squealed with delight as the news clicked, and she absorbed what he was telling her. Graham was going to be okay. The procedure had worked, and Graham would be coming home soon.

Pip clapped her hands together and let out a big throaty laugh. Her laugh delighted Joe's ears as he suddenly stopped swinging her around and set her down. She was standing on her tiptoes, and he was still holding her in his arms. He gazed down into her eyes. The flecks in her eyes were bright green as she looked into his eyes with a huge grin on her face. Her mouth grew still as she looked up at him wrapped in his arms.

He bent his head and slowly took her lips on hers. She seemed hesitant at first, but as her eyes fluttered closed, she seemed to draw him into her. His mouth was hungrily devouring hers, and his desire and need for her filled every inch of his being.

He wasn't slow or patient as he began to quickly pull off her blouse and unbutton her shorts. They slid to the floor and landed in a heap. He scooped her up and carried her to the bed. He laid her down and hurriedly undressed so he can join her.

Darkness had fallen outside, and the only light on was a bedside table lamp that cast a dull glow over the bed. The curtains twirled softly in the slight breeze that was flowing through the window.

"You're beautiful," Joe whispered to Pip as he joined her on the bed. He kissed softly down her neck until he came to her hard and erect nipples. He took them into his mouth and traced his tongue around them until he heard Pip moan with pleasure.

He then slowly kissed and licked his way down her taunt stomach until he found her inner wetness. She softly sighed and shuddered as he molded her into his hands and pleasured her with his tongue.

"I need you inside of me," she begged him. He slowly slipped into her as she spread her legs to take him deep inside of her. He found her lips again and plunged his tongue into her mouth as he continued to ride her.

She arched her back and was softly moaning as she began to come a few moments before he did. As he felt her tighten around him, he joined her and took them both over the edge together.

He flopped over onto his back and wiped away a bead of sweat that had collected on his brow. She rested her head on his left shoulder, and neither of them said a word for a few seconds.

"I love you, Piper," Joe softly whispered.

"Oh my god, Joe. What have we done?" Pip sat up abruptly and pulled the blanket around her to cover her nakedness, suddenly modest.

As the moonlight streamed into the room, it was hard for Joe to see Pip's blonde hair.

"You aren't my husband, and I am not Piper. We both let our emotions get the best of us." Pip stared at Joe with wide eyes.

"Pip—I am so sorry. I was so excited about Graham, and when I held you in my arms, you felt just like Piper. I miss her so much, and it just felt so right. I am sorry that I let that happen."

"It takes two, but, Joe, it never should've happened. I love my husband dearly. I just forgot for a few minutes that you weren't him. This can never happen again. I won't let it."

"I agree. I am sorry, Pip. Can you ever forgive me?"

"Yes. I do love you, Joe, just not in that way. We both let our bodies lead the way and didn't think about our hearts or anyone else for that matter."

"I'm going to go. I am sorry once again. I hope that you can forget that this ever happened." Joe snatched his pants and shirt off of the floor and quietly walked out of the room leaving Pip alone to her thoughts.

A few weeks had passed, and Pip still had not gone home. Graham was going to be coming home in a few hours, and Pip had spent the last few days cleaning and sterilizing everything as best as possible. She didn't want him to get any germs when his system was still in a fragile state.

She and Joe hadn't talked again about that night, but she couldn't stop thinking about it. She had such feelings of guilt that it was beginning to consume her. Her head knew all of the reasons that it had happened, but her heart ached for what she had done to her husband. She wished that she could go home and was starting to wonder if she would ever see her Joe again. Maybe she was going to be stuck in Piper's world forever.

It had been different between her and Joe. She wasn't trying to avoid him but found it easier to move to another room when he walked into the same one that she was in. She was trying hard to make it seem like nothing was wrong, for Arie's sake, but it was easier on her if she had her own space right now.

She shook her head to try and clear her thoughts and her mind. First she had to concentrate on getting the house ready for Graham to come home. At least that is one thing that she could feel good about was Graham. He was getting stronger every day, and it looked like he would go on to live a happy and healthy life. She knew that her part in that was a big factor and glad that she could fulfill that promise to Piper.

She felt a tear fall past her lashes, and she quickly wiped it away with the back of her hand. She arched her shoulders and rubbed her lower back. She stifled a yawn and realized how tired she was from all of the cleaning she had done to get ready for Graham's arrival home.

She headed downstairs and found Arie at the kitchen table making a welcome banner for Graham. Arie looked up when she saw Pip pad with her bare feet into the kitchen.

"Auntie, can you help me hang this up in the doorway so Graham sees it when he comes through the door?"

"Sure. He is going to love it. Are you ready to hang it up now? I think your dad will be pulling in any minute with Graham."

"Yep. Let me just finish coloring this picture of Toby." Pip looked down at the drawings that Arie had made on the banner. There were pictures of Graham and Arie and a picture of Pip holding hands with Joe. Piper was drawn floating above all of them. They looked like a big happy family. The picture pulled on Pip's heartstrings, and she felt sad for the little girl and boy that had lost their mother.

"I am all done now. Let's hang it up."

Pip stood on a chair that she drug from the table and hoisted the sign above the garage door. She fastened it with tape and had just finished securing it when she heard the garage door start to go up.

She hurriedly scooted the chair back to the table and put the tape away in the kitchen drawer.

"Arie, they are just pulling in. I heard the garage door." Pip and Arie stood by the garage door and waited until it swung open, and they caught Graham's mop of dark hair come through the door.

"Graham!" Arie ran to him and squeezed him in a giant hug.

"Careful, honey. He is still not feeling 100 percent yet."

"I'm sorry. I hope I didn't hurt you."

"I'm okay, Arie. Don't worry about it."

"Let's get him in and up to his room. You must be tired, honey."

"I'm a little tired, but I am so glad to be home. Hi, Toby." Graham reached down and scratched the dog between the ears making Toby shake his whole body in excitement to see the young boy.

Joe helped get Graham settled on the couch. He had decided that he wanted to be in the family room until after dinner. He was tired of being in a bed and was elated to have something new to look at.

Pip watched the small family all huddled together on the couch and smiled. She was in the kitchen cooking hamburger meat for the spaghetti they were eating for dinner. She sniffed the meat as it was cooking and began to get sick to her stomach. She instantly worried that she may be getting sick. She thought that maybe she should keep her distance from Graham for the next few days just in case. He couldn't afford to get the flu in his condition.

That night after all of the dinner dishes had been cleaned up and put away, Pip climbed the stairs and wandered to Graham's room. She paused for a moment because Joe was standing in his doorway silently watching the small boy sleep.

"You must have had the same idea as I did. I watch him sleeping, and I am just so grateful that he is going to be all right. Thank you so much for your part in all of this, Pip. I don't think he would be home right now if it hadn't been for you."

Pip smiled at Joe and just nodded her head. She turned and was comforted as she watched Graham sleeping peacefully with Toby curled up at his feet.

She placed her hand on Joe's arm and gently squeezed it.

"Good night," Pip whispered and turned away toward her room.

"Night, Pip," Joe watched her as she turned and walked down the hall.

Pip woke in the morning and felt sick. She was so nauseous that she felt as though she may vomit. She stayed in her room for most of the day because she didn't want to expose Graham and waited to see if the symptoms would pass.

She reached under the bathroom sink to change the toilet paper roll and noticed that there were some tampons sitting on the shelf next to the toilet paper. Seeing the tampons sent a shock through Pip.

"Shit! I should've gotten my period by now." She hurriedly went to her phone and looked back at the calendar. She counted back the days—she was nine days late. Her hand immediately went to her belly. Could she be pregnant after all of these years of trying after just one night?

Panic and fear started to rise up in her throat. She tried to calm herself down and tell herself not to jump to that conclusion just yet. She needed to go out and get a pregnancy test.

She told Joe that she was heading to the store to get a few things and would be back shortly. When she arrived at the store, she combed the aisles looking for the pregnancy tests. When she found them, she picked up two boxes. Each box contained two tests. She wanted to be sure.

She quickly paid for the items and climbed back into the car in a matter of a few minutes. She drove home without even having to think about what she was doing. Her mind was racing with emotions, and she couldn't get it to stop on just one feeling.

Pip jammed the brown sack into her purse and slammed the car door shut. She made her way through the kitchen and was glad that no one seemed to be around as she came into the house. She saw Joe and the kids sitting on the back porch, and Arie was laughing at something Joe said. She crept through the kitchen and made her way back upstairs to the guest bathroom.

She popped open the first box and peeled back the foil wrapper. She read the instructions carefully and, following the directions on the box, set the stick on the edge of the tub and sat back to wait for the longest three minutes of her life.

As her watch slowly ticked away, she began to go through the different scenarios in her mind. Would she be stuck in this world forever and raise this baby with Piper's Joe? Would she ever make it home, and then what would she tell her Joe? There wasn't really a good outcome either way.

She stopped thinking about both of the Joes for a minute and began thinking about if she really was pregnant. She felt a smile start to creep onto her lips. A baby. She had been trying to have a baby for more than five years. This was obviously not how she had planned to get pregnant, but she was already in love with the idea of being a mother. She had so many different thoughts running through her mind.

She glimpsed down at her watch. Time was up. Pip took a deep breath and held it for a moment. She slowly got up from the toilet and reached down and picked up the small stick.

Pip looked down at the results window, and there was a faint positive sign. Could it be? She held it up and peered at it in the light. She thought it was a plus sign, but she couldn't be positive.

She decided to take the other three tests to be sure. She looked down at the four pregnancy sticks all lined up neatly on the counter—all of them showing the faint positive sign.

She started to cry when she looked down at them. Big tears rolled down her cheeks as she sobbed quietly. She wanted this baby desperately as she laid a hand protectively on her belly. She had wanted this for five years, but she cried for both Joes, for herself, but mostly she cried for Piper.

She slunk against the wall and allowed herself to slide down until she was sitting on the floor with her knees pulling up against her chest. Her cheeks were wet with tears.

"Forgive me, Piper." She hung her head and lowered her forehead onto her knees and allowed the tears to fall.

The house was quiet and still, but Joe couldn't sleep. He lay in his bed staring up at his ceiling. He looked at the clock for the hundredth time and watched the minutes tick away. He couldn't lie in bed anymore. He got up and slipped on some pants and went to check on the kids. Both of them lay sleeping soundly in their beds. Toby was snoring softly curled in a ball at Graham's feet. He hadn't left Graham's side since he got home from the hospital. He glanced at Pip's door, and it was shut with no light visible shining underneath it. It looked like he was the only one that was having trouble sleeping.

He remembered that tomorrow was trash day. He was horrible at remembering to put it out on the curb. Piper had always done that, and he had to ask Arie what day trash day even was.

He sighed heavily and thought about how much he missed Piper. He thought he better collect the trash and get it out so it would be picked in the morning. He walked into the hallway guest bathroom and stooped down to pick up the trash can. It had a brown sack that had been folded tightly and lay on its side in the bottom of the can. Joe flipped on the light switch and pulled out the sack, curious as to what it was.

He opened the sack and pulled out a white stick with a purple lid. He knew what it was immediately and stared down at the positive sign in the results window.

"Holy shit! Pip is pregnant?" Not knowing how he felt about this but angry that she hadn't told him she was pregnant, he quickly went to her door and turned the knob to demand answers.

The full moon cast light on the bed that had been slept in but was empty now. Joe quickly turned on the light and went to the bed. He ran his hand down the sheets that felt warm to his touch. He looked around and felt panic rising in his blood.

She was gone. She had jumped home and had taken his baby in her belly with her. He plopped down on the edge of the bed and rested his head in his hands.

"What have we done?" Joe whispered aloud.

*   *   *

Pip woke with a start and found that she was shivering. She sat up and looked down next to her. Joe was sleeping on his side with his back to her. She was home.

She got up and quietly moved to her makeup table. She looked down at it and smiled sadly as she ran her fingers over everything that was in the same place she had left it all of those weeks ago.

She sat down on the small stool and looked at her husband as he slept, unaware that she was home. She would have to tell him about the baby but didn't know what she was going to say yet. She selfishly took this quiet time to try and collect her thoughts as she watched him sleep.

The room was dark except for the light that the moon gave off that streamed in through the small transom windows that were on either sides of the bed. Pip sat and studied the lines of Joe's peaceful face as he dreamt. Tears welled up in her eyes and began to fall down her cheeks as she watched Joe sleep.

Graham rolled over and fell out of bed and thumped to the floor. He sleepily rubbed his elbow and blinked his eyes as they tried to adjust to the dark room. He had been dreaming and was a little bit scared.

He started to make his way into his dad's room. He bumped into a piece of furniture in the hallway that he didn't remember being there.

Toby had been sleeping stretched out on the floor and began to growl quietly as he heard small footsteps approaching. Pip heard Toby's low growls and turned on her stool to look toward the door.

That is when she saw him—Graham was standing in his pajamas in her room, sleepily rubbing his eyes. She gasped and quickly wiped away her tears.

Graham heard her before he saw her. He opened his eyes widely as he looked at her sitting facing him at her makeup table.

"Mom?"

Hiding in Plain Sight

Kate Mathias

Prologue

Graham's eyes snapped open, and he slowly moved to a sitting position. He gazed up at the green canopy of trees that swayed slightly in the breeze with a few rays of sunshine separating the leaves with their light. It was midday, and the birds were sweetly chirping to one another. He moved swiftly to a standing position and began to take in his surroundings.

He knew that he had "jumped" to Pip's world, but upon closer examination of the area around him, he thought he recognized the field as the Miller's farm on Appleside Drive. He began to trudge through the knee-high grass and made his way up the small hill. He came to the dilapidated fence that had been painted a crisp white at one time, but now the paint peeled where the fence was still intact. He found that he was drawn toward the small shack that was about a hundred feet to his left. It was an old tool shed that at one time held all of old man Miller's tools and small equipment for the farm.

Graham began to wonder why he was here. He had gotten used to jumping into Pip's world since he had done it so often in the last twenty or so years of his life. He found that he was drawn toward the woman from a parallel reality that shared his mother's identical looks, except for her golden hair. He had begun to enter her world after his own mother had died, and Pip had saved his life with her bone marrow. He had jumped to Pip's world too many times to count and usually did so when Pip was hurt or scared. His mother and Pip had been connected when his mom was alive, and both women had been in each other's worlds numerous times over the years. When his mom died, Pip stopped showing up in Graham's world—Pip no longer had the connection of his mother.

He was easily lost in his own thoughts as he began to think about his mom and back to the day of the accident. A shrill scream penetrated the air and startled him out of his thoughts.

Graham's hand immediately reached for his Glock 23 that was in his holster that hung low onto his hip. His training as a police officer for four years and his current position as a DEA agent prepared him for situations of danger.

Graham drew his gun and swiftly began to race through the grass, closing the distance to the shack in a few seconds. He crept up quietly to the edge of the north wall of the run down shed and inched his way pressed against the wall. He could make out a man's voice clearly and muffled crying of a woman. He slid to the broken window and peered in, careful not to be seen.

He scanned the interior of the shed. On the right hand side of the room sat Pip bound to a chair with rope. Her blonde hair hung limply in dirty clumps around her face. Her mascara had left streaks down her tear-stained cheeks. Her eyes stared in horror at the man in front of her. Her body was visibly shaking as she sobbed and pleaded with the man to stop.

Graham followed her gaze toward the man with sandy blonde hair that was standing about ten feet from Pip. Graham shifted and moved to his left slightly, and that is when he saw her—his half sister, Palmer— standing in front of the man, with her hands bound behind her back along with her ankles. She was dangling on what appeared to be a meat hook, and her limp body was swaying slightly. Her blonde hair hung in greasy strands and fell around her face where a dirty rag had been shoved in her mouth. Her eyes were closed, and Graham thought that she was already dead until he noticed that her blue eyes fluttered open, and then closed again a second later.

"Pip, do you see what you are making me do? You were never supposed to have this child. You were supposed to have my baby. Instead that annoying husband of yours knocked you up. This girl never should have been born. How many times have you escaped me? All of those times you got away from me when all I was trying to do was be close to you. Why couldn't you see that we were meant to be together? This is all your fault, and now you will have to watch her die."

"Please, Chad, stop. Take me. You can have me all to yourself. Stop, please don't hurt her. Chad, look at me. You don't want to do this. Let her go and take me. We can go anywhere you want."

"That would be too easy, Pip. You are only agreeing to go with me because you don't want anything to happen to her." He motioned to Palmer with his knife.

Chad moved closer to Palmer so he was standing in front of her. He reached up with his left hand and gripped her face.

"Open your eyes and look at me." Palmer groaned. "I said open your eyes, you little bitch!" Chad spat on her face, and it rolled down her cheek, streaking her dirty face.

Chad took the knife that he was holding in his right hand and ran it down the length of her right side. Her shirt had been torn, and her right side was exposed. Chad ran the tip of the knife along her hip until a few tickles of blood began to drip down her thigh.

Palmer's eyes flew open, and she shook her head in an attempt to be released from his grasp. Her eyes were wide with fear as Chad got closer to her face breathing his hot whiskey-laden breath on her neck.

Graham adjusted his position and tried to see Chad more clearly. He aimed his gun at Chad's head but didn't have a clear shot through the broken window. He ducked under the window frame and began to inch his way closer to the door.

"So young, what a pity you have to die." Chad swiped the knife in a swift left-to-right motion opening the right side of her neck. Palmer had massive bleeding from her carotid artery and jugular vein that pulsed with each beat of her heart.

Pip screamed and began to violently rock in her chair in an attempt to break free, but she only managed to tip over until she was lying on the floor on her side watching her daughter bleed to death before her eyes.

The door burst open and startled Chad who turned sharply and faced Graham. Graham quickly pulled the trigger three times, pumping two bullets into Chad's chest and one into his head. Chad fell to the ground with a thud, and his neck rolled to the side with his eyes staring wide at the ceiling.

It had only been mere seconds since Chad had slit Palmer's throat, but to Pip it had felt like an eternity. She was still wrestling with the ropes that bound her hands.

"Untie me, Graham. Hurry!" she screamed at Graham.

Graham ran to the nearest table and dropped his gun and picked up a handsaw. He hurried over to Pip and quickly removed her ropes, and then rushed over to Palmer. He hoisted her off of the meat hook with ease and stripped off the black T-shirt he was wearing. He applied direct pressure to her neck to stop the hemorrhage.

"Palmer, Palmer. Stay with us. You're a fighter, baby. Don't you dare leave me." Pip was cradling Palmer's head in her lap, and she looked up at Graham, her eyes pleading with him to do something more.

The color was quickly draining out of Palmer's face, and her eyes slowly opened and stared into her mom's eyes. Pip looked down at her daughter's glassy eyes and felt the fear bubbling up in her throat.

"Baby, I love you. Stay with us now. Don't go to sleep," Pip pleaded with Palmer. Pip looked down at the blood-soaked shirt that Graham was still holding onto Palmer's throat. Palmer let out a small noise, and then her eyes slowly shut.

"No!" Pip's scream filled the air and deafened her own ears as she was left gasping for breath.

CPSIA information can be obtained at www.ICGtesting.com
Printed in the USA
BVOW071624190712

295694BV00001B/4/P